NINE
TENTHS

Books by Jeff Macfee
Nine Tenths

NINE TENTHS

Jeff Macfee

JABberwocky Literary Agency, Inc.

Nine Tenths

Published in 2022 by JABberwocky Literary Agency, Inc.

Cover design by John Fisk

Paperback ISBN 978-1-625675-49-1
Ebook ISBN 978-1-625675-48-4

The list of people to thank is vast, so a bunch of them get the short stick. If I didn't mention you, them's the breaks.

To my wife Karen, who endured numerous claims all the computer time would result in a book, and believed anyway.

To Sean, Rachel, and Riley, who put up with their father's distraction, as he tried to solve story problems when he should have been parenting.

To my agent Lisa Rodgers, who saw something in my writing and took a bet. May that bet pay off. Also thanks to Richard Shealy for copy-editing, John Fisk for cover design, Karen Bourne for editorial notes, Susan Velazquez Colmant for rights work, Patrick Disselhorst for ebook production, and the rest of the JABberwocky team for their support.

To the many writers and writer-friends who read this book in drafts or just supported me. Especially Stephen Blackmoore, Paul Garth, Hector Acosta, and my Viable Paradise crew.

To Mom, who just wanted to buy a book with my name on it.

To Dad, who never got to see this book, but always knew I could write one. I miss you.

CHAPTER ONE

I was sliding mini-jacks under Captain Nietzsche's jet-car when my phone went off. For half a second, I thought the damn vehicle was vibrating, the modified Firebird ready to blast off. Franklin Nicholas Elmore the Third—AKA Captain Nietzsche—was known to control his vehicle by remote. But the modified ramjets were silent.

My phone buzzed again. I glanced over my shoulder—the Elmore residence was dark. Butt against the curb, I dug out my phone and took the call. No telling when someone from Treasury would spot-check the repo process, looking for holes. When I answered, I didn't hear some officious bureaucrat. Instead, the voice on the other end shaved ten years from my life.

"Gayle Hardwood. How the hell are you?"

Geographically vague Southern accent. A casual familiarity assumed since our first meeting. And poor timing, always a specialty of the man. Donald Maxwell Spielman. Donny. My old boss and partner. I didn't answer him right away, and he assumed control of the conversation. "Not much point in ignoring me. You picked up."

"Donny." My voice cracked. "Been a long time."

"Only in dog years." He chuckled as if required. "Say, you got a minute for an old friend?"

"Kind of busy right now. Maybe we can catch up later."

"Are you working? Tell me you're not doing a recovery solo."

"It's just Nietzsche—his only power is the car, and that belongs to the bank. Besides, you used to do augment repo jobs by yourself all the time, if I recall."

"Back in my day, the Augments dressed up like bats and cats. Now they shoot you with armor-piercing rounds from three miles away."

At the end of the street a truck blew by, orange dome lights flashing. The stubble on my head prickled, my bald noggin sensitive to changes in the wind and Treasury Department entanglements. But the vehicle was just a tow truck.

"What did you need?" I asked.

"Recall when we first met? You were doing a civvie repo. I was after Translucence and the Nowhere Man."

"Donny, I don't have time for memory lane. Things to do."

I could feel him shrug across the miles. "I understand. Guess I'm lucky you even took the call."

I fished another mini-jack from the grass and squared it with the car, checking the undercarriage for tripwires. Nietzsche knew the bank was after the car—he'd missed three payments, and Liberty Trust had sicced another repo firm on him only last month. *Your so-called repossession is the puerile judgment of a moral system*, he'd told the bank. *I do not recognize it*. The other firm had charged in blind, subcontracting the work to chuckleheads who worked augment repo for kicks. One of them went to hook the tow yoke to the front tires, and Nietzsche ignited the liquid fuel. Poor guy suffered third-degree burns on his arms and chest. He was the only one to leave the hospital.

When I'd started in augment repo, I hadn't known about tripwires or mini-jacks or any other tools of the trade. I only knew what I knew because Donny had taught me.

"I'm listening," I said.

Across the airwaves, I could hear him crack a smile. "Damn if you aren't as stubborn as always. Reminds me how much I miss working together."

I pressed my back against the car and jammed my heels into the curb. Nietzsche had parked his jet-powered mid-life crisis between a Tacoma and a low-slung Caddy. Space wasn't an issue—the vehicle could take off vertically, and the state had licensed Nietzsche for flight. He'd figured we couldn't repo the vehicle if we didn't have room to pull up the tow. Sound logic, if you didn't consider the mini-jacks

I'd used to raise the car and slide the whole shebang out sideways.

"There's this job," Donny said. "The players are bigger than I usually care to tangle with. But circumstances make the encounter... unavoidable."

I pushed. The car started to move. "Didn't think you were licensed for augment repo anymore."

"Never claimed I was."

"Then that's not repo. That's theft."

"If Netherhouse does the repo, it's not stealing. The firm is still in good standing, I take it?"

Netherhouse Liquidation. My company. Donny's company, once upon a time. "Since you left, yeah."

"Then my departure was for the better. As I've always said, the good Lord had his reasons."

The good Lord. As if Donny ever believed in anything but Donny. "What's the job?"

"It's interesting you mention my divestment in Netherhouse. Do you remember the Dimension repo?"

I froze. The car almost rolled backwards over me.

"Doctor Dimension is dead," I said.

"The world believes he's dead, yes."

My thigh muscles shook as I replanted my feet and once again slid the car into the street. "A bridge fell on him. That's been killing Augments since the dawn of time. Believe me—he's dead."

Donny kept information close to the vest. He never told you what he was after until he had his gnarled old hands wrapped around it. Ordinarily.

"I think the ring is in play."

Hitching the jet-car to the tow became more difficult.

"You turned Dimension's ring over to the Treasury Department. It's long gone."

"We executed the repossession paperwork. You know as well as I the ring was never properly recovered."

A desk lamp glowed on the second floor of the Elmore household.

I couldn't be sure it had been lit a moment before.

"Still. Dimension's ring was lost. You said it was lost."

"Nevertheless, this is why I need you. There's a place on the lake—"

"Stop."

Saying no to Donny was a tall order. I lived in a world of powerful beings, where women swallowed star systems whole and men birthed suns. But these giants—these near-gods—even they had trouble resisting the heavy drawl of my former partner.

"No," I said. "I'm sorry, but no."

He inserted a long, deliberate pause. "Fair enough. Figured I'd ask."

Another light came on inside Nietzsche's house, and then another. The place blazed with the angry white light of imminent discovery. "I wish I could, but you know how it is. Can't risk the business."

"It's not a problem. You don't owe me a thing."

I hooked the jet-car's front end to the metal lifts and ignored the stillborn sense of guilt Donny had implanted in me long ago. I pulled open the tow truck door and hopped into the seat. My hand rested on the key as Nietzsche's front door banged open. Nietzsche himself barged out, black-and-gold suit unzipped and folded over at the waist.

"You know," Donny said. "I do remember a time you'd have fought to take this gig. For the thrill. To pull one over on the big guys. Government. Augments. Fool them all, good sense be damned."

Nietzsche tore across the front lawn like a boulder rolling downhill.

"Sometimes," I said. "The practicalities win out."

Donny's final words were lost in the full-throated growl of the tow's engine. The tires scrabbled at the road as I lurched away from the curb. Nietzsche leapt at the truck and snatched at the mirror as I pulled away, shearing the polymer housing clean off the screws. He was still running when I lost sight of him in the rearview. He clutched the mirror in his meaty fist and hurled it as I spun around the bend. He almost hit me.

Close. Too close. My heart thundered in my chest and I thanked a number of gods both real and imaginary that I had gotten away clean. By the skin of my teeth.

The road flew by. Warm July air blasted through the cracked windows. I sped away from the suburbs and popped on the radio and scanned until I found something released before 1990. Golden Earring. "Radar Love."

I drove. I felt pretty good about myself. Twenty-five thousand dollars in recovery fees hung from the end of my tow, last month's rent and payroll covered, and another big repo added to Netherhouse's resume. Life was looking up.

Still.

Why had Donny called about Dimension?

Why now?

I squashed those thoughts. To hell with it. Donny was always trying to pull someone into his web of lies. Let him jerk someone else around.

I turned up the radio. Let the lyrics wash over me.

Gotta keep cool now, gotta take care.

God damn right.

CHAPTER TWO

Nine AM was early. Repo boom time fell between midnight and five, when augmented debtors were away fighting crime or tunneling under banks or just plain asleep. Luck was found during those in-between hours—the hour of the wolf—and was our best window to swipe the spare laser visor, the jet-car propped on blocks, or the bulletproof suit hung out to dry. Most days, I didn't roll home until six, and usually I was so keyed up I didn't nod off until ten. Then I'd sleep until five in the afternoon and start the whole circus over again. This schedule suited the business. But doctors? Doctors' hours weren't so flexible. And I had problems that couldn't keep. Namely, my daughter.

Jamie was seventeen. For a teenage girl dealing with divorced parents, she wasn't too bad. Attitudinal, to be sure, but she didn't hate me and didn't call her mother a bitch, and she concealed her underage drinking to the point I barely noticed. When she raided the liquor cabinet, she refused to pour water in the bottles to disguise her theft. I appreciated the honesty.

It was my week with her, the weeks getting fewer as she contemplated college. I treasured those days, and ordinarily I wouldn't waste them in a doctor's office. But Jamie had leukemia. Acute lymphocytic leukemia.

In the waiting room of the Cancer Center, I considered how frustrated Donny made me. In the grand scheme of things, Donny was nothing.

They let me walk back to the infusion room. Banks of padded chairs flanked both sides of the room, the place flooded with bright morning light. Nurses in blue scrubs circulated among the patients, the unfortunates a sampling of Austin's diversity and proof positive cancer held no prejudice. The patients barely noticed as I passed, their faces buried in paperbacks or television, or their eyes closed, lost in thought. Jamie sat on the end, wrapped around her iPad, a needle and tube running into the portacath below her collarbone. She wore a beige tracksuit and a short haircut, and there were bags under her eyes.

I sat in the lime green guest chair. I watched her read.

"How's this one?" I asked.

She swiped at the screen. Kept her head down. "Same as the last treatment. I won't know until tomorrow."

"I meant the book."

"Oh. Not bad. Main character is kind of a dick, though. He's preachy."

"Hate that."

"Yeah. Me too."

I folded my hands in my lap and studied her. "How do you feel?"

"The Thing is being a bitch." She'd named her tumor. We watched the Carpenter classic as often as we could. Popcorn. Candy. Lights out.

"It's weird and pissed off, huh?"

She grunted. She didn't bite on my quote. "I feel bloated." Swipe, swipe. "I need more sweatpants."

Last month it had been a private tutor to help raise her math scores. She was retaking her SATs.

"You look great, honey."

Her eyes flicked up, then returned to her screen. "How's Mak?"

"Good. Asleep, I assume. We don't keep banker's hours."

"You don't have to be here, you know."

"That's not what I said."

She shrugged. Tongued a sore blossoming in the corner of her mouth. The silence dragged.

"How's Larry?" I asked.

"Fine. He's writing a book about *The Cloud*, but then, who isn't?"

I nodded like I followed. Larry and I couldn't talk. We'd start with sports and inevitably he'd drift into computers and IP and I wouldn't know if he was talking about intellectual property or something else. Plus the whole *fucking my wife* thing. His wife. Whatever.

"I got an email from administration, plus some stellar white envelopes." Jamie took a deep breath. "Apparently, you missed a payment."

She'd fanned three envelopes on the bedside table. The corners of the envelopes looked sharp enough to poke out an eye.

"What about your mother's insurance? Charlie used to get everything covered, including her damn back massages."

Jamie reached up and rubbed a spot between her eyebrows. A gesture of mine—one I used when I wished all life's hassles would disappear. "Do I really have to get in the middle of this? Now?"

The bills. Money. My ex-wife Charlene—Charlie—worked for the State, and Larry wrote technical books on spec. I co-owned the augmented recovery firm Netherhouse Liquidation, but throughout the years, Mak and I had taken a survivor's pride in our lack of benefits. A normal doctor's visit was nearly unaffordable, and as for augmented treatments, those were right out. Lady Laser cost six figures easy, and that's before you factored in her incidentals. I was closer to buying the Taj Mahal. The good vibes from last night's repo faded.

It occurred to me—Donny hadn't said what his repo would pay.

"We'll figure it out," I said. "Don't worry."

"Yeah. That's what Mom said."

The conversation died. Jamie kept her nose in her book and I watched one of the shared televisions and tried to ignore a garlicky stink I associated with the cancer. There was a moment, an earth-tilting *I can't believe this is happening* moment where the reality of my daughter's condition hit me right between the ears. I saw her in the hospital at birth, two days in the NICU, her veins collapsing under a barrage of needles. I saw her the day we learned about the cancer, her face distorted in a silent scream.

My daughter. Never not sick.

But other images bullied their way into my head. Jamie, dragging herself to the Cancer Center treatment after treatment. Religiously attending school. Talking about water polo in the fall.

My daughter. Stubborn as all hell.

Still, I couldn't make myself linger. I told Jamie I'd see her outside and slunk back to the waiting room. She never looked up from her iPad. I glanced at a clock on my way out and noticed I'd only been in the infusion room for fifteen minutes.

The lobby felt oppressive. All walnut paneling and low-backed wicker chairs and sound-absorbing Berber carpet. Even the grandfather clock had the pendulum muffled. It was the kind of quiet that made me sweat. I fled outside so the Texas heat could remind me I was alive. But clouds boiled on the horizon. Turned the air from a cleansing fire into a simmering stew. Nevertheless, I figured I could endure. Jamie was fighting the cancer by killing her body. The least I could do was suffer a little heat.

And then I saw the woman in the car.

CHAPTER THREE

She was a lump in an ill-fitting suit waiting in an Oldsmobuick the color of a dead elephant. She pitched Swisher Sweets into the potholes. Treasury Agent Barbara Cahill. She appeared to be alone, but a fed with a radio was never wanting for company.

Barb had seen me—there was no use hiding. I approached the car and she smiled, revealing mismatched yellow teeth. Even sitting, she had swagger. She was a pain in the balls, but less uptight than most of her brethren. Fun to drink with, although I wasn't excited to see her in the daylight hours. But she punched a clock for the Treasury Department, and the Treasury Department regulated augment repo.

"This is bold," I said. "Even for you. Maybe consider boundaries?"

"Elbridge wants to see you." She raised her hands like I'd demanded her purse. "Don't shoot the messenger."

Government hassling was part of the gig. Had been in Donny's day. Was du jour in mine. "I'm on a personal matter. Can this wait?"

"You got a hot date? If her name is Destiny, it doesn't count." She cackled.

"Respectfully, Barb, you can fuck off. You need contracted repo, call someone else. Netherhouse doesn't do sanctions."

Barb cleared phlegm likely percolating since the eighties. "Who mentioned sanction? This isn't a government contract. You're a person of interest. Boss asked for Netherhouse quite specifically."

If she was a cartoon, the alcohol would have radiated off her in waves. She must have started on the Bushmills at sunup. I could be sympathetic to her reasons, but not when she harassed me within spitting distance of Jamie's chemo.

"What if I say no?"

"Temporary injunction. Boss pulls your paper and you can't do repo until a judge clears you. Three-week backlog on that."

I thought about three weeks without any work. And the resultant lack in pay.

I could still smell the garlicky stink of the Cancer Center.

"Where are we going?"

CHAPTER FOUR

Barb drove in a way best described as approximate. Approximately within her lane. Approximately within the speed limit. Her badge excused her disregard for traffic laws. It did not excuse her taste in music. She drove the car with the volume cranked all the way. Bob Seger. "Like a Rock."

"Seeing as you're violating my constitutional rights," I said, "the least you could do is play some good music."

"Quit your huffing and puffing." She chuckled and bumped a knob with her finger, changing the volume not one iota. "Constitutional rights. You're a riot."

I regretted not staying with Jamie. My daughter claimed she'd call a rideshare—they had augmented rickshaws and stilt-walkers now, if the suburban comfort of a Toyota Avalon wasn't your speed. My departure had left her unsurprised if not unconcerned.

Bleary-eyed, I stared out the window and watched the grey smear of rain move over the city. Man still endured the whims of Mother Nature. Manhattan's fleet of weather-control drones was constantly on the fritz. LA's had gone rogue. As for Austin, we lacked the financial wherewithal and the will. So, instead of scheduled sun, we got another summer rainstorm. It was probably for the best—the politicians never would have kept the project in the black. They'd have owed billions to some corporation or nation-state, and commission aside, I didn't relish the idea of attempting to repossess several thousand semi-sentient flying machines from the City of Austin.

Once the rain started, Barb turned down the radio. "How's the family?"

This, after ambushing me at my daughter's chemo treatment. "They're great."

"Still divorced?"

"Yeah. You?"

She grinned into the rear view. "No man can handle me."

The wipers dragged across the window.

"You hear from your dipshit ex-partner?" she asked.

Barb and Donny. Two cigarette butts floating at the bottom of the same tin can. They shared a love for whiskey and western music, and either hated one another or were secretly fucking. Maybe both. *Dipshit* and *shitstain* were commonly exchanged terms of endearment.

"Why would I hear from him? *Ex*-partner."

"I thought he was working again."

I rubbed my chin, covering my lips so she wouldn't see the twitch. "Not that I'm aware. Why—what did you hear?"

She shrugged. "You know Donny. Man loves to hear himself talk."

After this revelation, Barb fell quiet for a while. The scenery around us changed, seventies ranch-style homes replacing five-bedroom, four-baths. Barb scrutinized the surroundings as we drove through.

"Didn't you work a case back in here?" I asked.

"Ladykiller." Underneath the cashed-out veneer, the cop stirred. "Eighty-one and eighty-two. He hunted and killed Augments. Only women."

"You caught the guy, right?"

"Nothing that stuck. Although I know it was the husband of the first victim. He never did sit right with me. SOB claimed he could hear what *they* really thought of him. The women. Like he actually believed it, said it was an augment power. Pushed him off his rocker. Course, none of the good old boys listened."

"Didn't you complain? Light a fire under them?"

"I was the only woman in the department. They only involved me in the case to *talk emotions with the females.*" Her fingers tightened on the steering wheel. "Motherfuckers never gave me a lick of credit."

"Now they got you driving me around," I said. "To god only knows where. Like a chauffeur."

"The fix is in. I get a whiff of a lead, and they take the case away from me."

"Like this thing today, right?"

"I'm always on the outside. If they put me on the team, I could tell them—" She caught my overly interested face in her rearview. She sneered at me. "Nice try, Harwood. Nice try."

We didn't talk much after that.

Barb put us on the highway headed south, bumper-to-bumper traffic made worse by the storm. At the split, she took the upper deck and swung her government-issue sedan off the first exit at MLK. We spiraled toward Royal Memorial Stadium. Huge banks of lights hung overhead, dimmed. The wind had petered out, leaving sad flags wrapped around their poles. There was activity at ground level—cops in rain slickers directing traffic, guys in dark suits pulling over cars and turning aside pedestrians. Barb steered past the bustle and under the shadow of the stadium and halted before a series of chained steel barricades. She flashed her lights. Three hooded figures peeled out of the grey. One stopped at the barricade while the other two approached the car. I zipped down my window.

"Look, officer." I produced my best *concern for authority* voice. "Can you tell me what's going on?"

A human skull appeared. Vacant sockets turned my way, and a gap-toothed jaw unhinged to let loose a low hiss. A giant black fly passed through her bottom teeth. I smelled fertilizer and decay. The threshold of Hell.

Scythe. The living Death.

Scythe was an Augment in the employ of the Treasury Department and rumored to have the power to steal life. She moved slowly, but she moved with purpose. They say if she hadn't agreed to work for the government, Treasury would have killed her on the spot. If they could manage it. If she could die.

I leaned back and rolled up the window before she could suck my soul into her gaping maw. I turned to Barb for an explanation, but she had her own problems.

Barb's augmented escort was Donna Holmes. Donna worked freelance, and I'd seen her around. She could replicate herself to a maximum of four copies. One of her watched Barb, and another stood near the barricade. They exchanged looks with each other, and I wondered how they communicated. Did she have one brain or two? Did one copy control them, or were they no more coordinated than a flock of birds?

The copy at the barricade had a nose ring and a pistol. The other did not.

These were the kind of Augments Netherhouse stayed away from. Miles away from. Scythe was a Spectral, an Augment associated with the afterlife. There were supposedly a few Spectrals floating around Austin, like rumors. The flower girl at the Driskell Hotel. Antoinette, the leaping lover at Mount Bonnell. The translucent figure taking potshots at tourists around the Governor's Mansion. The government took these ghost stories seriously—exhibit any one of the prohibited powers, and you went on a permanent vacation to parts unknown. You didn't mess with the afterlife. Or invulnerability. Or phasing.

I pushed Donny and his baggage from my mind.

Finally, Barb stumbled upon the magic words. Donna—whichever copy was in charge—approved our passage. She waved us through, her twin unchaining the barricades and dragging them aside. Scythe also pulled away from the car, leaving a dusty contrail in her wake. I felt as if bony fingers had reached for my soul only to stop short at the last moment. I figured that was the point and probably why Scythe was on guard duty in the first place.

Scythe. The living Death. On guard duty.

We drove. As we passed the barricades, I glanced out the window and watched the drizzle cut out as if on a switch, and suddenly the dark stadium blazed to life. Huge overhead lights bathed the pavement in a diamond glow. More standing floods burned white-hot near the stadium entrance and at the edge of the field. The place was lit up like Christmas.

We cruised to the edge of the concession tunnel and jerked to a halt. I sat in the back and waited until Barb came around and opened the door. We walked into the busy tunnel, Treasury agents marching to and fro, none of them acknowledging our presence. The concession stands were shuttered and the restrooms blocked by folding tables covered in paperwork. Standing next to the closest table was a familiar face.

"Hey, Mak," Barb said. "You ready for the big leagues? Got a desk at Treasury where you might fit."

Makareta Black flipped through a file she probably wasn't supposed to have. She was hard to miss. She stood six foot two. Displayed a proud mat of tangled black hair. She had big cheekbones and no makeup and a very direct stare.

And the spider moko. Blue swirls carved into her chin.

"Somebody has to babysit the old man," she said. "He'd be lost without me."

She winked at me.

One of the passing agents nearly tripped over his shoes to ogle my partner. As I looked at Mak in her jeans and baggy Cowboys jersey and the heeled boots she didn't need, I tried to fathom the appeal. She was a good four inches taller than me. A bit broad in the shoulders. She had two left feet. How would we have danced?

Mak felt the same. She'd once compared me to grapefruit juice. Oddly colored and sour.

A pair of agents wheeled a cart laden with tripods and recording equipment up a ramp and onto the field. Another agent came down the ramp cradling glass jars full of black dirt.

"What the hell is going on?" Mak dropped the file back on the table. "You dragged us all the way out here. What's the fuss?"

Barb nodded at the ramp. "Up there," she said, like she'd explained everything.

Mak and I exchanged shrugs. We marched up the ramp, Barb

trailing in our wake. I smelled ozone and burning motor oil but didn't hear a drop of rain. Royal Memorial was open-air, not domed. Considering the weather, a layer of fine mist should have coated us from head to toe.

We stepped onto the field and saw the bus driven nose-down into the turf at the forty-five-yard line. Stabbed into the grass like a knife into green cream cheese.

I stared at Barb. She gave me that *fuck you* grin backed by thirty-plus years of looking at the world through a cop's eyes. "Still think you can talk your way out of this?"

I didn't. Think I could talk my way out of it.

God help me if I was right.

CHAPTER FIVE

The floor of Royal Memorial was a madhouse. Agents in blue-and-yellow raid jackets labeled TREASURY swarmed the field. A cluster of them assembled a scaffold under the bus's rear end, while others lugged oversized garbage bags. More folding tables were arranged beneath the bleachers, their surfaces littered with bagged eyeglasses and phones. A loudspeaker erected at the fifty droned a constant stream of numbers and names. The acrid burning smell was strong. They'd have to bleach the field just to eradicate the stench.

I took it all in. I didn't know what to say.

"Check it out." Mak aimed a finger at the sky. "They hired a Bird."

Augment shorthand appeared not long after the Augments themselves. Instead of describing Contrail as a device Augment with a belt powered by jets of concentrated hydrogen peroxide, Joe Taxpayer said *Bird*. And there were more nicknames. Gills, Speedsters, Spectrals. A litany of goofball monikers. Boiling the beautifully complex down to cutesy references you'd expect from a four-year-old.

I watched the Bird. He circled the field with his cape snapping in the wind. Behind him, the sky was dark coffee, a blank canvas devoid of stars. I remembered the drive into the stadium. The too-static background, the limp flags, the slightly mismatched sky. There was a reason we couldn't see the stadium lights from the highway.

"Faraday cloak," Mak said. "Never seen one this big before."

"The whole point of a Faraday cloak," Barb said from behind, "is that you don't see it."

Royal Memorial was one of the largest football stadiums in the world. The complex sat one hundred thousand and end-to-end ran nearly a quarter mile. Hiding the stadium was impossible, but augmented devices routinely performed the impossible, and a Faraday cloak was no exception. Woven of charged conducting material, the Faraday cloak protected as much as a typical Faraday cage, and more. Television signals and RFID tags couldn't broadcast through the curtain's electrical field. But unlike a Faraday cage, the Faraday cloak blocked external radiation and altered it. A specific pattern of charges could produce images on demand—say the image of a dark and empty football stadium. The curious and the augmented curious were thwarted—no gamma or X radiation penetrated the barrier. The Faraday cloak was the perfect tool for Treasury to throw a blanket over this accident. If that's what it was.

Barb pushed me between the shoulder blades, in the direction of the bus's nose. As we walked, she reached into her jacket pocket and found her cigars. She fumbled one between her fingers and lit it with casual disregard, her knuckles disappearing into the flame of her lighter. She projected the air of someone who had seen it all before.

"What is this?" I asked.

"You'll have to ask the man." Barb walked through a smoke cloud of her own making. "I just work here."

As we drew closer, I began to make out details. Oil and brake fluid dripping into the field, seeping through the turf's fibers and infill. The accordion doors hanging open. Along the sideline, civilians sat with heads in hands, bloodied polos and pantsuits sticking to sweaty skin. A young man poked at his phone and furrowed his brow. The front of his T-shirt was covered in arterial spray.

Farther down the line lay a couple of stretchers and white sheets. What the sheets covered wasn't large enough to be bodies. Not complete bodies, anyway.

Yellow police tape and a crowd of agents obscured the nose. Barb herded us in their direction. We were stopped, wanded, and patted down. After Barb was cleared, she ducked under the tape and beckoned for us to follow.

"You ever seen anything like this?" Mak asked.

She wanted me to say no, but I was becoming convinced that would be a lie.

I needed to get away.

I needed to call Donny.

We moved through a crowd of agents. Up close, we could see where bus met ground, and the trough was far too shallow for a normal crash. Grey earthen slurry covered the front of the bus and extended outward in a ragged circle for three or four feet. The harsh smell of burning metal flooded my nostrils, again mixed with an ozone-like crispness.

At the circle's edge knelt a man. I knew him.

Barb put a hand on my arm and squeezed. "Stay here and be quiet," she said.

Andrew Bradley Elbridge, State Treasury Secretary, squat with his back to us, drawing one long finger through the dirt. Words dribbled from the corner of his mouth and the nearby agents nodded, soaking in his wisdom. The top of Elbridge's head bobbed as he talked, the combed-over black hair so waxed, it looked plastic. He shook his head at something, then drew his hand through the dirt scribblings and wiped them away.

Elbridge was Sherlock Holmes inspecting cigar ash. *Elementary, my dear Watson.* He was a giant ass.

The State Treasurer didn't notice our arrival. Barb was forced to stand behind him and wait.

Inside the circle with Elbridge stood an Augment I didn't recognize, a young lady wearing a gold-and-glass eyepiece over her right eye. Part of her skull was shaved to expose flashing circuitry, behind which dangled a butter-colored ponytail. The costume she wore was slick, an almost liquid platinum with three discrete gold eyes sewn into the right shoulder. A leather bandolier crisscrossed her chest. She was likely a Modjob, an Augment built with government dollars or by a rogue defense contractor.

Elbridge was talking to her. At her.

"And this will help you identify the man? This…procedure?"

She mumbled a response.

"You better speak up if you expect me to hear."

"No, sir."

"Clarity," Mak muttered. "She's new."

Clarity knelt and put a hand to her chest. She pinched the bandolier between her thumb and forefinger and extracted an eyedropper from a slit in the leather. It was clear plastic, not much bigger than my thumbnail. She shook it vigorously, then twisted off the cap. She licked her lips and squinted up at us nervously.

"You're all safe. I mean, so far."

I couldn't see Elbridge's face, but I could tell he was irritated.

"Right," she said to herself. "Get going." She tipped the dropper upside down and squeezed. Three clear drops ploinked into the shallow ditch at her feet. The earth darkened. After a moment, Clarity capped the dropper, pinched the bandolier, and returned the augmented chemicals to their pouch.

"Everyone okay?" she asked.

"You haven't done anything yet," Elbridge said.

Clarity nodded, then took a deep breath and put her hands into the damp earth. She kneaded, counting silently. *One one thousand. Two one thousand.* She recited numbers until she reached seven then spread out the remains, casting the dirt like seeds.

The crowd of agents watched in silence.

Click. Click-click-click. The Augment twisted at her eyepiece, the many sections rotating opposite one another. As the sections rotated, they popped and clicked like a swarm of beetles. I shuddered.

The process continued for a while. Clarity stood and paced, things crunching under her boots. Bones? Old stadium tiles? Clarity remained unfazed. She passed us and I noticed she wore no cape—her shoulder blades stuck through the back of her costume.

"Girl needs a burger," Mak whispered in my ear.

"We can't take all day, young lady." Elbridge said. "Lest you want to practice with the football team."

A couple of Elbridge's cronies laughed. Barb was right in there chuckling.

"I'm sorry, Mr. Elbridge," Clarity said. "I'll try to go faster."

"Faster than this shouldn't be any challenge."

The girl nodded. Her eyebrows knit together and she continued to pace around the impact zone. She muttered to herself. "Change in water content changes the pressure, changes the gas-exchange." Two steps. "Twelve-hour period for the biochemical reaction." Three more steps.

She stopped. She bent to touch the ground. When she spoke, she was a different person. Confident.

"I've found a signature. There's at least one identifiable DNA structure."

Elbridge smiled his tax collector's smile. "Go on."

Barbara Cahill had a hack's feel for timing. She laughed before the punchline. She arrived at parties too soon and left when the hosts were bleary-eyed. And right as I was about to catch a critical piece of information, she interrupted Elbridge to tell him we had arrived.

Elbridge leveled a stare that would melt steel. "What in the hell are you talking about? You brought Netherhouse here?"

Everyone seemed to notice Mak and me at the same time. Clarity aimed her googly eye in our direction, and the nearby agents stepped away. Elbridge rose, his head angled for the Stetson I'd seen him wear but today was absent. He approached slowly, as if he didn't trust the ground we stood on.

"Hello, Andy," I said.

"Hardwood." He'd always mispronounced my name. The joke stale from the word go. He scratched behind his ear. "I don't know whether to laugh or to cry."

"I said hello."

"I heard you." Elbridge lifted his chin toward my partner. "How you doin', Makareta?"

"Just fine."

I could practically feel Mak ramping up her augment powers. Mak was a Natural. Born with augment ability. She could lower a man's inhibitions—drop his guard in a mild buzz sort of way. But she wasn't invisible. In a crowd full of Augments and paranoid Treasury agents, she'd never get away with bamboozling the Secretary. Nevertheless, she furrowed her brow. Dialed in her power and set it on a hair trigger.

In some ways, Naturals were the scariest, as you couldn't revoke their powers. Not easily.

"You said you wanted to talk to them," Barb said.

"At the office, I said. At the office." Elbridge frowned at us, at Clarity and the hole behind him. He shook his head. "Everybody clear out. I need to talk to Netherhouse."

Clarity attempted to leave. Elbridge put up a hand. "Not you, young lady."

"How about me?" Barb asked. "Where do you need me?"

"I need you doing anything useful. I don't know. Go check the perimeter."

Barb retreated with shoulders hunched. I wondered if I treated her as dismissively as Elbridge. Thirty years of service, only to be shooed away like a stray. Why would you endure it? What would it do to you if you did?

Once the agents departed, Elbridge removed his blazer, making a big show of smoothing the wool and laying it out flat on a square of unchewed turf next to the bus. This was typical Elbridge. He'd spend two minutes fussing with his wardrobe but not two seconds tending to the feelings of those in his employ. He had a cherub's features, a mouth that wanted to settle into a smile, even as he delivered grim news. But the good humor never took root behind his eyes. He used his trustworthy face and cowboy stance and record of law and order to get elected. Reelected. There was even talk he'd run for governor.

Elbridge pulled reading glasses from the pocket of his dress shirt. The shirt was chalk white, starched, and monogrammed on the cuffs. ABE. Andrew Bradley Elbridge.

Governor.

He unfolded the glasses and hooked them over his ears. He fumbled his phone from his pocket and broadly swiped at the screen until he found what he was after.

"Just after five this morning, two unidentified witnesses observed a Capital Metro bus behaving erratically. The bus missed its stop at Dean Keeton and San Jacinto and continued south, driving over several medians and nearly totaling a guard station. The bus then, and I quote, 'pulsed in place for approximately five seconds, after which it completely disappeared.'"

Elbridge waved his phone at the bus. Continued reading.

"Metro dispatch confirms they lost contact with a seven-line bus between five and five-thirty. Bus 9805 failed to respond to repeated radio calls, and subsequent buses failed to spot 9805 on that route or any other."

He stopped and stared at us. When we didn't react, he unhooked the glasses and waved them at Clarity. "Give them what you found, honey."

Clarity flared her nostrils, and I wanted her to fight back. Instead, she steadied her eyepiece and took a deep breath. "I can't be one hundred percent certain, but there are strong indications of phase technology at work."

My stomach flip-flopped. Augment phase technology was rare, and not a single natural Augment with the power was known to exist. The last appearance of anything resembling phase technology was fifteen years ago. I knew the date. It was the date of the Dimension repo.

"Strong indications?" Mak asked. "You're not positive?"

"Not one hundred percent. I can only read indications. Patterns in the chemical makeup and vapor results from post-incident breakdown."

"Wait one minute," Elbridge said. "An hour ago, you tell me it's phasing, and now it isn't? What kind of game are you running?"

I watched Clarity blanch under the stadium lights and the heat of Elbridge's glare. "My powers don't work that way, Mr. Elbridge. I only told you what I thought."

"I wasn't interested in your opinion. I was interested in results. Law enforcement isn't a profession of opinions."

Clarity withered.

"Get out of the hole." Elbridge jerked his thumb over his shoulder. "Matter of fact, get out of the stadium. Get out of my sight in the entirety. You wander into another one of my crime scenes and I'll have all your equipment impounded."

She came topside with color in her cheeks. She walked past me with some pride—her head held high, her back straight as a board. The effort was wasted on Elbridge. He looked at me and shook his head, like I shared his frustration.

"Kind of a dick move, Andy," Mak said.

Elbridge folded his glasses and slid them back into his breast pocket. "You don't understand how often this happens. These kids come down here and promise they can do the work, and then we get them where the rubber meets the road and they fold. Media loves these augment types, but nine times out of ten, they're all flash and no substance." He looked at Mak and did that thing where he appeared to smile. "Present company excluded, of course."

"Of course."

I raised a finger. "Is there a reason we're still here? Other than the conversation?"

"You're not supposed to be here at all. I ordered Barbara to question you, not give you a tour. But since that cow is out of the barn." He moved closer. He smelled like burnt coffee. "Where were you this morning?"

"At five? Sleeping."

"Anyone verify that? Your wife?"

He knew I was divorced.

"No."

"What about your kid? You got a daughter, don't you?"

Mak looked at me.

"She lives with her mother. I don't see her much."

"Ah. Well. That's too bad." Elbridge shook his head. "Kids are wonderful."

Jesus.

"I wonder, Hardwood, what your daughter thinks about the work you do. The lies you tell."

"Again with this?"

"I'm not talking about a single white lie." His lowered his brow, drill-sergeant-style. "But an entrenched history in your entire industry. Lies and bribery and theft."

I was uncomfortable, and it wasn't due to the lights beating down on me. "Those other firms aren't us. Netherhouse is clean."

Elbridge licked his lips. Considered. "How about you, Mak? Where were you?"

"At the gym." She pumped her arms up and down. "Working out."

"You have witnesses?"

"There's a guy in a blue tracksuit always checking out my ass. You could ask him."

"That's all right."

"I think he's straight. More than likely, he won't check out your ass."

Elbridge winced. "We'll confirm with the gym manager. Don't worry about it."

"Who's worried? My ass looks great."

The Secretary was not amused. He looked like he'd swallowed a bucket of piss. "You know, there's a marked lack of respect here. This incident—I like you guys for this."

I kicked at the earth. "For the hole?"

"We're standing in the middle of phase debris."

Mak walked the edge, peered down between her feet. "I hate to agree with Gayle, but it looks like your garden-variety hole."

Elbridge persisted. "Fifteen years ago, Netherhouse repoed Doctor Dimension's phasing ring. Augment device serial numbers were compared at the site and all sixteen digits of the ADSN matched. But before the ring could be collected by Treasury, Dimension broke loose from holding, and there was that shitstorm down by Lady Bird Lake and the ring was lost."

Mak shot me a look out the corner of her eye but I didn't

acknowledge it. Couldn't.

Elbridge continued.

"I wasn't there, but I remember reading about it. Hell of a thing, Netherhouse cornering Dimension where every government agency failed. I'd always wondered how you guys pulled the thing off him."

"I didn't." The words stuck in my throat. "My partner recovered the ring."

"Not me," added Mak. "Before my time."

"Your partner." Elbridge stuck his hands on his hips. "You hear from him?"

"Who?"

"Donny. When did you last talk to him?"

The phone in my pocket radiated guilt.

"He's my ex-partner. And it's been ten years, easy."

"We're pulling his phone records. We'll know if you're cooking up a lie."

"Now you're just badgering me."

Elbridge cocked his head. "You seem uncomfortable, son. The question bothering you?"

Pause. It felt like even Mak was waiting for me to answer. "If he calls, I don't answer. The partnership dissolved. Our relationship was purely professional. There was no reason to talk after."

"He still in the business?"

"No." I pictured the turf beneath me as the surface of a frozen pond. Full of cracks. "Not last I knew."

"The Donny I remember loved repo. Considered it legalized theft. He held a particular contempt for those in public service and delighted in tweaking our noses. No way he quit."

There was history there. Donny beat a Treasury rap a dozen years back, a case built by Elbridge.

"Not to be a pain"—Mak watched me like a hawk—"but what does all this have to do with Donny?"

It felt like she was asking me the question. Fortunately, Elbridge answered. He waved his hand at the bus jammed into the earth. "Who do you think is responsible for all this hoopla?"

I watched him. Elbridge trying to lawyer me, lead me where he wanted me to go. "You telling me Donny had a hand in all of this?"

"Didn't he?"

"What makes you think he could move a city bus?"

A dark something flashed in Elbridge's eyes. "Suppose Dimension's ring was never destroyed at all. Suppose Donny kept it."

Not so much as a blink disturbed my face. "That's nuts. You're grasping at straws."

Elbridge produced a genuine smile. He approached the line of tables and flipped through the plastic bags. He found the one he wanted and chucked it into my hands. Inside the bag was an old-style clamshell phone.

"We've already checked," Elbridge said. "The number's his."

You remember the Dimension repo?

I think the ring is in play.

A chill raced up my arms but I shrugged and flung the phone back at Elbridge. The cell hit his belly and fell to the ground, forcing him to stoop to retrieve it.

"Maybe he sold the phone," I said. "You're familiar with Donny and his schemes."

Mak played spectator. Her chin swung side to side like she was watching a tennis match.

"I do remember his schemes, now that you mention it," Elbridge said. "Which is why we put the new girl on forensics. Despite her chickenshit performance tonight, she comes recommended. Puerto Rico sent her. She worked Maria."

"Worked?"

"After. Recovery and identification of remains."

I stared blankly.

"DNA," Elbridge said.

I looked down at the turf. At the dirt on my pants and my shoes. The smudges on Elbridge's hands.

"Donny was on the bus," Elbridge said.

CHAPTER SIX

After Elbridge released us, Mak bought a breakfast sandwich. Egg McMuffin with an extra slice of ham. She gnawed on the toasted muffin and dribbled bits of egg between her legs. I nursed a lukewarm cup of coffee and dug fingernail grooves in the Styrofoam.

The clock threatened to turn eleven, and I hadn't slept in over twenty-four hours. Donny was dead. Dimension's ring was in play.

"We should have asked for a lawyer."

"Only lawyer that will return our calls is Sandoval." Mak wiped her mouth with her sleeve. "And he's disbarred."

"Suspended." I stared out the window of Mak's truck, watching the nine-to-fivers swarm like locusts. "He's appealing."

"Whatever."

Elbridge had made it clear he thought Netherhouse was involved. He'd told us he'd get warrants for our phones and our office and the same went for our two employees.

"Were you actually asleep at five?" Mak asked. "Those are working hours."

"Not exactly. I was doing paperwork on the Nietzsche recovery. I was too keyed up to sleep."

"Why did you lie?"

"What?"

"You were awake at five. Why lie about it?"

I sipped at my coffee. "Sometimes, lying is easier."

Mak ripped another bite from her McMuffin. Swallowed. "Seems like keeping all the lies straight would be harder."

I let the remark pass without comment.

"You never said much about the Dimension repo," Mak said

between bites. "Anything I should be made aware of?"

"Nope."

"Remarkable. One of the most famous, nay, infamous repossessions in history, and you have no additional insight?"

"I told you Netherhouse executed the repo. What else is there?"

"The ring, apparently. Elbridge seems to think your buddy Donny had it." Mak dug around for more McMuffin but found only scraps. She tossed the empty bag in my lap. "Maybe we lay low for a while, until Elbridge finds a jaywalker to harass. Or a really complex case of graffiti."

When I knocked the bag from my lap, a small receipt floated out. Five dollars and twenty cents. That price included my coffee, which Mak had to cover.

"We can't lay low," I said. "We need paying gigs."

"So we cut expenses."

I pictured envelopes. Three crisp white envelopes.

"We won't make payroll. What about Dru? And Patrick?"

"You don't want to hear my answer to the last question."

Desperation squeezed the base of my skull. "What if we get Elbridge off our backs?"

She chewed on my answer. "I'm not sure I like where this is headed. You said *paying gigs*. Treasury considers us suspects, not contractors. And Donny is a pile of dirt. How's he paying us? There's not enough left to bury in a box of mints."

Donny would have appreciated the line, had the dead body been anyone's other than his. But then, Donny never thought he would die. For that matter, neither did I.

He'd given me my first shot in the business. Taught me how to stand with titans and act as if I was the most powerful person in the room. He'd introduced me to whiskey and bullshit. There was no Netherhouse without Donny. At the same time, he'd used me. He constantly left me in the lurch. One time in Bastrop, he'd left me with an Augment who controlled bees. Another time, he sent me in blind after a guy who threw thermite and laughed it off afterwards as *a little bit of hazing*. I felt bad he was dead. But with his last act he'd left me in the lurch. Again.

"Maybe I owe him," I said.

Mak bit her lip and closed her eyes. "This isn't about Donny, and this isn't about Dru or Patrick. This is about you and whatever you're not telling me."

I shook my head like she was being unreasonable. Prayed she didn't ask me more questions.

She sighed and stuck her arm out the open window. She drummed her fingers along the side. Finally, she shook her head, started the engine, and drove toward the office.

"The ring?" she asked. "You ever see it?"

"Once." I kept my eyes on the traffic, the folks in cars and trucks and mobile fiberglass exoskeletons. "It's black. Tungsten. Looks like a thousand other rings nowadays."

"You see him use it?"

Him. Doctor Dimension.

"From afar. Never up close. Donny ran point on that repo."

Mak kept her truck in the slow lane, not shifting even when a gap presented itself. "You must have seen something. Read the file, even?"

I shrugged. Glanced behind us. "You know there's room to get out this lane."

Mak stayed put. "I've heard the stories. He could teleport a little bit. Pass through matter. They say he slipped a mobster out of Rikers back in eighty-five. Killed an informant stashed in an FBI safe house. Even triggered a quake just east of San Diego. Three point two on the Richter."

"Sure. He was a bad guy."

Mak chewed her lip and looked at me as if I was trying to sell her Amway. "You see the body? Down at Lady Bird Lake?"

"No. But a bridge fell on him. Believe me, he's dead."

The cars started to move, but Mak kept her eyes on me. "Be a real shame if he wasn't."

The world believes he's dead.

Mak drove us to the office.

CHAPTER SEVEN

Netherhouse Liquidation rented a small office in a drab one-story strip mall next to Planned Parenthood. Of all our neighbors, the PP folks had lasted the longest—our experiences were similar. When their offices were egged or a brick sailed through their front glass, we could all empathize and laugh. Netherhouse had endured the literal slings and arrows of angry debtors. Of course, when Lady Ember set fire to our sign out front, the Planned Parenthood folks weren't laughing quite as hard. We never did replace the sign.

Inside, the office aspired to the level of barely functional. A hodgepodge of furniture filled the room. Mismatched chairs and lopsided desks salvaged from a sixties-era warehouse. The yellowed base to a water cooler but no water tank. And a giant corkboard occupying half the back wall, stabbed full of augment repossessions both in progress and upcoming. The lifeblood of our business.

Dru Sessions manned the desk closest to the door. She toiled away on our singular decent computer—a five-year-old laptop that she owned. She was petite and short-haired and granted the office a little respectability. She'd appeared on our doorstep with a grab bag of skills—she could recover files from a scrubbed hard drive, she'd picked the lock on our supply closet during the technical portion of her interview, and she'd unearthed supposedly sealed juvenile court records. Mak said I'd done quite well on diversity, hiring the only Black skip tracer to walk through our door, although Mak also stated I'd lost all my credit the moment I'd hired the whiter-than-white Patrick Riddle.

Our skip tracer greeted us with a cheery good morning and kept her eyes glued to the screen. She drank black tea out of a clear plastic water bottle and radiated the same freshly scrubbed glow she had since day one. "Patrick is out on Joe Franks. The Swiss Cliff."

"Keep wanting to call that guy Swiss Miss." Mak settled behind her desk. "God, what a horrible name."

I ignored my chair and instead stood under the corkboard. The damn thing wasn't near full enough. The Treasury Department squeeze was coming at the worst time. They could pull our paper or apply pressure on our banking partners. Make our financial position significantly less liquid. This was untenable. Cancer wouldn't wait or negotiate new terms.

We needed more work. Better-quality work. My eyes hopped from job to job. "Get Patrick on December Warrior. The recovery pays twice as much."

"You sure?" Dru asked. "He made it sound like a ten-minute job."

"Patrick always makes it sound like a ten-minute job. Put him on December Warrior."

"You just bagged Nietzsche. That's a fat payday." Reservations lined Mak's face. "Why not let Patrick grind the small stuff?"

"I didn't think you were a fan of Patrick's."

"Never said I was."

"So, what do you want me to do? Can him?"

"Why are asking me this now?"

Mak and Jamie were close. Over the years, they'd engaged in water-gun battles and constructed elaborate LEGO castles. Mak fed Jamie snacks I'd specifically prohibited. Aside from blood family, Mak was the only person Jamie allowed at doctor's visits and chemo treatments.

"The Thing," I said finally.

Silence.

"Shit. Okay. Yeah, pull Patrick." Mak pushed back her thick curly hair. "This is why you're worried about Elbridge?"

Mostly. "Yes."

Only the smallest tilt of Dru's head alerted me to her eaves-dropping. "Are we going out of business?"

"Nobody's going out of business," I said.

"You might get furloughed," Mak offered. "After Treasury yanks our license."

Dru's eyes swelled into moons. She was engaged, supposed to marry her massage therapist fiancé in three months. Skip tracers and massage therapists didn't retire to estates in the Hamptons.

"Nobody is getting furloughed." I abandoned the board and sought the comforting solidity of my desk. My hands found the grooves in the flattop, the frustrated gouges and dings of repomen gone before. "Elbridge is always trying to pin shit on Netherhouse. The State goes through a process before they pull an augment repo license, and the first step is proving the firm broke the law. Treasury has a city bus stuck in the ground at Royal Memorial, and they need a scapegoat. Beyond that, they have diddly."

"A city bus?" Dru asked.

Like I told Mak—sometimes lying was easier.

"I've got a target for you," I said.

The words calmed Dru. Once she had an assignment, everything else faded away. "Sure. Who are we searching for?"

"I want you to find out where Donny's been."

To her credit, Dru's smile never wavered. She swiveled around and started typing. "Your old partner? Last name Spielman?"

"That's him. Check known associates. Past jobs." Mak stink-eyed me. "Don't spend a lot of time on it."

Dru began digging through our computerized records, although I wondered how successful she'd be. Many of the older cases weren't digitized. Donny hated computers and kept paper records like he was constructing a bird's nest. Filing cabinets jammed with paperwork used to line the office walls. I'd stuffed most of that nightmare into boxes and shuffled it offsite years ago.

Mak sat in her chair, shaking her head.

"What?" I asked.

"You should have told Elbridge everything," she said. "Right then and there."

Dru searched tweets and social postings. She called the big tele-coms, fishing for account and billing information. She trawled the internet for Donny under a dozen different names and aliases. She even concocted a fake dating profile, on the off chance Donny had a profile too. *You never know*, she said.

I downed my coffee and paced like a caged animal. I thought about the Dimension repo, closed these fifteen years. The case's spectral fingers had reached from the past to snatch Donny from the living. He'd been careful. Avoided computers and hardly talked on the phone. Yet someone more clever than my partner had come back at him, and they'd used the ring.

The players are bigger than I usually care to tangle with.

I sauntered over to Mak's desk, the thing covered in memorabilia from her time in Iraq. Expended shell casings and sheathed knives and inactive landmines. I sat on the corner, careful not to disturb the sole picture on her desk, a four-by-six of her kid Nathan. I waited her out.

"This ring of Dimension's," she said finally. "Did you steal it?"

"No."

"But Donny stole it."

It wasn't a question. "Maybe. The man had a different idea of right and wrong."

"Him stealing the ring—you weren't aware?"

I didn't want to lie. "He called me, you know."

"Really?" Mak rubbed her hand against her leg, considering, not acknowledging how I'd ducked her question. "When?"

"Last night, during the Nietzsche repo. He wanted to hire us."

She threw back her head and laughed, the kind of full-throated outburst that drew stares in crowded restaurants. "Okay. Sure. Why not?"

"I told him no."

"You told Donny no? You've never turned the man down in your life."

"Maybe I should have supplied a different answer."

Mak rolled her eyes. "Listen to you. *Maybe I should have supplied a different answer.*"

"I'm sorry. You're always asking for full disclosure. I'm telling you the truth."

"You tell me what you have to. That's not truth." She leaned into the arm of her chair. "You put us in a spot. We spill on this now, and at best—*at best*—we get suspended. And if we hide it, we're culpable. Accomplices after the fact, to whatever bullshit Donny was involved in."

"It's been fifteen years. I thought it was dead and buried."

Mak selected one of her knives. Flicked splinters off her desk with the point. "This is just about the money? For Jamie?"

Images of Donny standing over me, leering, an envelope in his outstretched hand.

"And to make it right. For us. For Donny."

"To fill the Donny-shaped hole in your heart?"

I picked up one of the dead mines. An M14 with the charge removed.

"If we do this," she said, "and I mean *if*—this is a favor for you. I'm not doing this for Donny. I know he never liked me."

I fiddled with the mine. "He was a little sexist."

"He was a full-blown misogynist. And an asshole."

"Well, he's dead now. You got his half of the business. And his comfy chair."

Mak stared.

"Fine," I said. "Call it a favor. Help me figure out what happened to Donny. I repay an old friend. You get us squared with the government and free to work paying gigs. Win-win. You owe me anyway. Remember Pedernales Falls? That time I pulled you out of the water?"

"I pulled you out of the water."

"You can't swim."

A caught-stealing smile creased her face. "Oh, yeah."

Dru typed quietly in the background, well accustomed to our banter.

"We find who put Donny in the dirt," Mak said. "Then we call

Treasury. This isn't a skip trace. This isn't a recovery. We give them their suspect, and we go back to business."

"I hear you." I tried to yank out the safety clip. Failed. Smiled at Mak lamely and set the M14 back on her desk. "You won't regret this."

Mak watched me like I was her oldest and most irresponsible child. "Get off my desk."

After an empty hour, we realized Dru wasn't about to stumble across Donny's trail. She did provide his last known address, and rather than hover, Mak and I made ourselves useful. We drove out to Donny's place. Maybe we'd find him sitting in a chair, blue eyes dancing, flipping the ring like an old weathered coin.

No worries, Gayle, my boy. No worries.

Right.

CHAPTER EIGHT

Donny lived in a mobile home park just north of downtown, out by what I still considered the old airport, although the airport had moved years prior. A host of strip malls had sprouted in its place, but otherwise the area hadn't gentrified much. Still the domain of lower-income apartments, taco shops, and nail salons. A place where I felt comfortable. Donny would have felt the same.

The park owner seemed surprised to see us. Treasury had paid the place a visit only hours before. *Marlboro Man doesn't usually get so many visitors*, he said, Donny's nicotine-and-a-grin personality lending itself to such caricatures. Turned out Donny was also behind on his rent. The owner moments away from bagging Donny's shit and turning the place over to someone else. He let us into Donny's trailer without so much as a request for ID.

The inside held few surprises. It was spartan. An unmade bed and two piles of clothes and a refrigerator preserving canned beer and bad eggs. The frying pan had a couple years' film caked to the inside. There was a small television parked on the carpeted floor, but it didn't work. There was a radio on the kitchen counter. No computer. The place might have been tossed, but who could tell.

Mak picked up a fistful of creased betting tickets. Parimutuel betting. Retema Park down in Selma.

"I thought Donny was retired," Mak said. "Shouldn't he be playing golf?"

"Not exactly his style."

I found the baked bean–encrusted bowl in the microwave. Mac found the sun-faded picture fallen down behind. I was in the photo, me and Donny. The two of us in flannel and denim, out in the hills somewhere, in the midst of a fishing trip that involved more drinking than fishing. A third man stood between us. He'd be easily mistaken as a refugee from one of those World's Strongest Man competitions. A large hammer leaned against his muscled thigh. He was smiling, a rarity for Augments in our presence.

"Shit," Mak said. "Not that guy."

I felt an ache. A pang for a moment that would never come again. "There was a time we were friendly."

"He was always two-faced."

"You didn't know him like I knew him."

"Sure. It was *A River Runs Through It.* Boys becoming men through the magical power of fishing."

I plucked the picture from between her fingers. "Friendly or otherwise, he'd know about Donny. Or know someone that would."

Donny's parents were dead. His drinking buddies croaked or alienated after Donny pulled repos on them. There were rumors of a brother in California, but Donny hardly mentioned him, and when he did, he ended the sentence with *asshole.* Other than me and booze, Donny had very few friends left.

I stared at the picture.

Other than me and booze.

Mak was unhappy but civil. She hated being used, hated being used for her powers even more. But the place we were headed only allowed Augments. Mak and her Natural status opened doors that would otherwise remain closed.

After we piled into Mak's truck, we sat headstone-still, staring at the dilapidated trailer through the dirty windshield.

"You ever think this could be you?" I asked.

Mak side-eyed me. "Maudlin thought."

"Augment repo is not a yellow brick road. There is not a castle at the end."

"Speak for yourself." She tilted her head in an attempt to catch my attention. "I'm worried about money too, you know. You've seen where I live. I can barely afford that shithole."

"Are you good on rent? Maybe I can help."

She laughed. "How are you going to help? You're broke as me."

"I was being nice."

"Which I appreciate." Things were normal between us, until they weren't. "You're telling the truth, right?"

The words hung in the air along with the odor of stale coffee and butt-worn leather.

"Donny never told me anything about the ring," I said. "Never."

Mak hesitated, then nodded. She cranked the engine and we headed south at a good clip with the radio loud and the conversation minimal.

Funny the lies I could make myself believe.

I was protecting the business.

I was a good person.

Donny never told me about the ring.

CHAPTER NINE

Big Fight was an augment bar. The bar sat alone in a parking lot off the highway. It resembled a government office—squat, square, and only enough windows to meet building code. There were a handful of improvements. A stylish smoke-colored paint had been slapped over the prison beige. Tint covered the glass. The gravel lot was paved over. And there was the sign. An enormous black-and-gold totem flashing BIG FIGHT. Situated as it was near the airport, the bar was popular with Natural and device-powered Augments the world over. It was barely three PM, and the only parking space we could find was on the grass.

As we approached the entrance, I noticed words written in shoe polish on the glass. *Owned and operated by Woody Chaikin, the famous Oak Hammer.* There was a time Woody knocked over banks under the criminal nom de plume of Slinger. His full history must not have fit on the window.

A line ran along the side of the building. Warm sound leaked through the cinderblock. Music and conversation.

"Your buddy is doing well," Mak said.

I chewed my lip. "Before he went Augments-only, he bitched about shipping rates and state inspection fees. Said he couldn't afford to keep Donny and me in free drinks."

Mak gave the interior hubbub a listen. "Sounds like lack of customers isn't a problem."

We queued up. I scanned the line, always on the lookout for an augmented debtor on our rolls. I saw Rainmaker in his yellow slicker. The Scream with her mouth capped behind a soundproof mask. A couple of other Augments I'd never seen. Some costumed, some plain-clothes. Most of them looked beat. Often, they worked day jobs—waitresses and electricians and bank tellers. They had to make ends meet. They had to pay for their expensive augmented toys.

We waited in line until we reached the front door. And there we were stopped.

Under the shade of a canvas awning, a tiny red creature sat cross-legged on a high barstool. Pointed ears stuck out from either side of his head, and his clawed feet alternately curled and extended. Fangs extruded over his upper lip. His prehensile tail wound from his ass down around the stool legs, twitching idly an inch or so above the pavement, like a cat batting a fly. The creature was completely naked and without visible sex organs. Calling him *him* was arbitrary. But I'd seen him before.

Needle-sharp eyes darted our way. He didn't move or speak.

I reached for the door. The red tail flew up and slapped me across the back of my hand.

"No can do, pal," the red creature said. "Read the sign."

He pointed a long-nailed finger at a laminated sign taped to the upholstered door. AUGMENTS ONLY.

"My partner isn't very bright." Mak moved closer to the little red devil. "He doesn't read too well."

"He does look dumb, that's for sure." The tail relaxed. "Why keep him?"

"Maybe I'm not too bright."

The red guy smiled and his blinding white teeth peaked like the Himalayas. "I don't think so."

Again I set a hand on the door handle. "I know the owner. This is all right."

Red guy stood on the stool, grunting with the effort. He burped, spat a little fire. His tail whipped back and forth but didn't strike.

"Nick Holiday." He extended his small hand. "And you are?"

Calluses covered his palm—it was like shaking sandpaper. "Gayle Harwood. This is Makareta Black. Woody knows us from way back."

"He knows lots of people from way back." Nick sniffed the air. "Makareta? You're a Natural."

Mak hooded her eyes. "Yeah. Neat trick. How'd you do that?"

Again the pearly-white grin. "I'm not Natural, if that's what you're after. Gained powers via an injection of my own special sauce. With the following side effects." He spun around slowly. "Not much of a downside, though. Keeps me employed."

I squinted at him. "You used to bounce over at Gadget."

"I remember that place. Real shithole."

"Yeah. You were bigger then."

The smile slipped. "Hey, man. Science is the hills, not the plains. Up and downs; you know what I'm saying?"

"You've found the Grand Canyon."

Nick's sharp talons scraped against the wood stool. "You know, Makareta, your friend has a big mouth."

"Call me Mak. And yes, he does." Mak squinted, a tiny crease lining her forehead. "If you let us in, he's out of your hair."

Nick's toenails stopped scratching. "The conversation is wearing thin."

"Woody isn't going to mind," Mak continued. "We're telling the truth. You can tell."

"Maybe." He sat down and crossed his legs. The blood pumped slowly through the veins crisscrossing his calves and thighs. Almost as if he was relaxing. Putting himself at ease.

Mak was using her power.

She'd never used her augment powers on me, but I'd heard the effects described. Drink three beers, then try to resist the temptations of a pretty lady or whatever your poison. And it didn't have to be sexual—I'd seen underpaid security guards walk off the job after Mak talked to them, nothing more than frustration in their eyes. I'd seen exhausted cops admit they just wanted to go home and sleep. I'd seen an Augment with balls of electricity in his hands confess he was tired of the game and then turn over his high-voltage gloves. Mak couldn't make these people do what she wanted. She made them do what they wanted.

Nick didn't blink. His eyes drifted over the parking lot, like he was looking for new customers to aggravate. Mak helped him remember we weren't his problem.

"We're not your problem," Mak said.

"Yeah." Nick rubbed his face. "Go on. I got work to do." He used his tail to yank open one of the large padded doors. "You and your dumbbell partner skedaddle."

Mak nodded. She placed a hand on his arm and paused one last time to drench him in power. As we walked away, Nick was already forgetting us.

There were days I wondered if my partner and I were truly equals.

CHAPTER TEN

Inside, Big Fight was almost classy. Hardwood floor. Naked Edison bulbs hanging from the ceiling. Red velvet curtains partitioning the space, making it seem bigger than it was. Framed photos of local celebrities adorned the walls, and I recognized some of the augmented musical acts—Empowered Armadillo, Wrath, Carter the Electric. Woody knew a lot of people. He'd even bagged photo ops with our last mayor and the city's youngest congresswoman. He had the congresswoman smiling. Everyone loved a redemption story.

The air smelled of whiskey and fried chicken, a mélange that made me hungry and long for home. It was a room crafted to have impact. Maybe augment-enhanced. Maybe damn good feng shui. Last time I was in Big Fight, peanut shells had littered the floor and it cost a quarter to use the pisser. The scene had changed. But the customers hadn't. Augments packed the joint. Augments on fire, Augments made of ice, Augments walking on stilts and Augments flying with butterfly wings. Most of them in shirts and jeans but plenty in sparkling gold or silver lamé. One Augment paraded around in full plate mail armor, and another pulsed inside amorphous green gas. An amber-colored man drank beer from within the protection of a robotic exoskeleton, and I saw an octopus swirling in a tank of oily black water.

"Never get used to it." Mak watched me watch them. "Do you?"

A greeter with a shrunken head and the body of a dancer glared at me as we showed our IDs. I smiled. Her tiny black-and-yellow eyes narrowed to slits.

"No," I told Mak. "No I don't."

Woody Chaikin worked the bar. He wasn't the Woody Chaikin

of old. He was still tall, and his tree-bark eyes were still sharp, but his stick-figure arms had wrists I could wrap my fingers around. A bald dome had replaced his once-proud mane. He wore a brown suit fitted for a man with a size fifty chest, and his jacket shoulders dropped halfway to his elbows. The only thing that fit was his bolo tie, an exclamation point on the man's once-striking appearance. The Oak Hammer had been a giant. This man was a husk. When his hammer had been repossessed, everything changed. Nonetheless, he knew a bible's worth about this town and the people in it. Everyone owed him.

Almost everyone.

We threaded through the crowd. Woody was polishing twenty feet of oak bartop with a black microfiber cloth. The rag looked so sleek, the devil could use it to wipe his ass. As we approached, he made eye contact but pretended he hadn't spotted us. Instead, he disappeared into the back before I could raise a hand in greeting.

Mak and I looked at each other and shrugged. We elbowed into a space and one of Woody's staff took our order. I selected a no-name gin with a thumbnail of tonic. Mak chose an American beer I could have mistaken for piss. We sipped our drinks and waited for the next thing to happen.

Two guys with electrodes on their skulls slid up next to me without comment. One of them ordered whisky while the other glared at me.

"You guys come here often?" Mak leaned into the bar. "Ever see Donny Spielman?"

Captain Hostile frowned and looked away. The other electrode guy asked the bartender if she could pour faster.

"I'm looking for Donny Spielman." Mak said the words louder this time. "He's in augment repo. Ever heard of him?"

More dark looks. A few additional heads turned our way. The bartender drew her mouth into a thin line.

"Nobody's heard of him? Guy probably repoed trinkets from half the Augments in here." Mak pointed at the blinking lights that danced around the electrode guys' wired skulls. "You get those on credit? Donny loves an Augment with a credit card bill."

Electrode guys looked at each other, grabbed their drinks, and melted into the crowd. They didn't leave a tip.

"Friendly place," Mak said.

The bartender didn't waste any time. She vanished into the back room, and not long after, Woody reappeared, black cloth in hand, Hollywood smile frozen in place. He strolled over.

"Nice vibe, Wood." I put my elbows on the bar. "What happened to the peanuts?"

"I prefer to leave the past in the past." He stuffed his luxury rag under his arm. "Surprised to see you here. Nick didn't announce you; otherwise, I'd have fixed Shirley Temples."

"Got some of your best house gin. I'm doing fine." I rolled my head around like his was the first bar I'd seen. "How's tricks? The giant sign out front says business is booming."

"You saw that?"

"Was I not supposed to? It's twenty feet high and blinks. Kind of hard to miss."

Woody fished a toothpick from his breast pocket and stuck it between his molars. "Not my idea, you know? Investors." The grin got less friendly. "So, what do you want?"

"We came for the company." I took a sip of flat tonic and well gin. "And the drinks, of course."

He found a glass to polish. "And?"

"Since you asked, I'm also wondering if you've seen Donny in here recently."

Woody smiled the way a guy does when he's got a splitting headache. "I've told you before. I run an Augments-only place now. You and Donny are no longer my target demographic."

He burnished the glass like a genie might pop out of the mouth.

"Target demographic?" Mak took a sip of her piss beer. "You read that on a PowerPoint slide? Subscribe to *Forbes*?"

Woody sighed. He positioned his extremely clean glass on a shelf. "You know, you haven't changed at all, darling."

"Thank you."

The shrunken-head woman approached Woody with a clipboard and some paperwork. She looked at me like I'd crawled out of her soup.

"You didn't really answer my question," I said.

"I'm sorry, Gayle. Was I not helpful?"

"Not especially. It's disappointing, considering all we've done for you."

Woody signed his name to the paperwork with a flourish. I could see the *W* from across the bar.

"Donny doesn't even drive anymore," he said. "I was picking him up, sometimes twice a week. You want helpful? Try being Donny's personal chauffeur."

Woody finished the paperwork and handed it back.

"I got tired of his bullshit. I had enough of Netherhouse."

Shrunken Head stomped off into the crowd. She snarled and flashed one tiny curved fang at me as she passed. Maybe a threat. Maybe a come-on.

I turned my attention back to Woody. "What's the matter? Rough day?"

"Lopsided arrangements tire me, is all."

Back in the day, Woody had fallen under the influence of Blue Sunday, a hypnotist covered in Russian tattoos. During the second of their two titanic engagements, Blue Sunday managed to lock eyes with the unalterable, salt-of-the-earth Oak Hammer. Woody quit the fight and dropped off the radar. He turned up eight months later. Rebranded. Realigned. He called himself Slinger and opened his bank-robbing spree by leaving two guards in a coma and a fourteen-year-old kid with a broken arm that never did heal. Almost a year went by with Woody hip-deep in crime. Augmented supergroups. Impractical secret hideouts. The whole nine yards. Eventually, he hit hard times and couldn't make ends meet. Austin Mutual wanted back payments on Woody's augmented hammer, not to mention relief from Treasury's pressure to seize the device. The bank contracted Netherhouse to collect.

On the day Netherhouse took Woody down, he'd bowed his proud head low. *Help me*, he'd said. *I'll do anything.*

We'd made a deal. The price to be named later, although everyone involved knew it meant favors to be played against the Augment community at large. Seemed better than the alternative, which was government sanction and jail. Once Netherhouse repoed the hammer, the bank—at our request—pushed back on Treasury. The bank had more pull than we expected. Woody Chaikin was detained briefly, then released on a technicality. Probation—time served plus community service. Depowered, but a free man.

The longer Woody tasted freedom, and the more Netherhouse leaned into him for favors, the less appealing the deal had seemed. Fishing trips became a thing of the past. As did free drinks and information on local Augments.

Another monument of hope ultimately crafted from shit.

I stirred my gin and tonic with a swizzle stick. "You hear what went down at Royal Memorial last night?"

"Couple of folks didn't arrive for their usual medicinal, if that's what you mean. Probably working the scene for Treasury. You coming down on a few folks because they took a job?"

"Wasn't judging. Just asking."

"You know my rule. I don't talk about my customers."

Mak dug out her wallet and put her elbows on the bar. She flopped open the wallet and cast a critical eye over Woody's clientele. "You got customers that can phase?"

"Phasing's illegal. I run a square bar."

"People trust you." She looked Woody in the eye. "You've got a friendly face. Everyone talks to their bartender."

"I'm trusted in the community because I'm not an informer. Not everyone is as loyal."

Mak flipped the wallet closed. Raised her eyebrows. "What's that supposed to mean?"

"Don't get ruffled." He took an order slip from a waitress, looked it over, then pulled strawberry schnapps and lime juice from the bar.

"Like the man said. I'm not judging."

I sighed. Spun my glass between my hands.

"Since we're just talking," Mak said. "What do you think Nether-house does? An augment device bought on credit is just that. Credit. From a bank. Anything less than paying the loan is theft."

Woody mixed the schnapps, lime juice, and some shaved ice into a blender. "You guys are going to do what you're going to do. Like you always have."

Mak rubbed her index finger and thumb together. "Tiny violins, Wood. Tiny violins."

Woody flipped on the blender. "I'm going to let you two finish your drinks," he said. "But then you'll leave. Before I have Nick throw you out."

"Throw us out?" Ice banged against my teeth as I threw back my drink. "Used to be you looked out for your friends."

"Friends?" Woody shut off the blender. Slow poured the drink into a glass. "Interesting."

"Seemed friendly, all those years ago."

He paused. A bit of strawberry schnapps fell on the immaculate bar. "That again?"

"You feel I'm harping on something, by all means let me know."

He wiped the strawberry blob from the bar with a slow sweep of his finger. Flicked the castoff onto the floor.

"You're not the bad guy anymore, Wood," I said. "You're not Slinger."

He rubbed the blob into the floor with the tip of his boot. "Gayle?"

"Yeah?"

"You didn't save me."

The gin soured in my stomach.

"Matter of fact," he continued, "you drag me back to the bad times, with every visit. You never let me forget. Ride me like a damn horse and screw me like an augmented whore. In a word, Gayle, you're a user."

He swirled the strawberry mixture in its glass.

"Calling us friends is a real fucking stretch."

He plunked an umbrella into the drink and delivered it to a waitress. Then he turned to face me. "I changed my mind. Mak can come back any time she wants. She's an Augment." He nodded toward the front. "You can get the hell out."

Mak and I exchanged a look. She shrugged and hopped off her stool. Then, in a move so casual I almost missed it, she pushed her beer across the bar. The bottle toppled over the edge and shattered on the floor. Woody jumped but not fast enough. Beer foam and glass splashed against his slacks.

"Thanks, Woodrow, but I like drinking with Gayle. And I'd hate for you to have to make any exceptions."

Woody preserved one exception to his no-Augment policy. Himself. The terms of his probation prohibited him from holding so much as an augmented toothpick.

Leaving Woody to dab at his ruined pants, we walked away from the bar. I felt the torpedo looks of the augmented customers. As we filed past their hostile stares, Mak whistled "The Imperial March" from *Star Wars*.

"That was fun," she said between bars.

"Woody seem keyed up to you?"

"Keyed up? He was downright hostile. Usually, he at least fakes civility."

"What's changed?"

Mak's eyes roamed the bar. She lingered on the velvet curtains and hardwood floor. "New money?"

Not my idea, you know? Investors.

"From where, I wonder?"

"My bet—nowhere good."

I glanced at Woody doing his shtick behind the bar. He was pretending not to watch me.

"I don't know. Maybe the Oak Hammer is finally tired of paying his debt."

Mak rolled her shoulders, hugged herself. "Let's get out of here.

I'm an Augment, and this place gives *me* the heebie-jeebies. Too many of us in one place."

"Heebie-jeebies? You sound like my grandmother."

"Screw you. How old are you now? Fifty-five? Sixty?"

Suddenly, Nick Holiday appeared out of the crowd. He wore a look politely described as cross. He planted himself in front of Mak.

"What the fuck, lady? I don't appreciate being played."

She stopped and threw up her hands, as if to say *What did I do?* The gesture failed to mollify Nick. He launched into a tirade about augment abuse and what he usually did to people who crossed him, female or no.

I shook my head. Best to let my partner handle Nick. She'd talked her way into Big Fight; she could talk her way out.

I pushed open the big front doors and walked out into the cooling afternoon. Outside, the sky was clouded again. Dark. Heated Austin air pushed the color out of the horizon. It was the last gasp of the day. Or the calm before the storm.

I heard a growl. Felt the approaching rumble. Looked behind me and saw a beast.

Desert-sand camo. Meteorite tires. More armor than Fort Knox.

The beast hurtled through the parking lot.

The Humvee came straight at me.

CHAPTER ELEVEN

The Humvee skidded and did a ninety-degree into the entrance canopy. The vehicle tore through the steel support poles like a rhino through gauze. Canvas exploded and sheared metal flew through the air. Augments fled, streaming back into the bar or out into the parking lot. Tinted windows plowed toward me like the dark eyes of an angry god. I tripped over the fallen barstool and landed on my ass as my brain screamed at me to get up, to get on my feet, to run. But the gears in my brain locked.

The Humvee door opened, the bolts in the armor flying at my face. I felt a dull pain like a ballpeen hammer rapping against my forehead. When I put my hand to my face, I felt blood.

I was yanked to my feet. A gas mask swam into view, the twin eyepieces bugged out like an alien. A side-mounted filtering canister swung back and forth as the stranger frisked me with cool professionalism.

"You're clean," he said.

Gas Mask punched me in the throat.

The sucker punch knocked me to my knees. My eyes watered and I vomited half a gin and tonic and the milky remains of two cups of coffee. The stuff burned coming up.

Scarred knuckles wrenched me to my feet. A wiry arm pinned me against one of the remaining support poles. The man throttling me was dressed in camo pants and a tan shirt and smelled of mothballs. He put a gun to my temple as I struggled for air.

"You the one asking about the ring?"

The words came out muffled. He pressed his arm into my

esophagus and repeated the question. "You the one asking about the ring?"

I gargled a non-answer. Behind my attacker I saw another masked man exit the truck. Same attire. Bigger. He had a shotgun that he swept over the few Augments still rubbernecking.

Gas Mask lightened the pressure a fraction. "What's your answer?"

I found enough air for a response.

"Go to hell," I said.

He threw me to the ground. Got down on one knee and popped me on the forehead with the butt of his gun. My vision blurred in one eye as blood ran across the pupil.

"You listening now, smartass?"

A nod. Anything more hurt too much.

"We know about the money."

That hurt. More than his arm in my windpipe.

"We know about the money, so you stay away from Dimension's ring. You see so much as a wedding band, you run the other way, you got that?"

I opened my mouth. Vomit and drool spilled out. Gas Mask waited while I puked, and when I finished, he knelt and wrenched my head around so he could look me in the eye. "I'm not convinced you got the message."

He put the gun to my temple. Pressed until I thought my skull would cave in.

And then an airplane hit him. Or a safe. Or an anvil. It was big.

Darkness. Blood spilled behind my ears and down my neck, and it felt cold.

There was a roar, like a lion or a T. rex. Guttural and primal. Close.

Something big and hairy stormed overhead, and then everything went black.

CHAPTER TWELVE

As a kid, I never dreamt of getting beat up for a living.

My first job was at the corner grocery. I bagged white bread and white zin and fat bottles of white pills. Whatever the blue-hairs living in our lower-middle-class neighborhood wanted. That job drained the life out of me, and fast, so I quit. My parents busted a gasket and acted like I'd taken a shit on the porch, but I moved out and took whatever work I could find. I flipped real estate for a while. Played at day trader before the market tanked. And eventually, I found good, decent work. I delivered packages. Small packages, not much bigger than a toaster, wrapped in butcher-block paper. No names or addresses written on the outside. I was told an address. I dropped the package at that address. I got paid. And then I did my best to forget everything.

Ask me no questions and I'll tell you no lies. The perfect job. Until the truth became too much to bear.

He wore Dockers and a green polo and he stood six foot five. He called himself Tech and he needed me to deliver a package. He was the first Augment I'd seen up close. A great silver watch sat on his wrist, names and numbers flying by like a stock ticker. Social security numbers, he bragged. Bank accounts. Alarm codes. The watch had access to every government database in existence, he said. Almost.

I'd come recommended. Like a cola or new kind of deodorant. I didn't like Tech, but the money was big, and Charlie and I wanted to get married. At the time, I found it hard to say no.

The lure set, I delivered the package. A twelve-story office building full of clockwork people. The place reminded me of school, fresh faces charging in and out of tiny rooms every sixty minutes. Lemmings. I left the package with some suit in a room full of computers. I couldn't escape the place fast enough.

The computer room exploded ten minutes after I delivered the package. The suit almost lost an arm. The computers fried. The company never recovered.

Afterwards, I met Tech at the mall. He ordered at Orange Julius. He left his watch face unlocked, social security numbers and sexual orientations flying by on the display. The cash sat just inches from my fingers. He'd thrown out stacks of banded bills, maybe twice what he'd promised to pay.

My fingers on a crisp one-hundred-dollar bill, I pictured the moment of the explosion.

Heat. Licking flames. Maybe a daycare in the basement.

I asked Tech why, if he had access to every database, he needed a bomb. He looked down his nose at me, the way you can when augmented and standing six foot five.

It's about value, he said. The office workers had access to the same information as Tech. And that couldn't be.

People jumping out windows. An old man trampled when he fell on the stairs. A mother who might never regain the hearing in her left ear, and counted herself lucky.

I told Tech to go.

"I don't need your blood money," I said.

He took his money and left.

Lesson learned, I moved on. Don't trust Augments. They lie, cheat, and steal. I promised myself I'd work in a business that steered clear of their machinations.

The great irony—I fell hip-deep into augment affairs and found myself corrupted by a man without so much as an augmented toothbrush. Good old Donny blue eyes, everybody's favorite repoman.

I never dreamt of getting beat up for a living. But since I'd met Donny, it happened all the time. These two jerk-offs in gas masks were just the latest to dole out the punishment.

CHAPTER THIRTEEN

Bigfoot clomped through my head in high heels. Dull pain thumped against my skull and threatened to push my eyes out of their sockets. My head felt somewhere south of migraine territory and it hurt to swallow. But I was alive.

I sat on the bumper of an ambulance parked well away from the shattered front porch of Big Fight. Butterfly tape covered the wound on my head, and a couple of ibuprofen sat in the palm of my hand. Despite the attack, the place was still busy. Austin PD patrolled the scene, talking to uncomfortable witnesses and checking their watches. Treasury swooped in on most cases—they had jurisdiction over almost any augment case they wanted—but somehow, these poor uniformed bastards had received the call to clean up the mess. I'd have felt sorry for them if I wasn't in so much pain.

Mak squatted on her heels. She lifted my chin, checked out my eyes. "Pussy," she said.

"Where were you?" I croaked. "I had them distracted."

Her smile drained away. "You're lucky to be alive."

"I got hit by a truck, punched in the throat, and pistol-whipped. I'm goddamn blessed."

PD had questioned me briefly. My answers hadn't satisfied them. *I saw a gas mask. I saw a gun. I saw a big truck.* I'd skipped the bit about Dimension—his name had come up far too much as it was. It went without saying that I didn't mention the money.

Back when the ring disappeared, there was talk someone knew where it was. Maybe Donny. Maybe me. But the theory never played out. If Netherhouse had stolen the ring, where had it gone? Surely, we'd have sold it. Surely, there'd be a new Augment with silver spandex and a cleft chin. Not many people knew the answers. I knew a bit. Donny knew a bit more. Beyond that, things got murky. Maybe the bruisers in masks had the ring, although why they'd opted for old-school intimidation instead of phasing me into mush was an open question. Sadly, my masked friends weren't around to ask. They'd split after I'd blacked out. Scared off by my mysterious benefactor.

I inspected my arms and legs and wiggled my fingers. My head pounded. My throat ached. I remembered an avalanche of noise and muscle. "Did the cops bring a Heavy? I feel like a punching bag."

"No." Mak pulled me off the bumper. "First responders said you have a mild concussion and you should check yourself into a hospital. You'll be fine unless your liver quits on you."

"You're a ray of sunshine." I popped my neck. "Who do I thank?"

She squirmed like I'd proposed. "What do you remember?"

"Something big. Like a shark shot out of a cannon." I remembered the hair. "Or a grizzly bear."

"I don't think she'd find either comparison favorable."

"She?" I looked around but didn't see anyone I knew. Augments and cops and gawkers. Nobody big and hairy and female and…

Shit.

"Skylark?" I asked.

Mak nodded. "Skylark."

Skylark was Ellen Clovis's driver. Ellen Clovis ran Texas Recovery, the largest augment repo firm in the South, if not the country. Our competition, and not a rivalry one would classify as friendly. If Skylark was lurking, that meant Ellen was lurking, which was the last thing I wanted. I pictured my hollowed-out daughter showing me bills she knew I couldn't pay. That I certainly couldn't pay if my business was hobbled.

Treasury. Masked Augments. Ellen Clovis. Too many circling wolves.

Not all of them wolves. Skylark was half-gorilla.

Mak escorted me to her truck, keeping a wary eye on the police.

"We're attracting quite a bit of attention. Ellen Clovis isn't Jessica Fletcher. She's not out here solving mysteries on a lark."

"I don't give a shit what Ellen is doing."

Mak raised an eyebrow but didn't say anything. She approached the passenger door and I thought she was going to open it for me. She didn't.

I opened my own door and settled into my seat. I took a couple of breaths. "For all we know, Skylark was here on her own. She probably thought it would look good, pulling my ass out of the fire."

"She did look good. She flung that guy with the mask a dozen yards." Mak smirked. "Made him look like a rag doll."

I swallowed. My throat burned like I'd chugged bleach. "He was considerably stronger than that."

"And what about your friends with the gas masks?" She produced her keys but didn't put them in the ignition. "They just here for a beer?"

We know about the money. "I don't know. They didn't say anything."

Mak made a noise. She jammed the keys into the ignition and started the truck.

She paused.

"What about the ring?"

"What about it?"

She looked at me like my fly was open. "Aren't you afraid of it?"

I'd barely seen the action that day at Lady Bird Lake. I'd never encountered Dimension before Netherhouse seized the ring. But I'd heard stories. One in particular stuck with me. The whacked mafia informant—it's not like Dimension shot the guy in the head. Dimension didn't use guns, not after he left petty crime behind. According to testimony by the FBI agent—the one who survived—Dimension reached into the informant's chest, squeezed, and pulled out his heart. Then he walked out. Right through the wall.

Dimension had killed three other FBI agents first. He didn't bother to remove their hearts, just stuck his phased hand through their skulls.

"I'm afraid we'll run out of time," I said to Mak. "That's all."

Mak drummed her fingers on the steering wheel. She didn't seem convinced. "What next, then?"

"We wait on Dru," I said. "Check in tomorrow, see what she's found."

My partner watched the cars stack up on the highway.

"I gotta relieve my mom," she said. "You coming along or what?"

I considered staying at Big Fight. Waiting for the next truckload of goons or troop of augmented monkeys to come beat the secrets out of me. I thought about Donny and money. I thought about Jamie.

Mak had a kid too.

"Let's go see the family. They love me."

That finally got a laugh. "Sure." Mak drove out of the parking lot and into the fat of Austin's rush hour. "You're like the son my mother never had."

CHAPTER FOURTEEN

Aroha Black was a party in a floral-print dress. Squat. Tufts of hair sprouting from the sides of her head like horns. Laugh lines on her face but no telling how they formed because all she graced me with was cold judgment. Mak's mother had always assumed I'd cheated on my ex-wife Charlene, and made sure to tell anyone who would listen. She hated that Mak and I were partners. Two years had passed since we'd signed the papers. Aroha still went on about it.

We pulled into Mak's apartment complex and parked. Aroha waited in the lot, holding Mak's son Nate by the hand. He was seven. He thought his mom was the strongest and smartest person in the world.

As I approached, Aroha kept her eyes trained on me. She didn't say hello.

"Ms. Black." I stuck out a hand. "How are you?"

Aroha frowned. "Why did Makareta have to leave Nate so early this morning? Was this due to your incessant text messaging?"

"That wasn't me."

She pulled Nate closer, as if I might snatch him. "Phones are for talking, not typing."

"Whatever you say, Ms. Black."

"Don't humor me."

Mak watched the exchange from afar. She sighed and rubbed one of her shoulders.

"Hey, Mom."

"Makareta."

Nate peeked out at me shyly from beneath the shield of Aroha's arm. He was tall for his age, coming up to his grandmother's shoulder. Despite potentially being the shortest member of the family, Aroha still inspired the most fear.

"If you came for something of mine," Aroha said, "I would shoot you."

She said this unprompted. Much like my parents, Aroha Black considered repo akin to stealing.

Mak came in closer and gave her mom a one-armed hug. She tousled Nate's hair. "I'm taking him for tacos and a movie. You want to tag along?"

Her mom scowled. "No."

"Suit yourself. Mind if I drop him at your place tomorrow?"

Aroha grunted. She didn't say yes. Instead, she lifted Nate's chin and patted his cheeks. She told him to be good. Then she waddled off to find her Mustang. I tried to make eye contact, to crack wise, but she wouldn't meet my gaze.

Mak told Nate to stay with the truck and then followed her departing mother. She squared her shoulders like she was marching into a firing squad. I wondered what kind of relationship they'd have if she didn't need her mom for babysitting.

Nate shuffled over to the truck and kicked one of the oversized tires. He wanted to ask where Mak and I had been. My partner never told her son about our cases.

"You don't have to stay," he said.

"I can't leave. That would be rude."

"Mom says you're rude sometimes."

Nonplussed, I turned my attention to Mak and her mom.

Aroha hadn't stopped to talk. Instead, she'd wedged into the front seat of her Mustang. She'd started the car and waited for her daughter to move aside. She stared coolly out the windshield as if she was pondering life's great mystery. Of course, Mak wasn't moving. She waited with her arms folded and stood behind the car until her mom rolled down the driver's-side window. Mak's mess of tangled hair blew in the wind as they talked, and she constantly pulled it from her face. Underneath the rippling black cloud I could see the creases in her forehead. She and Aroha were arguing.

Her mom shook her head. A short angry twitch, and then another. A statement punctuated by a finger in my direction. Then the window zipped up and the car jerked into reverse. The conversation was over. Mak walked back, her chin on her chest. She stood next to Nate and watched her mother peel out of the parking lot.

"I get the impression your mother doesn't like me," I said.

"She doesn't."

Mak banged her keys against one leg. She worried the bottom of her lip.

"You okay?"

"You ever try to use logic and reason on your mother?"

"Once. But only after she was dead."

Nothing. Not even a blink. I could have been talking to the nearest tree.

"My mother was a teacher," I said. "She taught history and science and math. She held an array of facts at her disposal. I can't say she ever used a one of them to win an argument."

Mak's eyes crinkled, and she flicked hair from her face. She was pissed I was making it difficult for her to stay pissed.

"She won't let me bring Nate to her place." With a free hand she tugged her only child closer. "It would be as if she approved of the situation."

I assumed *the situation* meant partnering with me. I said nothing.

"She can't commit to staying here every day," Mak said.

"Maybe I can help."

She looked at me as if I'd begun barking. "Are you running a daycare on the side?"

"Jamie can watch her. The house is close. She has her license. We'll have to work it around her chemo appointments, but Jamie likes kids. She loves Nate. Hell, she'd pay you."

"I can't. She's sick."

"Don't let her hear that. She'll want this. She doesn't want the cancer to define her."

"Charlie won't have a problem with it?"

"Me she can say no to. Once I make it clear this favor is for you, you're golden. You she still likes. For some reason."

"The sun shines out my ass."

"Please. I've already been assaulted today."

Mak laughed. "Thank you."

Guilt ate away at my stomach lining. She thought I was her hero. "Don't mention it."

The sun dipped lower on the horizon. Mak hugged Nate tight. Smoothed his hair. After a few minutes, she told him to get his butt inside. She watched him as he ran, proud and concerned. She didn't turn back to me until she heard the deadbolt slam home. She looked every bit the apprehensive mother.

"What if someone big is looking for the ring? And I don't mean Elbridge. Dimension worked in that augment supergroup for a while. Any one of them might come sniffing."

The League of Six. An augment criminal organization and one of the few to go public. Dimension, Arsenic Insanity, and a rotating cast of characters. They fell apart just before Dimension failed to bench-press a bridge and died.

"This doesn't have to be super-criminals," I said. "This could be normal schmoes. Imagine Donny did steal the ring. He'd need help. A partner. No way he unloaded a dangerous augmented device all by himself."

"Yeah." Mak raised an eyebrow at me. "That's what I'd been thinking."

"Screw you."

Cars filed in and out of the parking lot. Normal people going about their lives. I hadn't seen normal since I started working for Donny.

I almost told her what Gas Mask said. Almost unburdened my soul of the lie and offered the truth we could investigate together. I don't know if I really would have done it. But my phone buzzed and sent my world off the rails. It was Charlie.

"I'm reminding you about dinner," she said, without preamble. "You don't have to dress nice, but you should be on time."

Each individual word pushed one of my buttons, but the sentences strung together stopped me cold. Dinner meant dinner with Jamie. Jamie and Charlie and Larry.

My head began to throb.

I should have thrown myself under the Humvee.

CHAPTER FIFTEEN

Charlie had suggested a fish place for dinner. She knew I hated seafood. I'd listened to her reasons and tried to keep an open mind. *Jamie knows the sous chef.* Sous chef. As if we could afford a place with a sous chef.

We'd made a habit of eating together after Jamie's chemo treatments. Me, Charlie, Jamie, and Larry. The complicated math of four to a table and me not wanting to sit by two of the guests. During the first meal, I'd allowed myself to get righteously drunk, and the fallout had taken weeks for my lawyer to settle. Had Jamie been any younger, I'd have lost visitation. As it was, I had to use the cancer against Charlene.

The seafood place had a kid's burger. I ordered it dry and said no thanks to the drink menu. Larry ordered a fish I'd never heard of, Charlie got the salmon, and Jamie picked a salad at random. When I asked Jamie if she felt okay, she stared at me through bagged eyes. The waiter left us bread and water, and then fled as fast as he could.

We tried chitchat. We covered the weather and the Spurs. We speculated as to how much the University would spend on improvements to the stadium. Maybe it was mention of the stadium that threw me off. Too many visions of a bus jabbed into the artificial turf. Whatever the reason, I wasn't ready for my ex-wife's follow-up. She dropped the line on me just as the waiter delivered Jamie's salad.

"Someone from the Cancer Center called for you."

Charlie despised when people called her home looking for me. Like I still had a flag planted in the bedroom. *I claim this boudoir in the name of Gayle.*

"They called the house?"

Charlie tore a thin strip from the communal loaf of sourdough. "That's what I said."

I waited for her to finish chewing.

"She asked for you by name," Charlie said. "She said, '*Is Gayle there?*'"

Silence. I didn't know what to do with my hands, so I kept them tented in front of my teeth.

"Getting friendly over there at the Center," Larry said, "huh, Gayle?"

Larry thought he was cute. He used a knife and fork to cut some bread for himself, as if Charlie had germs he didn't want to catch. I was tempted to spit in the basket.

"I could have dropped something at the last visit. One of my business cards, maybe."

"You gave some woman a card at my chemo session?" Jamie picked a soggy green tomato from her salad and held it in front of her like a fly's wing. "Wow, Dad."

"I didn't give anyone anything."

Larry rolled his tongue into his cheek and swallowed a grin. Had we been alone, the innuendo would have been thick.

Charlie let the silence drag. Her usual way to make a point. She tore off another strip of bread but didn't eat it.

"Do you want to know why she called?" she asked.

"Sure. Why don't you tell me?"

"First, she asked if you were at home, and I said no, you'd long since left. Over ten years I've been paying the mortgage, and somehow my house is still your home."

Jamie paused with a piece of lettuce hanging limply from her fork. "Mom."

I put a thumb in my eye and rubbed the orb until the muscles in my face unlocked. "Well, how much of the mortgage does Larry pay?" I asked.

Clank. Jamie dropped her fork on her plate. "*Dad.*"

Larry drank his water. He was no fool.

Charlie took a breath. She chose to ignore my comment. "Anyway. The woman was very polite. Once she discovered I was Jamie's mom, she felt comfortable explaining certain things. Like how your card went through but was declined at the end of the day. There was a message from the credit card company on the Center's answering service. Apparently, this happens all the time."

"That's not possible," I said. "I'm paid up on that card."

"Gayle. I'm not asking you about the card."

"You're not listening. The card is paid up."

Charlie sought help from Jamie and Larry. "Do you hear this? I'm not asking about the card."

Silence. The table behind me burst out laughing, and the difference in atmospheres was stark.

"How was work today, Gayle?" Larry cut a few atoms from his slice of bread. "Anything exciting happen?"

Larry always asked about work, hoping I'd namecheck a famous Augment. He was usually disappointed.

"I spent the day getting grilled by the Treasury Department. Bunch of starched shirts who smoke crap cigars. Tomorrow, I'll probably go through the whole routine all over again. Does that count?"

The words were out of my mouth before I could consider them. To Charlie's credit, she didn't mock me. She touched a spot on her forehead, mirroring my wound. "And this?"

"Nothing," I lied. "Doesn't even hurt."

Her face indicated disbelief. She'd heard such lies before. "Treasury doesn't have to assault you to hurt you."

"They're a government agency. There's a process to respect. They can't shut us down, touch our phones, or access our computers. Not without a warrant."

Larry found entertainment in my pain. He laughed. "Send them over to our place. We've got boxes of your old shit."

Charlie shushed him. She looked at me with guarded concern. "Was it Elbridge?"

The man had been after me for years. I nodded. "And Barb. She actually followed me to Jamie's treatment. I know the woman lacks tact, but Jesus. Can you believe it?"

Charlie appraised me from across the table. "Do I want to ask?"

I shrugged. "It was one of Donny's cases."

"Still? How long are you going to haul that man's water?"

"That's not what I'm doing. And he's—" She wouldn't know about Donny's untimely demise. "You shouldn't say things like that."

"It's the truth. You never say no to that man. You do whatever he tells you."

Fear grabbed me, a ghost hand around my heart. *Coward*, the ghost whispered. *Liar. Thief.*

"Why do you always assume I'm guilty of something?" I said. "Jesus. Nothing's changed."

"Exactly." Jamie dropped her fork into her limp salad and pushed the plate out into the middle of the table. "Nothing ever changes." Her skin was the color of clay. "Happy chemo day to me."

"Honey." I leaned over and reached for her hand. She pulled away.

"Don't," she said. "Just. Don't."

The order took forever. My burger had mustard and a pickle on it and was stone-cold. Larry said his fish was the best he'd ever tasted.

The pain in my head never quite went away.

CHAPTER SIXTEEN

Outside, a hazy twilight had fallen over the city. Late rush hour filled the streets. Lights twinkled overhead, airplanes and helicopters and the occasional Augment in an FAA-approved flight suit. There were also stars, somewhere, the final dying light of solar systems with the good sense to explode thousands of years prior.

On my way back to the office, I called the last number I had for Donny and listened to his slow Texas drawl.

I'm indisposed at the moment, but let me know what you need. I'll get back to you with all alacrity.

All alacrity? Who talked like that? I wasn't sure if the phrase was some joke or Donny being Donny. You never knew what the man was up to.

After a few seconds, I realized the voiceover had ended. In its place, a rolling silence as some automaton waited for me to leave a dead man a message. I ended the call and realized how cliché it was to call Donny's phone.

The mess he'd left me.

The mess I'd made for myself.

The office was occupied, harsh light streaming through gaps in the blinded window. Dru banged away on her laptop and drank tea. Patrick sat in my chair with his feet on my desk, eating a popsicle. No shoes.

"Hey, brother." He dripped cherry-colored sugar water on my leather chair. "Didn't think you were coming in."

Patrick was a big dude. Two-fifty to two-eighty of soft muscle. The kind of guy who kept free weights in his garage and a gym membership he rarely used. He had thin, white-blond hair. Blinked frequently through tiny round-rimmed glasses too small for his ham-hock head. A button-up blue silk shirt spilled over his belly and covered the belt with his name on the buckle. He wore painter's jeans and a friendly popsicle-smeared grin.

"Why are you here?" I looked at Dru. "Why is he here?"

"The Atomo repossession went sideways." Dru blew over her mug. "Apparently, Patrick nearly got stabbed."

"What *nearly?*" Patrick held up his arm to display a faint red line. "Dude went psycho on me. Tried to rip me apart on a cellular level."

I closed my eyes. "That's a paper cut. You'd get hurt worse making copies."

"Whatever, dude. Police moved in and it was sayonara, Netherhouse; know what I mean?"

Atomo could flatten himself to four one-thousandths of an inch. Slide under doors. Fold himself into envelopes. He used the power in a couple of hostage rescue situations, really got the local cops out of a jam. But like most Augments, Atomo didn't profit from his powers. He worked twelve-hour days struggling to get fourteen-year-olds to give a shit about *The Iliad*. PD didn't pay much for the occasional consulting gig, and Atomo's day job vanished when the public schools cut back on teachers. His supply of molecule-flattening grog had been bought on credit.

"I don't suppose," I said as I leaned against Dru's desk, "you got his compression cocktail first, did you?"

"Dude was violent, like I told you. Thought he'd slice my jugular."

"He'd agreed to hand over the bottles. Did you show him the authorization to repossess?"

"Didn't really go down like that."

"Why didn't you wait for him to leave?'

Patrick slurped at his popsicle.

"I told you," I said. "He's working nights at the grocery, selling cigarettes and scratch-offs. After seven o'clock, he'd have been gone for nine hours."

"You never told me that."

"We talked about it." I pointed at the corkboard. "The notes are right there."

"Not in my email. Modern age is mobile; know what I'm saying?"

I stared at the empty chair where Mak should have been. She'd have gone mental by now, listening to Patrick's bullshit. The Atomo job was worth three thousand.

"Get out of my chair, Patrick."

He moved over to Mak's desk, leaving a popsicle blood trail in his wake. I considered going apeshit on him and then remembered Patrick was the only one working a paying case. The only one keeping the firm going.

Donny didn't found Netherhouse. He'd signed the papers on our lease, but Netherhouse started long before Donald Spielman came along. I'd never unearthed much in the way of background. Apparently, Donny wasn't the only owner who'd lived in fear of paperwork. A casual search of Netherhouse Liquidation didn't reveal much, only the occasional arrest report. Early eighties for Donny. 1970s for some guy named Tom. Sixties and fifties and even a mention in the forties. Before that, who knew. The firm had endured for decades. Before I came along.

I checked in with Dru. "You find anything?"

"Unless Donny became an accountant or a high school track star, no. I've got the trailer park, no car, no tax records. He's not licensed to practice repo. He'd be easier to find if he'd gone Spectral."

I pictured the slurry at Royal Memorial. Changed the subject.

"I have something else for you to work. No names, just descriptions."

I described the two gas-mask Heavies who knocked me around outside Big Fight. Dru typed notes into the computer, picking up speed as I described the Humvee and the camo wear.

"That's fairly distinctive," she said. "And they do sound augmented. I'll take a crack tomorrow. I need to get home."

Hard to complain when the woman gave me a plethora of night

and weekend hours. She packed up her laptop and bid Patrick and I good night. I watched her walk out the door with our singular piece of modern technology, less our damn phones. Only now would Donny be comfortable in this office. Netherhouse dialed back to his preferred paper-based stone age.

We've got boxes of your old shit.

I sat up in my chair. The secrets of Donny's past weren't hiding on our computer. The files needed searching. The paper files hiding in the dusty confines of the garage attached to the house of my buddy Larry. My house, before Larry cuckolded me out of it.

Outside, the night blazed brightly. A full moon graced the city, deserving or no.

The perfect couple would still be awake.

CHAPTER SEVENTEEN

Larry stood in the doorway to the garage, wearing his pajama bottoms and an undershirt with yellowed armpits. Toothpaste crud lined his mouth, and he smelled like he'd chugged a couple of beers and then fallen asleep. He squinted and scratched his belly but otherwise remained silent. Charlie had refused to come to the door.

The overhead fluorescents flooded the garage with light. Narrow pathways wound between organized towers of stuff, the entire space given over to storage, the family cars parked in the street. I had to navigate the maze before I found what I was looking for. A dozen boxes stacked in the corner behind one of Jamie's old Schwinns and a dusty set of golf clubs. My name was written on each box in large strokes. GAYLE'S SHIT.

I unstacked the boxes and pulled off the cardboard tops. Piles of carbons and receipts and scribbled napkins filled each box to the brim. Donny's filing system. Twelve different pits of despair.

"This the case you were talking about?" Larry asked.

I grunted.

"Must be important, if you had to come out here at this hour."

I looked at my watch. It was nine forty-five.

"You don't have to wait on me," I told him. "I'll let myself out when I'm done."

Larry put his hands on his hips. He frowned and tilted his head to the ceiling. After consultation with his god of choice, he stepped back to close the door. He left it open a crack.

"It's my house, Gayle," he said. "Don't forget that."

He walked away.

I sat on my heels and examined the haunted array of files. All of this crap had accumulated when I was still married to Charlie. She'd always said the work in these boxes had helped destroy our marriage. The accumulation of all things Netherhouse. The hours. The people. Donny. Me.

I crushed one of the cardboard box tops without realizing it.

The paperwork wasn't sorted in any meaningful way. Years, cases, and assignments were all mixed together. I created two piles—relevant and not relevant—and pulled everything from the year of the Dimension repo and before. When my back hurt, I stretched, and when I had to take a piss, I held it. There was no way I was walking back into Larry's house. When the time came, I'd leave out the garage.

Augment names bled together as I sifted through the paperwork. The Red Penguin. The Tuner. Fulton the Magician. Not all crooks, but treated by Netherhouse as if they were. Some heroes—or so they thought—but also teachers and shop owners. Husbands and wives. Everyday people with a jones to be better, and no hint in the paperwork of their eventual fate, just a litany of closed cases I hadn't spared a second thought because Donny taught me not to look back. Work the case, get your scratch, and move on. If you bent some rules, skirted some laws, that was only natural. Just, even. We were chasing thieves. What was the harm?

Somewhere in this house, my exhausted daughter chased sleep, deprived of her goal by stress and steroids and nausea. The consequences of her very expensive and life-saving chemotherapy. Should I not manage to keep Netherhouse clear of earlier harmless decisions, her insomnia would be the least of her problems.

One box remained when Charlie wandered into the garage. She didn't say anything, just swished in behind me in her terry-cloth bathrobe and bare feet. She fished an old plastic chair from the stacks and settled herself behind the last box. With a sigh, she pulled up her feet, crossed her legs, and regarded me with weary suspicion.

The house settled. Wood popped and metal groaned. An old thing, that house. I'd wasted a lot of time, trying to repair it. Like the boxes in front of me, a chunk of my life I'd never get back.

I'd almost forgotten Charlie was there when she spoke.

"Do you remember the night you found the phone bill?"

The night I found the phone bill was the night I discovered Charlie was sleeping with Larry. Almost thirty calls to his number, and those were just the conversations she initiated. She never mentioned that night. Ever.

"Rings a bell."

Charlie hugged herself. "You know I still think about that night? How I could have done it different."

A donut-shop receipt sat curled atop the last pile. I twisted it between my fingers.

"But by then, it was too late to do anything different. The phone bill was coming. And even if it wasn't, you'd have found out some other way. A smell. Coming home early on the wrong day. An email sent to the wrong address. In the end, something would have tripped us up."

I turned my back on her. "You could have stopped."

"In the beginning?" Her voice wavered. "Sure. But that's my point. By phone bill time, it was too late. The lies were already out there. They were always going to come out."

Under my fingertips, more papers waited. Gas receipts and credit contracts and voided checks. Some of them signed by Donny. A few of them signed by me.

"They were always going to find the ring." Charlie put her feet down on the concrete, the bare pads scraping against the concrete. "You should never have taken the money."

I closed my eyes.

* * *

On the night of the Dimension repo, Donny ambled into the office, his all-denim ensemble dirty and frayed. His eyes held the same frost-giant mystical quality they always had, but the ice within had cracked. Slid off center. After the botched attempt to claim Doctor Dimension's augmented ring, I'd been detained by Treasury but almost immediately released. Donny had been sequestered and driven away to an undisclosed location. Hours had passed. Part of me had contemplated the fact he might never return.

"Not sure if you know this," he said upon appearance, "but the Treasury office doesn't serve whisky." He threw himself into his chair, the upholstered mahogany groaning under the weight. "Going to steal a man's soul, least they could do is provide anesthetic."

I stared at him, wondered if he'd wandered off to get drunk instead of spending the last six hours with government agents. "Did they pay you?"

"Their position was without Dimension's augmented ring, there was no sanction to be paid."

"They signed a contract."

"Their position was, unfortunately, supported by the contract."

Rent. Groceries. Pediatrician appointments and ER visits and a new pair of kid's shoes every six weeks. Lots of pressure piled on my shoulders. Reasons I needed the money. I put my head in my hands.

"I'm not worried," Donny said.

"Sure. You never worry. Why start now?"

"I don't think you're listening. Look at me."

I looked up. His grin stretched from ear to ear. Idiot I was, I asked him why.

"Lost," he said. "The ring was lost. Doesn't mean the ring was destroyed; doesn't mean it's powering another freak. Dimension doesn't have it; Netherhouse doesn't have it. To that extent, Treasury is satisfied."

My head hurt. "Speak English. What are we talking about?"

Donny rolled the words around his tongue, as if he had a mouthful of golf balls. "Say someone was grateful—grateful to benefit from the confluence of events that satisfied our friends at Treasury."

Whatever I told myself later, I knew. I knew right at that moment what had happened. And I said nothing.

Donny stood and dropped the overstuffed manila envelope on my desk. "I'll bet you have concerns. You're a family man, whatever Charlene might think. You worry about your little girl. But you're out there every night. Doing the work. You deserve to be done right."

"Donny. What's in this envelope doesn't have anything to do with me."

My partner shrugged, his teeth disappearing behind tight lips. He stared out the front window, considering his words.

"The place needs cleaning," he said. "Tomorrow, I think. First thing."

I blinked at him.

"Anything you leave on your desk, I'm tossing out." He nodded, agreeing with himself. "So, if you need something, you should take it with you."

My mouth opened and closed. Words brewed in my head but failed to spill out.

"Buy yourself something nice," he said. Then he turned and shouldered open the door and disappeared into the night.

The envelope sat on my desk. When I bent back one of the metal braids, a hundred-dollar bill slid out.

There were dozens more inside.

* * *

Charlie left me alone. There was still a fistful of mismatched papers to sort through and countless lines of Donny chicken scratch to parse. Besides, she'd evened us out. She had the guilt of an affair, and I had the guilt of a bribe. Neither of us better than the other.

She'd locked the door. Either because she knew I wasn't coming back inside or because she didn't want me to.

I'd confessed to Charlie only after I'd given her the money. After she'd spent the cash on clothes and food. I wasn't proud of it, although at the time, I'd felt pretty good about coming clean. She'd shot down my Man of the Year nomination right away. Complicit, she'd said. I'd made her a criminal after the fact. Worse, I'd stolen our future. *You can't build a house on a foundation of lies.* Words both of us could and should have heeded.

Sometimes, I imagined I'd reached into that envelope and traveled through time. Stuck my grubby fingers in and lifted cash right out of future Gayle's pocket. Money Jamie needed to live.

I flipped through the paperwork and shook out the dead flies and crickets. Focused on the things most official—copies of bank receipts and stapled authorizations for augment sanction. The items most likely to have names and dates. The closest thing to a paper trail Donny had left behind.

When I found it, it was obvious. I'd have noticed the name mentioned one time, let alone eighteen. She was relevant to Netherhouse Liquidation, and apparently always had been. Her Jane Hancock signed right across the bottom of eighteen repo authorizations.

Barbara Cahill.

CHAPTER EIGHTEEN

Five after seven and my phone danced on the table. I ignored it the first time, grasping at a dissolving sleep. The second time the phone rattled, I peered at the caller ID and answered.

"They're in the office and I can't keep them out." Dru threw words at me a mile a minute. "You need to get down here."

Earliest I'd managed to nod off was 2 AM. But the urgency in her voice jolted me awake. I imagined faceless men phasing through the walls. "Get out of there. Get out of there now."

I heard voices in the background and Dru shouting. *Put that down.* There was echoed conversation, and then something heavy crashed to the ground, and I was pulling my pants on when I heard the ringleader up close and personal. I stopped worrying for Dru's safety and began worrying for my own.

Andrew Elbridge was inside Netherhouse Liquidation.

* * *

A black sedan sealed the entrance to our parking lot. The feds raiding our office were dressed business casual. Pressed khakis and navy T-shirts labelled TREASURY in yellow print. Little badges on their big belts, so everyone knew who they'd be fucking with. One agent emerged from our office, toting Dru's laptop and the few file folders we kept on active cases. Another pair carried out the corkboard.

Dressed for the office, even in the heat, was Elbridge. He leaned against the grill of his F-150 and talked down to a distracted Dru Sessions. She had a cell phone pressed against her ear, and one eye watched Elbridge like she wanted to crush him beneath her heel. She spotted me as I approached and gestured to the Secretary, as if to say *Now you're going to get it.* I wished I could deliver on such promises. Elbridge watched me approach, and when the linebackers manning the perimeter stopped me, he waved me through.

"My taxes pay your salary," I said. "Don't you have a real job to do?"

"That taxes line—I've never heard that one." He accepted the laptop from his stone-faced agent and tucked it under his arm. "We have your computers. In-progress casework. The forensics guys are analyzing trace from your office and the dumpster out back. By this time tomorrow, we'll know everything. This is serious business. I suggest you come clean now, before the situation gets worse."

You should have told Elbridge everything, Mak said. *Right then and there.*

I couldn't breathe. The truth fought hard to push past my teeth.

"This is BS," Dru announced. "Just like I said."

My skip tracer wasn't concerned. She was pissed off. Elbridge suppressed a minor stroke.

"I've explained to this you, Ms. Sessions. We have a warrant."

"Not good enough." The cell phone remained at her ear. "Sandoval, I'll call you back. Check your email." She ended the call. "Our lawyer confirmed. There's no augmented rider. None of this is even legal. If you refuse to vacate, we will bring suit on a number of fronts. Federal tort. Official misconduct. Augment Registration Act. Every second you stay only strengthens our case." She used the same phone to snap pictures of the agents, including Elbridge. Most turned away or used file folders to shield their greedy little faces. Only Elbridge tolerated the impromptu photography.

"Think of your family here, Hardwood." His jaw muscles worked beneath his sallow skin. "Or your employees. This investigation could expand in scope. That would be unfortunate for all involved."

I tried to embrace his suggestion. To believe a confession would save us all. But I saw a vindictive Elbridge crushing the Netherhouse he'd always despised. I saw very sympathetic doctors informing my daughter she could no longer receive treatment at their facility, because the checks from her jailbird father just wouldn't cash.

"Lawyer," Dru repeated. "Vacate the premises. Now."

Elbridge counted on breaking our backs right here. He'd be under pressure—from the governor, from the media—to wrap this case quickly. It wasn't every day the Secretary visited the crime scene. Personally served warrants.

He looked at me.

"I'll make a stink," I said. "You know I will."

The words rankled. He licked the film of failure from his teeth, then handed the laptop back to Dru. "Leave it," he shouted.

The agents stared.

"All of it. Leave it where you stand."

File folders went to the ground, papers fluttering free. The corkboard leaned against a wall, where it slid and crashed to the earth. Agents walked to their cars, bristling.

"This investigation remains active." Elbridge leaned in. "You made this personal. I'll have you under a microscope. You have no idea."

"You're making a scene," I said. "At my place of work."

There wasn't any conversation after that. Official Government Vehicles peeled out of the lot. Elbridge shook out his blazer as if he was covered in dust. He got in his truck, alone, and drove off after his agents. Dru and I were left to retrieve scattered paperwork and right the toppled corkboard. A few local pedestrians stopped to gawk, but most of our neighbors were familiar with our kind of chaos. The Planned Parenthood folks just shook their heads.

Once inside, Dru produced disinfectant wipes and scoured the desks, chairs, and her laptop as if they were covered in bubonic plague. I went through my desk drawers and scrutinized every paperclip and stick of gum. When you're hiding the truth, you see incriminating signs everywhere. In your handwriting. In your emails. In the words you say and the words you don't. Dru couldn't make things clean enough.

Mak arrived after we'd largely restored order. She held one of those executive stress Zen-garden things in one hand. The tray contained river rocks and a rake and a tiny content buddha but no sand.

"Found this in the street," she said. "Patrick will be crushed."

She dropped the remnants on his desk. Parked her keister at her own. "Seems we dodged a bullet. Thanks to Dru."

Dru was on the phone with her fiancé. She raised a hand in greeting.

"She called Sandoval?" Mak asked.

"We're lucky Elbridge backed down. Sandoval's disbarred."

"Funny. I heard he was only suspended."

I wiped nonexistent dirt from the desktop. The office felt wrong. Like Treasury had left something behind. Or taken something I needed.

"Elbridge was pretty steamed," I said. "We made him look bad in front of his people. He's gunning for us. You should watch your back."

"He should watch his back. *White Male Elected Official Hassles Minority Business Owner*. I'll eat him for lunch."

I didn't have a snappy answer. Mak frowned and propped her feet on the desk. "I take it you didn't mention your suspicions? About one of his more-female team members?"

After I'd returned to my apartment, I'd sent a photo of the repo paperwork to Mak, suggestive Barbara Cahill signatures included. Mak hadn't responded, but I knew she'd seen the photo. Repomen didn't sleep before midnight. Not if they were any good.

"He seemed uninterested in my insights."

"That's your theory, though? Donny steals the ring, and Barb whitewashes it?"

"Or vice versa. It would explain their love-hate thing."

Mak stared at her shoes. "Not really what I would call evidence."

"We're not cops. We don't need evidence."

"We need enough to redirect Elbridge. No way we go to him peddling the idea one of his own is dirty unless we're sure."

I watched Dru try to reassure her fiancé. She was fine. Everything was going to be fine.

I needed her words to be true.

"Goose chase or no, I'm not waiting for Treasury to come back. Cops always find what they're looking for, even if they have to change what they're looking for." Mak hopped to her feet. "Let's see what kind of donuts Barb eats."

I sighed. Minimal sleep. A Treasury wake-up call. And now the prospect of tailing Barbara Cahill all damn day. God knew I deserved punishment, but this felt cruel and unusual. "She seems more the kolache type."

"Pigs in blankets."

"What's that?"

"Texans. They get everything wrong. What they call kolaches are actually pigs in blankets."

"Do you want share that with Elbridge? He was born in Amarillo. I'm sure he'll be excited to hear your low opinion of the natives."

Mak walked toward the front door. "My truck's low on gas. You're driving."

I told Dru to keep Patrick working and followed Mak out the door. Hoping I'd left nothing incriminating behind. Praying I wouldn't discover anything incriminating ahead.

CHAPTER NINETEEN

We parked a block away from Barbara's house. She resided just north of campus, wedged into one of those exclusive old neighborhoods like Tarrytown where no one could afford to live anymore. She'd bought the house years ago, before speculation and *Best Places to Live* articles drove up the prices. She talked about selling and moving to the coast, buying a nice two-bedroom out in Port Aransas. But Barb was a creature of habit. Every morning, she smoked a cigar, and every night, she drank Bushmills, and on her birthday, she took herself up to Dallas and checked into a nice hotel and ate room service all weekend. Same routine, year in, year out. She'd die in that house.

Unless of course she was dirty. In which case all bets were off.

We'd been watching the house for three hours. Barb must have been working nights, as her car remained parked in the driveway. I'd managed three pages in a Scandinavian crime novel, and Mak nominally played some game on her phone that involved squashing colored dots.

"You think she killed Donny?" she asked.

I stared at the closed blinds. The house was sealed. I'd expected her to be asleep, but the woman still rattled around inside. Earlier, I'd snuck around the patio and caught the faint sounds of last night's basketball game on the TV. The Knicks. Barb yelling over the announcers the whole time.

"She's capable. She shot a guy last year, down at the Magnolia on Lake Austin. It was a good shoot, but she pulled the trigger."

"Barb always seemed like a lot of talk. A real windbag. I don't know how you stand her."

"Of all people, you ought to understand. She's a woman in a good-old-boy business. They've had her answering phones and making coffee for decades. It takes nerve to swallow all that bullshit without it changing you."

"Maybe it did change her. And maybe Donny got between her and what she felt she was owed."

I remembered a manila envelope full of dirty money. Suppressed another twinge of guilt. "You think Barb stole the ring from Donny? You saw where he was living. Where did he keep the ring—in a Folgers can? And why didn't he use it? Why was he living in that shithole?"

"Don't crawl up my ass. This wasn't my theory."

We continued to watch the house. I drank my third Mountain Dew and ate leftover ramen from a Styrofoam bowl. I listened to Mak curse at her game and rubbed the grit from my eyes and tried to convince myself this wasn't a tremendous waste of time.

Just after noon, Barb appeared on her front stoop. She stood on the porch and scouted the street. We'd parked far enough away, we couldn't be spotted. Once Barb satisfied herself she was alone, she produced her keys and hustled to the car. She pulled away from the curb, and we slumped down until she passed. I ditched my food and Mak quit her game and we U-turned to follow.

Barb worked her way west through nice but claustrophobic neighborhoods. The central part of the city didn't facilitate surveillance—narrow lanes and a packed rush hour made it easy to lose a tail. One old lady contemplating a slow left turn and we'd lose Barb.

Mak told me I was too close. I eased off the gas and made myself sit back one car.

We worked our way across town. Barb drove erratically, just like the night she took me to the stadium. If I didn't know better, I'd have thought she was trying to throw a tail.

I dropped back another car length.

We crossed the narrow two-lane bridge of Redbud Trail and passed over the dammed might of the Colorado and slipped into West Lake Hills. Million-dollar homes stared down from above.

Anglo-Saxons walked dogs with papers and brandished enormous coffees. Barb wasn't headed to the office, but Treasury agents worked cases in the field, too. Just because she headed away from downtown was no smoking gun.

At the first major intersection, she stopped outside a market. She parked close and threw a blue handicapped hanger on the rearview and then shuffled into the store.

"She's a peach, your Barbara," Mak said.

"Her front door's unlocked."

Mak nodded. "Drive past, then stop."

I did as instructed. Once I slowed, my partner hopped out and ran to Barb's car and slid herself into the driver's seat as if she'd done this dozens of times. Which she had. So many middle-aged men with augmented cars they couldn't afford. Mak must have repoed three cars a month.

While my partner worked, I situated the truck so I could monitor her via the sideview and the grocery door from my rearview. Mak was leaned over the center console. She'd produced her phone and appeared to be taking pictures.

Soccer moms and personal assistants cycled through the grocery doors. No Barb yet, but this had the feel of a quick stop. I doubted she was stocking up for the week.

Mak stayed in place. Rooted through the contents of the center console like she was entitled.

Off to my left, a clerk negotiated a centipede of carts through the lot. One of the carts had a busted wheel and logjammed the entire train. I'd bagged groceries as a teen. Suffered long hours and low pay and a boss with short man's disease who'd once announced he could fire the lot of us and replace every one by day's end. The teen girl wrangling the carts had my sympathy. None of the customers stopped to lend her a hand.

Mak leaned way over, one hand buried in the glove. I imagined ice scrapers and honest-to-god paper road maps.

Back on my left, the clerk had detached the back half of the train only to have the carts separate and spin off into the lot. Brakes slammed and horns sounded. The girl jogged back and forth, pursuing carts like they were runaway calves. I had half a mind to exit the truck and lend a hand.

I looked at the sideview to see Barb standing at her car.

"Jesus."

At that range, it was impossible Barb hadn't seen Mak. There was no use in signaling. No use climbing out and making a scene. Barb wasn't dumb. Spying me in the parking lot would be a tell.

Mak was a pro. I'd have to trust she could talk her way out of it. But if she was caught, no natural power in the world would convince Barb this was all some misunderstanding.

I watched the inevitable unfold. Barb had her singular cup of coffee in hand. She yanked open the door. Plunked into the driver's seat.

No other head was framed in the windows. Only Barb was parked in front.

Mak was nowhere to be seen.

Behind me, the store clerk rounded up the carts. One of them slipped loose again and plowed into a Lexus and triggered the car alarm. The blaring racket drew more stares, the noise an offense in this quiet neighborhood. Even Barb gawked.

I checked the rearview. Turned all the way around to use my own two eyes and saw only shoppers pushing carts laden with specialty Ethiopian coffee beans and Tuscan kale.

If Barb had spotted Mak, she wouldn't be sitting calmly in the front seat. She'd have Mak pushed over the hood, fitting her for cuffs. She'd be on her phone calling Elbridge.

The car door opened again. Barb looked unhappy. She trudged back into the store, talking to herself. She steered around one of the rogue carts and disappeared inside.

I opened my door and got one foot on the ground before stopping myself. About the time Barb returned and saw me standing within spitting distance of her precious ride, I was, as Donny used to say, *in Dutch.* Tailing a federal agent, on top of my involvement with the

Dimension case. I might as well rob a bank and live-tweet the process. I pulled my leg back into the truck. As my door closed, the passenger door opened and Mak slid in next to me.

"Barb takes four sugars in her coffee." She checked the side mirror to see if she'd been spotted. "She's going to get diabetes."

"You were in the back seat?"

"Thank the young lady with the grocery carts for keeping Barb distracted. I'm a big girl. There's not a lot of room on the floorboards."

"Why she'd leave?"

"Must have forgot something. Or my power got stronger. Believe me, I was wanting her gone something fierce."

Our target returned just as the clerk unstuck the carts and got the train moving. Barb whistled as she walked, a fresh cup of coffee in her hand. She shot the clerk a thumbs-up, as if together they made miracles happen. I kept the engine running but stayed in our space until Barb reversed and cruised out into the street. I didn't want to underestimate a twenty-five-year law enforcement veteran. She might keep one eye on her rearview out of habit.

"She left her phone in the car. I got pictures." Mak swiped through the images she'd captured. "Recent calls—all numbers, no contact names. The email was a work account—I left that alone. Otherwise, some receipts stuffed in the glove. Very few augmented rings."

We cruised through additional neighborhoods of sprawling oaks and dormered roofs and drives barricaded to prevent our entry. Just past the last sealed enclave, Barb hung a left, her car passing moderate-but still lower-seven-figure domiciles. The homes armored with plantation shutters and sporting yards big enough to host a small soccer team. But the neighborhood felt familiar. The Cancer Center was just northwest of here. I'd been through this zip code more than once, and Barb had driven me through here only yesterday.

Mak rattled off some of the numbers she'd captured from Barb's phone. I didn't recognize any of them.

"Not a one?"

"Who remembers phone numbers? That's why I have my phone."

Barb's car slowed. I had to stay farther back to avoid discovery. We passed the residences of tech executives and former athletes and at least one congresswoman. A few retired Augments and celebrities with third homes. No Willie Nelson, but the Red Headed Stranger couldn't be everywhere, not since he'd decommissioned his clones.

"There's nothing back here," I said. "What is she doing?"

"Maybe she knows I was in the car," Mak said. "And she's jerking us around."

But Barb didn't spare us any attention. She puttered down the center of the road and nearly rolled to a stop. Her eyes scanned doors and windows. She leaned back to scope backyard fence lines. It was as if she was searching for holes.

"God, she is desperate," Mak said. "She's robbing houses now."

But Barb didn't stop. She accelerated and pushed south. She eased the car through sweeping turns until we left modern-day excess behind and welcomed older homes built in the seventies. The price tags fell. The homes grew more densely packed. Barb parked in front of a ranch-style with a freshly cut lawn, and we pulled over three houses down. She lurched from her car with twinned coffees in hand and went up the walk toward the front door. An old woman answered the door. Frizzy hair. A sweater even in the heat. A little dog stood at her ankles and watched as Barb and the woman hugged. The women and their coffees went inside and closed the door.

"Barb have a sister?" Mak asked.

My stomach sank. Barb and I had passed this house on our way to Royal Memorial. "Type in the address."

"What's that?"

"Google this neighborhood. Tell me what you find."

Mak was better with technology than I. She had an answer in seconds. "Holy shit. Ladykiller was up here."

"Barb worked Ladykiller. Dollars to donuts that's one of the survivors."

Mak blinked. "She worked that case?" She looked at the distinguished grey-haired man checking the air in his tires. Two men jogging, bumping each other in a familiar, perhaps intimate way. At the two kids skateboarding on their bellies down the driveway and the manicured hedges and the painted fences and perfect families. The lifestyles a bit more diverse than two decades prior, but still a neighborhood populated by people who felt safe, just as they would have back then, before Ladykiller ripped the facade away. "Shit. She checks in on the neighborhood. And the victims."

"We got our evidence, all right." I slammed the truck into Drive and jerked away from the curb. "Barb is a good cop."

CHAPTER TWENTY

We drank fast-food coffee at a plastic table outside the fenced-in playland. A toddler wandered the landscape, wonder on her face, a nanny alternating between her phone and watching the kid. Mak and I probably monitored the situation better than the nanny, for free, no less. A rate we could not afford.

"You remember that age?" I asked Mak. "With Nate?"

"It wasn't that long ago for me. But I never let him play on these things. I saw a kid poop on the slide once. Children are dirty, but there's limits."

The toddler found a knob that noisily cranked. Her face lit up. She turned the knob again and again, giggling at the racket.

Mak pulled the lid off her coffee. "Jamie would have been right in there. She'd have bumped that kid aside."

"Shoved, more than likely. I had to watch her like a hawk. She wasn't ever in danger. She was the danger."

The girl's laugh was pure love. Even the nanny watched her with something like jealousy on her face.

"How far in the hole are you?" Mak asked. "On the treatments?"

My coffee wasn't very good, but it was hot. I let a bit down my throat. "Netherhouse hits its best month, and I'm just making it."

"I take it Charlie and Larry can't make up the difference?"

"New alternator last month. She's still paying off his carpal tunnel surgery. Same story, different chapter."

Mak stared into her coffee, as if she expected answers to surface. "We need to give Treasury something."

"I can give them a sense of guilt. They've driven one of their agents into alcohol and depression, and she's still out there doing the job. On a decades-old case." My brain circled the truth. "I'm running out of practical ideas."

Inside, a harried dad in wrinkled dress shirt and loosely knotted tie attempted to coax a lunch order from his recalcitrant ten-year-old. Probably a divorced father juggling his job and his week with the kid. The man feeling like he was failing as both a provider and a parent. Maybe he'd fucked up in his past, embezzled a bit, tried to cover a bad stock trade. The kind of mistake that followed a man and never let go.

"I did the legwork for the Dimension repo," I said.

"A young Gayle Harwood? Dashing through the street in his newsboy hat? You must have been excited when they repealed Prohibition."

"You may respectfully cram it." I cupped my hands around the warm paper cup. "Dimension was connected. You mentioned that augment supergroup. He also did team-ups. One-shot partnerships. He had a handful of assistants and henchmen that went out on their own. There was a time half the augmented criminals in this town owed their start to Dimension."

"A real gentleman. Aside from all the murder."

"Honor among thieves, maybe? All I know is I couldn't get anyone to flip on his location. Not back then."

"You think revenge? A Dimension loyalist who's been nursing a grudge against Donny all this time?"

"Could be someone who just got out of prison. Had the ring squirreled away for safe keeping. Now they're squaring accounts."

My partner mulled over the theory. "I can run down Dimension's known associates. Free you up to work."

The idea Mak might turn over a rock with my name on it filled me with dread. "Or the other way around."

Mak side-eyed me.

"I worked the case," I said. "I know the names. I understand the relationships. Besides, it's my mess."

She chuckled without humor. "You're right about that." She sat in silence for a moment and watched the toddler, now bored with the crank, wander back to her guardian with arms outstretched. "You know I love Jamie like she was my own, right?"

"I do. Never a doubt."

Mak downed her coffee and stood. "Make sure I'm doing this for the right reasons."

Inside, another man joined the harried family. Dressed in a *Stars Wars* tee and cargo shorts and the entire software-developer ensemble, he kissed the man and slapped the kid's back, and everything was right as rain. No embezzlement. No broken family.

Ramen and coffee boiled in my stomach. "I've got your back."

Mak's smile was hard to read. "Let's hope there's no trouble from that direction."

* * *

Augments keep all kinds of hours. Most are average janes and joes and have regular lives in the daytime. They don flashy costumes after they punch a clock and limit their extracurriculars to hoisting junkers at monster truck shows or competing in local wrestling competitions. Others do get the occasional hankering for crime or crime-fighting. They're more likely to sleep through the day and fight for evil or good when the sun begins to fall. A narrow window existed around five o'clock where a man like me could contact those in the second category.

Ray "The Bad Man" Oldham. An early running buddy of Dimension. He'd chewed isotope tablets and used his resultant Olympian physique to keep the riffraff at bay while Dimension carried out his scores. But, over time, the radioactivity wreaked havoc on Ray. His skin sagged. He lost his hair. Bumps erupted from his skin. I found him out back of his domicile, smoking a chicken.

"Like I told them Treasury folks yesterday"—he dumped wood chips into the open loader—"Dimension is good people. He got me off them 'topes before they ate my insides. Hooked me up with doctors I couldn't afford. Not everyone looks out for their fellow man like that."

"You see him at all?" I asked. "Toward the end?"

"No, sir. His company changed. And I didn't want to bother him none."

"He ever let you hold it? The ring?"

Ray straightened, squeezing the bag of wood chips tight. His hands were still big. The knuckles like acorns. "If I had the ring, last person I'm goin' to tell is some repo man just off the truck."

"I didn't say you had it."

"Doctor Dimension died with that ring on his finger. No one else man enough to handle it."

"Well, surely—"

Ray shook his head slowly. "You'd best get off the property. Before my son gets back. He's taking the 'topes now. He's not much for company."

I had a lot of interviews along those lines.

Madelaine Mosley, "The Night Knife." She'd teamed up with Dimension for two years. They'd been rumored to be an item. Madelaine stood six two and seemed in good shape. She'd been doing Pilates. She told me Dimension was a good man and she missed him and if I didn't vacate her doorstep in the next sixty seconds, I'd never darken another.

Gaspar Hernandez. No augment moniker but still feared, he'd been in the League of Six at the end, before infighting and law enforcement pressure split them up. He simmered in his hot tub during our interview. Brave, considering he was once 35 percent robotic parts. They'd carved out the augmentation before putting him in prison, replacing the extendable arm and laser eye with depowered prosthetics. When I asked him about Dimension, he told me I could *go suck donkey dick*. I demurred.

Lockjaw. The Astonishing Alice. Scotsman. Over the next two days, they all told me to take a hike with varying degrees of politeness. If any of them had the ring, their means did not reflect the wealth such a treasure might bring. And if they'd held on to the device purely for revenge, they hid their smug satisfaction, and well. Associates seemed a dead end. But Dimension's criminal running buddies weren't the only options. Every Augment needed a friend with at least one foot in the real world. Doctors. Lawyers. Mechanics.

George Baikov sat in a chair in his garage with the door open and smoked a cigarette. His hair was grey and wild with a Dracula hairline. His skin had the elephant-skin cast of a lifelong smoker. He stood abruptly and stubbed out the cigarette when he saw me coming, like I was the school principal. "Get off my lawn," he said.

In all my years, it was the first time I'd heard the phrase.

"Mr. Baikov." I kept my hands where he could see them. Normals might not have augmented devices, but guns were just as easy to acquire. "I wanted to ask you a few questions."

"Last repoman said the same thing. Then he towed my Plymouth."

I didn't have the Netherhouse logos adhered to the truck. "How'd you know who I was?"

"Old George wasn't born yesterday." He squinted as if the sun had dropped into his eyes. "You got papers?"

"No. I'd like to ask about a friend of yours. Doctor Dimension."

The squint deepened. "You're not here to steal my property?"

"Scout's honor."

Baikov coughed and laughed. "Sure. Okay. He and I go way back. George knows lots of people. The good doctor is no longer with us, however. Pancake city."

"You worked on his car?"

"Back in the day. 1999 E-Class. Paint was a bit faded but that sucker was heavy. Germans put some weight in them back then. Like a tank. Ate gas but the Doctor didn't seem to mind."

"He like the car?"

"Told me she'd saved his life more than once. The whole car-as-a-woman thing. Myself, I'm not that sentimental."

"But he trusted you with his things?"

He spread his hands. "George has a trustworthy face."

"You ever see his ring?"

"Of course. Never leave home without it."

"He trust you with that?"

Baikov frowned. He looked up and down the street. "What are you here for? Really?"

"It's a past job. Government paperwork, you know how it is."

His eyes lingered on me. "Uh-huh." He eased back into his chair. "This is how they got me last time. The main guy smooth-talked me. Then, while I was distracted, his partner hooked up his tow and took my car. The augmented neverflats were on credit, not the entire automobile—they could have pulled the tires if there was any truth to the con, instead of taking the whole kit and kaboodle. When I drive out to the tow yard to get my car, I find a chassis, no tires; all my shit's gone."

"What did they take? The Creedence tapes?"

He frowned at me.

"Was it valuable?" I asked.

"It was my stuff. Ten years of driving that car, I kept a number of augmented personals in there. Things valuable to me." He shook his head. Brushed me off. "You can amscray. I'm done talking."

Pressing Baikov about the ring seemed a waste of time, but something he'd said drew my curiosity. "These other guys, the ones you say stole from you? When's this?"

"Why?"

"Maybe I know them. What you're describing sounds crooked."

He considered. "Showed up back when the good Doc still walked the earth, matter of fact. Two of them. Tall guy looked like he walked out of a John Ford western. I liked him, at first. Other guy I didn't like. The junkyard guy. He was a little Rodney Dangerfield for me. He's the one towed my car."

The western description didn't pass unnoticed. "You remember names?"

He kicked out his feet. "George has seen a lot. I've got pills for my ticker and those damn cheaters for reading. Can't remember every damn thing from ten years back." I reached for my wallet and he laughed. "I'd extort you if I could. But that's not what this is. I don't remember names, if they ever gave me names to begin with."

"The cowboy-looking guy—he smoke? Wear blue jeans and denim jacket? Go by Donny, maybe?"

Baikov snapped his fingers. "Marlboro Man. That's what he reminded me of, yeah. Bummed a cigarette off me."

"And the guy he brought with him. Kind of short? Pudgy?"

"Could be. Used his hands when he talked. Never trust a man like that."

I hadn't found what I was looking for. But maybe something in the neighborhood. "You've been very helpful."

He laughed. "George Baikov for president." He Nixon'ed his hands. "Now get off my lawn."

CHAPTER TWENTY-ONE

I'd recognized the junkyard guy's description. Back in the Donny days, we couldn't afford a wrecker. To fill the gap, we'd partnered with a handful of small-time towers. One I'd never particularly liked—he reminded me of a car salesman. He'd been in tight with Donny, but funny enough, we'd stopped doing business with him right around the time of the Dimension affair. Hank Ruiz, of Ruiz Salvage and Disposal. The business trafficked in standard and augmented recovery. They repoed trinkets mostly and made their money through volume. Per public records, the place still existed, a flyspeck festering just north of Buda. Seemed Hank had passed in the last year, but according to probate, the property now belonged to his brother Rick Ruiz.

Mak and I stopped at a drugstore on the way out, acquiring a half-case of Mountain Dew and a bag of powdered donuts. She gazed longingly at a frosted six of beer but left the cans in the cooler. Better to stay sober. Successful repomen assumed a collection could go wrong a dozen different ways—if it went south in only three of them, you were pleasantly surprised.

Looping Mak had felt right. If I pursued Ruiz solo, her suspicions would have been raised. Correctly. I was walking a fine line between friendship and backstabbing. Truth be told, I was just trying to alleviate my guilt. It wasn't working.

"You think the brother knows something?" she asked.

"The mechanic said Donny and Hank cleaned him out. I figure they were towing vehicles, then stealing the personal belongings and selling them. If Hank was involved, maybe he recruited Rick."

"Background check didn't show much. Rick has one pickup for

grand theft auto when he was eighteen. Since then, straight jobs in New York, Philly, Detroit, and Chicago. Pawn shop. Gun store. Nothing that says he's acquired one of the most powerful augment devices in existence."

"He's our best lead."

"That's what you said about Barb, and look how that turned out."

We drove south under a grey sky and popped donuts, the silence filled by road noise and comments about the vasectomy billboards along the side of the highway. We let the radio drone on about cybernetic troops in Syria and the latest batch of Wall Street indictments. There was a report on the increasing violence between the Augmented and the non-Augmented, the stadium mentioned in passing and referenced only as DKR, with few possessing any tangible details of the actual goings-on. This morning, someone had taken shots at the car of Rita Pham, a local congresswoman known for her pro-Augment views. Some were suggesting curfews. Others increased Augment tracking. Mak and I agreed on hardly any of these issues, and soon enough, she snapped off the radio.

The trip to Rick's place took us out of Austin proper and south of the city. Downtown high-rises receded in our rearview, and statuaries and tire shops sprung up ahead. We passed a couple of ramshackle roadside stands. Melons. Pecans. A guy claiming to sell love charms. The love-charm guy had the most cars. After thirty minutes, we reached our destination. A signpost staked in the weeds along the access road, emblazoned with one word and an arrow. RUIZ. The red arrow pointed down a rutted one-lane road. Mak eyeballed the narrow track that disappeared under the interlaced arms of giant live oaks.

"We go this way, he might see us coming." Mak rubbed her moko like a man might stroke a beard. "Might already be waiting."

"Why would he know we're coming?" I spit the words around my donut. "You think he casually hangs out in the trees?"

"We could park here."

"And what if there's another road out?"

Mak frowned. Eased the truck forward. We rattled down the

road, kicking up dust and rocks.

On the other side of the trees, a long gate blocked the main drive, a NO TRESPASSING sign posted front and center. There was a buzzer but it stood in high weeds and leaned drunkenly close to horizontal. Yards of chain link ran around the outside of the compound, enclosing a couple acres of crushed cars and rusted-out jets and motorboats with no motors. Coiled razor wire topped the chain link, fanged and mean. A motionless camera was bolted on a metal pole behind the fence, fixed in place and staring out over the entrance with one dead eye.

We parked and got out. The clouds spit rain. Less a downpour and more a drizzle.

"The camera is fake." Mak stared down the electronic eye while snarfing the last few donuts. "We could hop the gate, no problem."

"The camera may be fake, but the concertina wire will rip you to shreds." I waded into the weeds and pressed the buzzer. The post fell over. "I say we sit on the property until he shows."

Mak squinted through the fence. A weathered A-frame house rose out of the garbage on the other side. "What if he never shows? Ten bucks this place is deserted."

"You want to leave?" I high-stepped from the weeds and reached for the donut bag. Mak pulled it away.

"We're all the way out here," she said. "We'll try it your way."

Back in the truck we went. Mak eased out into the grass and drove until we represented an oddity on the horizon. The sun fell and the rainclouds accelerated the process of night. We kept our headlights off. Mak occasionally ran the wipers. As things went inarguably dark, a light came on inside the A-frame.

"You owe me ten bucks," I said.

"You didn't take the bet."

"There's an implicit acceptance assumed when you make a bet."

My partner failed to produce the agreed-upon Hamilton. But over the sound of rain hissing against the earth we heard the front gate shriek. Then a set of headlights, and the black torpedo of a car exiting the property. After a ten count, Mak started the truck and moved us from grass to dirt while keeping the lights killed. The taillights of our quarry winked as we followed.

"Be a shame if that's not Rick," I said.

"I'll pass him when he makes the highway, then drop back. You know what he looks like?"

"Dru has a friend in Illinois Secretary of State, sent the driver's license photo. Skinny dude. Glasses and a combover."

"You know what I hear, bald man? Jealousy."

"Speed up. You'll lose him."

Mak caught the car—a Monte Carlo—once it made 35 going north. I managed a glance without making eye contact. Glasses. Combover. A face only an accountant could love, or maybe a member of the ferret family. Mak changed lanes and drifted back and followed from a three-car distance.

"Looks like him," I said.

Mak grunted. "You owe me ten bucks."

"Really. Why's that?

"He's not home."

We drove for twenty minutes. The rain gave up as we reached downtown. The Monte exited the highway, then took Sixth to Lamar. Austin traffic crowded the street as the young gave a finger to public transportation. Rick seemed confused by the construction and one-way streets. Mak knew the terrain and shadowed him well. Traffic uncramped. He found Lamar and turned left and again we crossed the Colorado River. After a bit of driving, he exited and plunged toward the heart of Zilker Park. We quit the main road and Mak extinguished her lights yet again.

"Park will be closed at this hour," she said.

"Could be he's going through the park."

"Driving through the park doesn't take you anywhere except the park."

The park was closed, so said the sign, but Rick drove on, unconcerned with the rules. No guards stopped us. It was dark and Zilker was populated only by the rebellious and the stoned. I didn't peg Rick as either.

Eventually, the Monte veered into the bike lane and jerked to a stop. Mak braked a good forty yards behind. Rick's car remained dark and I couldn't tell if he was still inside or coming toward us with a gun. We waited. An ember flared in the dark, and I caught a whiff of smoke. Rick Ruiz had exited, leaned against his driver's-side door. The man was cool. He spent five minutes smoking while my legs fell asleep. Then he flicked the ember into the dirt and went around the back. He popped the trunk and pulled out a rifle. Thus armed, he walked out across the grassy field of the park.

"Trees to the right," Mak suggested.

Overcast skies didn't equal invisibility. With great care, I followed my partner into the thick clump of shrubs and trees hugging the field. The pecans shook as we entered. The crickets quieted. Mak led, deftly avoiding the branches I found with the soft parts of my face. Mosquitos swarmed and a larger something jumped over my boot. I certainly made enough noise. Treasury should have thrown a Faraday cloak over me.

The roads inside the park split the trees into clusters. We heard Ruiz leave the field, his boots meeting concrete. He took the two-lane that ran from the front of the park toward the pool. Off in the distance I heard voices, but out here, the activity was more likely kids sneaking a drink than a talkative security guard.

I pointed at my eyes and pointed at Mak. She made a masturbation motion and kept moving.

We left the woods and followed. We stayed in the grass, sneaking across the concrete only when necessary. Ahead I saw a wraparound fence and a long low building flanked by benches. We crossed a small railroad track with no cars—the Zilker Park Zephyr was a popular target for theft and vandalism. I tried to catch a whiff of the flowers at the Botanical Garden. Roses. Maybe the faint odor of azaleas. Instead, I caught an unfortunate waft of shit stink. Porta-potties. Austin was getting too big.

When Rick reached the building, he leaned his rifle against the wall, where it couldn't be seen from the other side. Then he disappeared around the corner. Off to the left, a rise overlooked the path ahead. We crawled up the incline and lay on our bellies just short of the top. From there we could see Rick where he stood in a sprawling playground. He'd stopped at the sandy perimeter before the swings. Someone waited for him there.

Barbara Cahill.

I was disappointed. Barb worked my last nerve, sure. But I knew what she'd been through. What people thought of her. I'd wanted to see her succeed. Believing in her allowed me to believe in myself.

Barb didn't rise from the swing. She said something to Rick, and he responded. We were too far away to catch the dialog. Barb pointed our way and Rick looked over his shoulder. His voice carried. *Bottom line, lady—you missed.* Then he turned back around and his words were lost. The two kept their distance from one another as they talked.

"Rick and Barb and Donny?" Mak whispered. "What does that mean?"

"I never met Rick; it was always his brother." Barb wore a jacket, although it hadn't cooled past 82. Rick stood rigid, like a squirrel before flight. "Shakedown? Donny and the Ruiz brothers steal the ring, Barb finds out, demands a cut?"

"There's a buyer in there somewhere." She watched the two converse. "We should be on the other side. I can't hear a thing."

"You could always waltz down there and ask Rick what he's doing. Drip a little honey in his ear."

"Is that why you brought me along? To play pet Augment?"

"Who said anything about powers? Blow in his ear and he'll go home with you, no problem."

Mak smiled. Then made a fist and nailed me in the shoulder.

Down on the playground, Barb was losing her cool. She'd come off her seat. Her voice carried. *Don't do a damn thing until I tell you.*

"Sure would be nice if they did something illegal," Mak muttered.

More conversation. The clouds broke and moonlight reflected off

Ruiz's glasses, giving him a slightly inhuman presence. I watched the starch go out of Barb's attitude. An envelope exchanged hands. From Barb to Rick.

Shades of Donald Maxwell Spielman. Everyone around him handling envelopes.

"Not the direction I was expecting," Mak said.

There was no handshake between the two. Their business concluded, at least for the time being, Barb took her leave. She left the playground and passed the Zephyr without seeing the rifle and kept hiking until she disappeared. Rick thumbed through the envelope and let out an audible cackle. Then he tucked the envelope into his pants, retrieved his rifle, and steered back toward his Monte Carlo. Mak and I followed from a distance.

I wasn't sure what was next. Maybe we had enough dirt for Elbridge. We could put him on Rick, leave Barb out of it, and let him track his way to the possibly corrupt agent on his own payroll. I'd never met Rick Ruiz. I was reasonably sure I couldn't be tied to any of this. Reasonably.

The goddamn dog gave us away. We weren't the only people breaking park rules. 350 acres, and we find the one stoner who had to walk his pit bull. The dog was leashed but machine-gun barked when we cleared the building. Rick was maybe twenty-five yards away but turned around immediately. He spotted the three of us, four if you counted the pit.

I don't know what got into me. Maybe it was the number of intangible uncertainties swirling around me. So many things I couldn't fight. Treasury. Augmented muscle. Jamie's cancer. But Rick I could see. He breathed and blinked. He was a little five-foot-nothing of a man, and on a good day, I could cover the distance between us in ten seconds.

No. Nine.

I took off while Rick was still flatfooted. I covered five yards. Ten. The burn felt good. Adrenaline pumped through my veins and the injuries of years past melted away. Rick came to his senses and bolted from the grass like he'd been struck by lightning. I sped up. We sprinted across the open field and toward the road. The Monte sat where he'd left it, the driver's-side door swung wide open. Rick pumped his arms but the rifle was unwieldy, the butt slapping him in the thighs. As we plowed downhill, I started to reel him in.

He reached the car first. Dove into the driver's seat and tried to yank the door shut. I reached him just after he tugged on the handle and threw myself between the closing door and the chassis.

They knew how to make cars back in the seventies. Big. Heavy. The door slammed into my left hip and crushed my thigh, then bounced open. My leg collapsed beneath me but I managed to pull Rick from the car as I fell. With a yelp, he popped clear of the seat. We wrestled in the dirt until I got him pinned under me. My leg throbbed and made it difficult to keep the wiry man still. He was strong.

He also still had the rifle.

The weapon's stock blindsided me. He'd grabbed the rifle by the barrel and swung it around in a wide arc, clocking me just outside my left eye. The world exploded. I fell over as he scrambled to his feet. I heard scuffling and the giant groan of the car door. Then a deep-throated growl as the Monte Carlo woke up. Dirt filled my nostrils and sharp pain stabbed at my skull. I hurt. But the car weighed almost two tons. The pain I was in now would be nothing compared to the crushing finality of the Monte Carlo running me over.

Hands under my arms. Mak had arrived.

"Move," she said.

I didn't need the encouragement.

I stumbled to my feet, nearly toppling Mak in the process. I turned to run. And that's when the car's headlights washed over us. Over Mak. She was half a step behind me and there was no time. Rick was going to hit her.

There was no time.

I lurched. Plowed into Mak and shoved her to one side. Her feet tangled underneath her and she fell into the dirt, landing on her face. I stood alone in the path of the Monte. The lights grew huge and I closed my eyes. The world went dark.

Nothing.

More nothing.

I opened my eyes.

Rick had yanked the wheel around to the right and spun the car down the road. A cloud of dust rose in his wake. He weaved back and forth across the pavement before disappearing out of sight around the bend.

Mak picked herself up off the ground. Her sweatshirt and jeans were covered in dirt. She didn't bother to clean herself. "You didn't have to knock me over."

"The car was about to hit you."

"Says you. I wasn't the one all starry-eyed after eating the wrong end of a rifle."

I blinked hard. My ears were ringing. "Is there a right end?"

Mak came to stand at my shoulder. "I could have talked to Barb. I was just kidding about the augment-pet thing."

"I know."

"You're old and slow. No way you were going to catch him. You should have let me chase him down."

"You're probably right."

Mak watched me shift my weight from one foot to another. Wince as I settled on the left leg.

"Pushing me out of the way," she said. "You could have been killed."

I didn't say anything.

"Thank you," she said.

I nodded, not quite looking her in the eye. She thought I had her back. She thought I was pushing her toward safety instead of quietly dragging her toward disaster.

I wished the car had hit me.

CHAPTER TWENTY-TWO

Near-death experiences exhaust a man. For once, Mak spared me questions and suppositions, and we drove home largely in silence, agreeing to meet tomorrow shortly before normal repo hours. Then we'd address the fuzzy threads connecting Donny and Barb and Rick Ruiz. I dropped Mak at her apartment and took myself home, eager to grab some sleep. Spots swam in my vision, blending with the cars and Speedsters and occasional lost souls stumbling along the highway in the dark. After not enough sleep and the chase and a gun to the face, I was dead on my feet. But as the traffic thinned and I neared my apartment complex, I realized I wouldn't be getting sleep anytime soon. Headlights filled my rearview. I eased onto the soft shoulder just outside the front gate and the headlights remained nailed to my bumper. The lights belonged to a stretch Town Car.

My legs sagged like wet toothpicks, but it wasn't the time to show weakness. I exited my truck and shuffled toward the car.

Blacked-out windows absorbed the lamplight and cast my dim reflection back at me. The car's owner cared a great deal about the windows. No augmented siloxane resins to repel the water. Instead, old-fashioned elbow grease. Wiping away the mud and the crushed bugs and the fine spots of dried rain. All for moments like this—when her opponents could peer into the window and face their worst fear. Themselves. Or maybe she just liked clean windows.

After I stood there long enough, the driver's-side door opened. A gorilla got out of the car. Literally.

"Skylark," I said.

"Gayle." Skylark's jaw stuck out a good half-finger farther than mine, mandible extruding past the maxilla, but her tongue and palate worked like a normal's. "Lady wants to talk to you."

Skylark, born in South Korea as Chan Sook Teng, endured what you'd expect coming out half-gorilla. Abandoned at an early age, she endured a series of unwelcoming foster homes and geek shows that could have warped a psyche for life. Could have, if she hadn't escaped to North Korea, where the government propped her up as a model of communist acceptance and thus moral superiority. The state showcased her around the country—aiding humanitarian efforts for flood victims, speaking to the Supreme People's Assembly. What then changed isn't clear, although many point to North Korea's weaponized augment program—the process of decanting power from a Natural and pouring the essence into molds approved by the North Korean government. Whatever the reason, seven years ago, Skylark defected to the United States of America, and by the next year she was on Ellen Clovis's payroll.

All that life experience, just to play the heavy in front of me.

She walked around the stretch and stopped at the back door. Stood there in a broad-shouldered steel-grey suit with a single black button. A mauve pocket square peeked out from her breast pocket.

"Nice suit," I remarked. "Custom?"

Skylark looked me up and down, eyes lingering on the bruises at my face and neck, finally settling on my weathered ostrich-skin boots and frayed jeans. "Texas Recovery has a dress code."

"Sounds restrictive. You ever consider changing firms?"

Her eyes flicked up to mine. "No."

Skylark stood on the balls of her feet. Her animal eyes watched me watching her. Despite her size, Skylark moved nimbly. I'd seen footage of her in action against augmented debtors—she built up a head of steam and charged, running her quarry down from behind as often as not. I figured sixty-to-forty against making it to my truck before she caught me. Maybe seventy-thirty.

I remembered the blur of her flying overhead at Big Fight. Wondered what Gas Mask had figured his odds to be.

I pointed at the rear door. "I don't want to talk to her."

Skylark was unmoved. "So?"

"So maybe I won't."

Skylark held her ground and kept quiet.

I feinted to the left. Skylark shuffle-stepped to block me, her breath chuffing in bursts.

My legs felt good. Fat bruises purpled my thighs, but the energy was there. Head a little foggy, throat a little sore. But I had gobs of willpower. And sheer cussedness.

I could take her.

"Stop it. Both of you."

Ellen Clovis had rolled down the rear window and dangled one small hand over the door. Clear polish covered her nails, and her fingers flushed pink like a newborn's. Misleading, as the woman wasn't new at anything, including being born. She had been a force on the repo scene for years, passing up other business opportunities and rejecting lucrative offers to sell Texas Recovery at above market value. She'd taken the firm public, endured the fickle highs and lows of the market, and taken the firm private again. Powerful, in both the normal and augmented sense, although interestingly, no one seemed to know what her power was. Invisibility? Telepathy? A permanent air of superiority? Her federal augment records had been expunged. Barely five feet tall and typically clad all in black, she was noticeable in any crowd. Life treated her well. Most of her clothing labels read Gucci.

"That was quite a display you were putting on, Mr. Harwood."

"What? Tailing another repo firm like an ambulance chaser? Yeah. That was embarrassing."

"Embarrassing would be letting Skylark tear you limb from limb. It's something she's been known to do, when asked."

"Really?" I swept my hand around in a magician's wave, highlighting the empty parking lot. "You going to order a beatdown in front of the drunks and the stoners? Please. You need the attention. After all—who brought the gorilla?"

Ellen sighed as if some internal load-bearing support was nearing collapse. "Get in the car."

Her hand disappeared as she retreated. Skylark popped open the door and glowered as I eased myself into the back seat.

Inside the car was all pale leather and burled walnut. Glossy flat-screen televisions were built flush into the back of the front seats, which were partitioned from the rear by a Plexiglas screen. After Skylark closed the door, the drone of the nearby highway was silenced, high-end acoustic baffling rendering the interior soundproof. Wrap-around bench seats filled the space, and a collection of the day's news-papers was tucked into the web mesh at each door. Ellen liked her information old- and new-school. The world poised at her fingertips.

As for the woman herself, she sat nestled in the corner, the *New York Times* folded and sitting on the lap of her pantsuit, her body emitting the faint powdery odor of lilacs. A gold cross hung at her neck, her finger idly rubbing the braided chain. A chilled glass of white wine hovered within reach, the thin-stemmed glass clamped in a modified cupholder designed to hold the narrow flute. I thought of Nether-house's two trucks, both purchased on five-year loans. I thought of Jamie's chemo treatments. A sick taste like vinegar scorched my throat.

Ellen offered me a glass of sauvignon blanc and I refused. The throbbing returned in my head, like Rick had left his rifle buried in my skull.

"I hope you won't find it bold of me to say"—Ellen cast her appraising eyes my way—"but you're not looking very well. Are the late nights disagreeing with you?"

"We all get older."

She flicked out her fingers and acquired her glass of white. She sipped in carefully measured doses. "Not all of us. The All-American Man fought in World War One, and he finished second on that ridiculous reality program last year."

"Must be the steroids."

That fouled the taste of her wine. The corners of her mouth twisted. I watched ridges form in her expensive designer lipstick.

"I'm wondering if you aren't up to this business any longer."

"I'm fine."

"I wouldn't blame you. Financial concerns. A family member in ill health. I'd hate to see Mak dragged down by a partner whose head wasn't in the game."

Her voice was a low rattle with a nasty rasp, like a snake in the bushes. She knew about Jamie. What else did she know?

"What do you want, Ellen? Why were you following me?"

As we'd talked, Skylark had dropped back into the car, wedging into the front seat and staring into the rearview with her red-tinged eyes. She caught me watching and raised the partition.

"I don't care for the implication," Ellen said. "Why couldn't I be out for a drive? Barton Springs Pool is beautiful at night. I'm sure the view is what brought you there."

The look on my face was meant to convey the polite interest of a man visiting the sandpaper museum. I couldn't let her provoke a reaction. Maybe she'd only followed us back from Zilker.

"Ellen Clovis with her Jimmy Choos dipped in Austin pond water?" I said. "Drinking a PBR under the stars?" I scanned the car's interior. "Please."

With a smooth motion, Ellen brought the gold wine to her lips and allowed a trace of a smile to soften her features. "I suppose I could tell you what I'm doing." Another sip, then she settled the glass back in its elegant holder. "I'm looking for Doctor Dimension's ring, the same as you."

I tried to keep a bland expression, but I knew my eyes had settled into something resembling an angry bear. "You think Netherhouse is looking for a ring we already returned?"

Ellen laughed. Almost cackled. "Such games. You didn't honestly expect me to ignore the most significant Treasury investigation since Sister Chaos stole the Moontowers in 2004? I'm well aware of your involvement in the activity at Memorial Stadium."

"You're fishing," I said. "This is a snipe hunt."

Ellen stared at me.

"You know what a snipe is?" I asked.

"The impossible or imaginary. Otherwise known as bullshit." She reached for her glass but didn't drink. "Bullshit is something I'm very familiar with, as was your former partner. This stinks of him. Lies were his forte. That and a penchant for skirting the law."

"Look who's talking." I nodded at Skylark hulking in the front seat. "How did you get her out of North Korea? I mean, it was you, wasn't it? How did you do it? Bribes? Teleportation? Tell me it was teleportation. That would be so cool."

Teleportation was up there with phasing. Munitions. Government-restricted. Akin to carting nuclear materials up and down Pennsylvania Avenue.

"The North Korean government treated Chan Sook like an animal." There was a schoolteacher quality to her, the way she arched her back and steeled her eyes and rubbed those quick, dry fingers together. Despite my dislike for Ellen Clovis, I felt a compulsion to pay attention. "Gorillas in the zoo are given more dignity. She was paraded about as if she were nothing more than a communist token. Behold the great democratic empire and how it has leashed the beast. Propaganda of the worst sort."

"Oh, yes. You'd certainly never march her down the promenade like she was first-prize pig at the fair."

"Tripe. She is an Augment—she is superior. Every interview, every broadcast opportunity, raises us up. North Korea attempted to turn her into a commodity, no better than boys with toys."

The famed disdain for anyone achieving superior ability through an augment device. She said *boys with toys* so often, she was a caricature of herself. "Discriminate much?"

"I simply speak the truth."

Ellen's fingers kept returning to the gold cross. I'd heard of her quite-public church attendance, a rarity in a world where the Pope condemned Augments as immoral. "Sermon on the Mount?"

She lifted one leg and crossed it over her knee. She was enjoying the conversation. "The augment crime rate is twenty percent less than that of weaponized humans. Twenty percent." She puffed out her lips, and I smelled the wine on her breath. "You'd use my faith to dismiss me, but perhaps God is sending us a message."

My eyes went to the partition and the gorilla on the other side. "And Skylark? She sign on for this augment public service? The Ellen Clovis hype machine?"

She caught a fresh dollop of wine on her tongue. "They are employees, not partners. That's not how it's done."

"I'm sure the organ grinder never asks his monkey about pay equality either."

Ellen's knuckles blanched against the stem of her wineglass. "You're being rude."

"I'm sorry. Who was following who?"

"Not following. Saving."

I frowned. "Excuse me?"

"Why am I not surprised to find ingratitude among your many flaws? Have you forgotten Big Fight? The expected response when someone saves your life is *thank you*."

I stared at the gorilla in the front seat. Skylark didn't move, but her neck tensed.

Ellen put a hand on my knee. "Who do you think fought off your attackers?"

The blur of muscled hair, the echo of an animal's roar. I didn't like being reminded of my debts. Particularly when owed to a rival.

"It's clear there are people of significance interested in Doctor Dimension's ring. I'd suggest these people are out of your league. They can be damaging, physically and otherwise."

"That sounds like a threat."

"Not from me. I have no legal authority here. I cannot pressure banks to turn over their records simply because they do business with Netherhouse Liquidation. It would not be me asking the types of questions that make your clients nervous. Exerting influence to impact your business. Your ex-wife. Your daughter. Your partner."

The car was cold. I rubbed my arms. "My mistake. You're Mother Teresa."

"We can help each other."

"Netherhouse doesn't subcontract."

Her smile could have cut glass. "Amusing. But not the relationship I had in mind."

If she knew everything, she wouldn't have me here in the car. If she'd wanted to crush me, she'd have done it in a room with no windows and far away from neighborhood busybodies. "Let's hear it."

"Texas Recovery has been engaged by Treasury to find the ring. It would appear a few others have a certain itch for the device as well. Between Andrew's desire to shut you down and those chasing the ring, you need all the help you can get."

Others. Did she mean the gas masks who attacked me at Big Fight? I didn't dare ask.

"Tell me what you know. Connect the dots between your thieving former partner and Mr. Hank Ruiz. You worked with Donny all those years. You must know something."

She knew about Ruiz. I didn't react, only stared at her *New York Times*. Rumor had it she read it front to back. Every page of every section. "And then what?"

"My firm recovers this dangerous item. Texas Recovery once again leaves the government satisfied, and everyone walks away happy."

"Leaving Netherhouse where exactly?"

"I would imagine if your role in whatever occurred was not significant, your firm would be cleared. In my experience, Andrew won't chase a loser. He's regaled me before with his case methodology. I can see him now, on his back porch, nursing his Macallan 18, one hand stroking his mangy border collie. He'll say *That dog won't hunt* or offer similar cornpone wisdom. In that event, Netherhouse could continue to chase augmented bicycles and other fare more appropriate to your business."

Mention of Elbridge's scotch and dog. Reminding me of her influence with the local power players. "I give you Dimension's ring, and you keep us in business?"

"I arrange it such that there's no point in Treasury pursuing you.

Or anyone else with a mind to." She looked me in the eyes. "If trust is an issue, I can have my lawyers draw up binding papers before end of day tomorrow."

Any satisfaction I felt knowing Ellen needed us to *connect the dots* paled compared to the bitterness of realizing she'd capitalize on the publicity of the recovery. TR succeeds where Netherhouse failed. At long last, Dimension's ring brought to light. Even if she failed to uncover the ring, she'd bring the perpetrators to light, and in such a way she'd benefit.

No way she wouldn't take her shots at Netherhouse.

What would Mak have me do? Take the deal? Not take the deal? This was Ellen Clovis, and we were talking binding legal arrangements. Oaths signed in blood with a woman who'd—per Donny—tried to wipe us off the map since before I'd even met her. She was our Ragnarök. Our end of days.

Then again, maybe she was something else. A port in a storm. She could be protection from a very big storm.

They are employees, not partners.

I returned Ellen's stare. Felt the words back up behind my teeth and realized they were never coming out.

There'd never been any doubt in my mind Mak would one day be my partner, not from the moment she walked into our office for an interview.

Ellen didn't do partners.

"I don't think we'd bring anything to the table," I said. "Like I said, the ring was lost years ago."

Her eyes lit up with wicked fire. "You're refusing my offer?"

"The deal is all downside."

Ellen drained the last of her glass and parked the empty in the elaborate holder. She took a deep breath. "I know you're involved."

I felt a bone-deep cold. As if the air conditioning had been cranked down to Antarctica.

"I wasn't quite sure who had the ring," she said. "At first, I assumed Donny. Then Hank Ruiz. But with the pair expired and you still scrambling so fiercely, the answer became obvious. You have it."

I put my elbows on my knees. "Why would you think I have it?"

"No incidents involving the ring in all these years, until now. Then your recent hardships. You intend to sell the ring, Donny isn't in agreement. A quarrel on a bus. Circumstances head south. You might argue self-defense, I suppose, although my interest in any particular outcome for you expired moments ago."

"I held the ring all these years for no reason?" I was so ready to eviscerate her pet theory. "Kept it in a cigar box?"

"You were holding it. For Doctor Dimension."

Ellen swirled her wine in the bowl of her glass, the name reverberating in the silence. I'm not sure she realized what she'd said. I'd seen Doctor Dimension pancaked under an avalanche of concrete and steel.

"You think he's coming back for it?"

"I'm not sure how you expect him to escape the confines of Bonnell Prison, but yes, I imagine you were compensated to hold it for the man. With a sum that seemed adequate at the time. But once you take a bribe and break the law, it's likely a short trip to blackmail and fencing stolen goods."

The United States government denied the existence of Bonnell, the fabled prison lying within the mathematically unproven dimension known as N Space. Thousands of Americans requested information on the alleged super-secret augment holding facility every year. Documents had been released, but the evidence was a mobius strip of references to other agencies, a trail of paper eating its own tail. NSA. CIA. Treasury. Anything near the truth fell under Above Top Secret, a rating in and of itself said not to exist. But then in 1919, when the first Augments showed themselves, the government denied them too.

Ellen thought Dimension was alive. Alive and confined to an impossible prison.

"It will all come out in the end," Ellen continued. "We'll expose you and Donny and the late Hank Ruiz. We'll recover the ring, and when we do, the blowback will be messy. It always is."

Ellen traded a look with Skylark via rearview mirror. The locks popped open. Skylark heaved herself from the bowels of the front seat.

"I'm afraid I don't have time to fight your battles, Mr. Harwood," Ellen said as Skylark tugged open my door. "Thank you for the conversation."

I stepped out of the car. Outside, the moon had clouded over, and the sky was a blue-grey wall of cement. It appeared another squall was blowing into town.

"And tell your partner I'm serious." Ellen leaned over, making sure I could hear her. "About the job offer."

"Yeah?"

"We provide ample salary, full health benefits, and a 401(k) with match. Even transportation."

I hated that I was listening. "Mak has a truck."

"How about a motorcycle? A 1958 Manx Norton."

On the weekends, my partner rode. She suited up in a blue-polyester-and-black-rubber road jacket with zippers at the sleeves and extra cushioning at the elbows. Then she climbed aboard a used Honda CBR, an inexpensive street-legal racing bike that got her from point A to point B. And she rode. She'd invited me to ride on the back, but I'd always turned her down, begging off the bitch seat but really more concerned with the top speed of 160 mph. The coward in me avoided Mak when she talked motorcycles and ram-air ducts and inverted forks. Despite that, I had captured one salient fact. Mak would love to own a 1958 Manx Norton.

"Bullshit," I said.

"Featherbed frame. 495cc."

Ellen produced a 4x6, which she offered me with a smile. "For your partner."

The number 31 mounted on the front. The bike's polish so vivid, the photo alone nearly blinded me.

I backed away. Left the snapshot in Ellen's hands. "Try the post office."

She smirked, returned the photo to the recesses of her mobile lair. "Think of Mak as your friend, not your employee. When Netherhouse is shut down by the state, what then? My offer may not be nearly so generous."

Skylark pushed herself between me and the stretch. Ellen started to roll up her window.

"Now get away from my car."

The wind howled as Skylark returned to the driver's seat. She jerked the car into reverse and darted into the road, performing an illegal U-turn as she plowed toward the highway with nary a care. It was funny. Skylark was more graceful on her feet than she was behind the wheel.

After I finally reached my apartment, I texted Mak to make sure she'd made it home in one piece. She rang me back immediately.

"I got a black eye when you went all chivalrous." Mak was chewing loudly into the phone. "Mom saw the shiner. She said only a coward hits girls, and she'd appreciate it if you stopped knocking me to the ground."

"Jesus. You told Aroha?"

"She's my mom. Of course I told her. It's not like she caught us necking on the couch."

The thought made me shudder.

I told her about my chat with Ellen. I described her partnership proposal and my none-too-gracious refusal. I mentioned the job offer. Mak laughed.

"Join the Ellen Clovis collection?" she said. "Like a fucking Hummel figurine? No, thanks. Makes me wish I'd been there to tell her off in person."

"Yeah," I said. "Me too."

I didn't mention the motorcycle.

CHAPTER TWENTY-THREE

Rain soaked the Austin streets. A heavy grey curtain that washed away the trash and the dirt. Many cultures found transformative power in rain showers. Considered them a blessing or a sign of new life.

If I stepped outside, would I feel clean or just wet?

"Earth to Gayle." Mak said. "Got someplace better to be?"

It was the day after my tete-a-tete with Ellen. We were at the office, strategizing our next move. I stood at the window. Mak sat at her desk with Dru's laptop, doggedly trying to reconcile our finances. Every now and again I'd heard her grunt, like she'd touched a bruise. The pained results of last night's near encounter with the car, or a reaction to our dwindling capital.

"Just trying to make sense of it all," I said.

"I can't believe Ellen thinks you have the ring." Mak shook her head. "I love what you've parlayed that power into."

Her tone sarcastic, but the words landing on me like the bridge I'd seen crush Dimension. I didn't say anything.

"If it helps, Dru identified the two douchebags who roughed you up at Big Fight."

Of course our skip tracer had never stopped working. She was as reliable as Austin traffic. "Really? Do tell?"

"Denis and Isaac Traden. They're small-time muscle-for-hire. Soldier-of-fortune types. Denis is the big one, but he and Isaac are both Naturals. Augmented strength, although a lethal oxygen allergy, thus the masks. Treasury has busted them before, but they always get kicked."

"We know who they're working for?"

"Like I said, they're for hire. Could be anybody."

The lunch-hour rush flooded the streets. An eighteen-wheeler flew along in the rain. A cyclist popped the sidewalk and gave the big-rig driver the finger. The driver was a robot and didn't much seem to care.

"You think he's really alive?" Mak asked.

"Who?"

"Doctor Dimension?"

"No." I didn't hesitate. "Bonnell is an urban legend. A deep-state myth. There's no such thing. And even if there was, Dimension died."

"People say that. So-and-so died. But really, how often do we really see a human being die? Take their pulse? Verify that Elvis has left the building?"

I had seen the bridge fall. Watched slabs of concrete and steel collapse. In the eyeblink before disaster, I'd spotted the tiny figure of Dimension on the far shore, the man looking up as the inevitable crashed into him. His remains were claimed by Treasury, his burial site kept secret to avoid tributes from his disturbed fanbase. So the story went.

"Ellen was drinking. She plays mind games. You know the woman."

"I do." The laptop's glow leached the color from Mak's face. "Where does that leave us?"

"We could consider the less-outlandish portions of her story. Donny steals the ring. Barb covers it up. Hank Ruiz fences the ring to an unknown buyer, not me. Proceeds are distributed to our three participants. And all's well that ends well."

"Until what? What changes?" Mak shut the laptop. Her eyes traveled the office until they landed on the desk she occupied. The one that used to be Donny's. "Someone died. Hank Ruiz died."

I pictured the envelope traveling from Barb to Rick. Envelopes were passed to keep people quiet. "Hank Ruiz died, and his brother Rick inherited his effects." I rubbed my head and put myself in the head of an enterprising individual with reduced moral boundaries.

"These junk guys—they're pack rats by nature. They can't help themselves. If there was evidence of the arrangement to sell Dimension's ring, Hank couldn't have brought himself to destroy it. He'd have kept it."

"And Rick found the evidence when he took possession. And figured, hey, where's my cut?"

"Enter blackmail. He blackmails Donny and Barb."

"And the buyer." The chair groaned as Mak leaned back. "The person with the ring—they don't appreciate the squeeze. More to lose, maybe."

I turned to face my partner. "*I'm not paying*, they say. Or they pay once, and Rick hits them again. Regardless, there's too many loose ends."

"So, they have to tie off the loose ends." Mak made a fist and aimed it my way, like she was about to shoot fire from her knuckles. "Or phase them into oblivion."

The joke did little to ease my nerves. "The buyer is covering their tracks. They killed Donny because he knew too much."

"That's our theory." Mak watched me. "It's certainly enough of a story to feed Elbridge."

The concept of Elbridge pulling threads I had not thoroughly explored filled me with dread. I slow-walked to my chair and eased into it. "Not very concrete."

"We've charged into repos with less intel."

"This is Treasury. If we sell them a bridge, they'll be up our ass forever."

Mak spread her hands. "Why do I feel like you're stalling?"

"I'm not stalling. You know I need this resolved. I'm suggesting the best way to do that is to provide proof."

Mak glanced at Patrick's empty desk. Dru was also out of the office, chasing records at City Hall. "You'd better hope those two are earning us money."

"That's what we hired them for."

"You hired Patrick."

Some days, the jokes about Patrick—not always jokes—didn't land. "What'd you want me to do? Hire Skylark?"

"Worked well enough for Ellen."

"Great. Maybe you should go work for her."

Mak shook her head. She spun her chair away from me and picked up one of her inert grenades. She turned it over in her hands as if she might discover a way to make it explosive again.

Usually, I was difficult to anger. But every now and again, something changed. It wasn't so much I ran out of patience. Instead, a little alarm went off inside me, saying *It's time*. The fury simply waiting for its turn. Even with friends and family, my anger would spike white-hot and I'd yell words I'd barely considered or recognized, venom with an intensity that surprised even me. Jekyll and Hyde, a me I barely knew.

Like the man who'd taken the envelope. Angry at the world for denying him *his*.

Mak replaced the grenade but didn't let go. "I'm sorry."

"You? What are you sorry for?"

My partner didn't conjure emotion often. Her voice quavered. "The Ellen thing. That's my fault."

"I don't see how. She followed me, not you."

"She wouldn't be interested in the firm except for me."

"Well, she does seem keen to claim you as the latest trophy. But I don't think—"

"I applied for a job."

The world tilted on its axis. "You did what?"

She squeezed the grenade. "Last year. After the Rundberg Eel job."

"We didn't get that guy. He escaped into a storm drain."

"I needed the money, is what I'm saying. The recovery fee from that job wasn't just another couple hundred bucks. I couldn't make rent. Mom had her hip thing—she couldn't help out. Nate's ear got infected. The truck broke down. This shit happens all at once and you tell yourself you're going to get through it. One foot in front of the other and you'll make it through the minefield. Only, the field was all mines. There was nowhere to step."

She didn't see me or the office, lost somewhere inside her head. I recognized the look.

"I went to Ellen," she said. "I took a bus and walked to 5th and Brazos, like I was afraid of being followed. I spent an hour in the first-floor lobby drinking coffee, telling myself that was all I was there to do. But then I went up and she saw me, no appointment. She was perfectly polite. She offered me a job on the spot, the compensation package everything I could ever want it to be."

I waited. The story poured out of her.

"She has this glass office, you know. Fifteen floors up, so far. Every year, she watches the leases on the higher floors, moves the firm up to bigger and better when she can. But on fifteen her office is all glass, and I can see the people working for her. Black Tornado. Narita Helmy—she's got that Everything Bag—almost nothing she can't carry off. The shark guy. Big-deal Augments. I watch them trudge back and forth while Ellen and I are talking reserved parking spaces, and I realize any one of them might have been me. They could have walked in here, thinking this was the path to making their life better. The money and the flash. A future guaranteed. But all you had to do was take a good look at them, bent and broken. The money gone. The flash faded. Ellen wasn't offering anything that lasted, certainly nothing like a partnership. Nothing to build, nothing to care for. Not unless you cared to build and protect Ellen."

She finally released the grenade.

"I walked out. I'm sure it stuck in her craw. I took the stairs down, all fifteen flights. Shame or penance, I don't know. And Ellen has been chasing me ever since."

She bowed her head. "I'm sorry."

My partner was tall. A lot taller than me. She looked small, bent in on herself. "Stop it."

"It's easy to blame you. You're a walking target. And I take every shot, every time. Like I'm so much better."

"Mak. Stop it."

"You don't have a Vegas lifestyle. I've seen the chateau you live in. Moving boxes and milk crates. You've got a kid, same as me." She looked horrified. "Only not the same as me. Jesus, the shit you have. That beautiful girl and what the two of you have to endure. I'm such an asshole."

"None of this is your fault. You have to stop blaming yourself."

"I betrayed you."

"Fuck. I did it, Mak. I did it."

She stopped talking. Broke off her thousand-yard stare and looked at me. "What did you do?"

"I took the goddamn bribe. Donny paid me to look the other way and I did. I took the money, Mak." Fifteen years of history and I ran out of words after three sentences. "I took the money."

The muscles froze under her skin. Her eyes sank.

"I never saw the ring. Donny arranged the whole thing. I never knew he had partners; I didn't know about Barb. He didn't tell me a thing until after; he just shows up in the office with this envelope of money and—"

Mak shot out of her chair. She squeezed her eyes shut. "You told me you didn't know."

"It was a long time ago." My voice came out soft. "I'm not proud of what I did. I convinced myself I had to take it. If I could go back—"

"But you can't." My partner was all flint and steel. "Don't give my your if *I could go back* bullshit. All the augmentation in the world can't change the past. You made your fucking choice. There's consequences." She looked around at our sparse surroundings. "There should be consequences."

I wanted to come out of my chair and reach for her. We weren't the hugging type, but I was afraid she'd walk out the front door and never come back. She looked angry. She looked disgusted. The reflection of myself in her face nearly drove me to my knees.

"Don't call me," she said.

Then she walked out the front door.

CHAPTER TWENTY-FOUR

I saw a lot of the moon. Normal sleep was always a tall order, made no easier by the baggage I carried. I tossed and turned for ninety minutes. My tongue felt like I'd been chewing a cat. Brain tissue swelled against my skull and threatened to split the bone open at the seams. It was possible my condition was the result of head trauma. A pistol-whipping and rifle beating in the span of a few days. Or the aches were my body's way of punishing me for bad choices. Many years of bad choices.

My firm teetered on the brink. My friendship with Mak was in tatters. I tried to remember what I'd bought with the six thousand Donny used to buy me. A wagon for Jamie? A house payment? A new washing machine and an oncologist bill? Or had I simply handed the cash to Charlie and gone on living? Did we own a single thing bought with those ill-gotten gains?

When ten AM arrived, I'd slept only fitfully. I ran warm water over the nicks and cuts in my arms. Splashed cold water on my face. Looking in the mirror, I resembled an over-the-hill boxer too dumb to take a payout. Or just dumb enough.

I made some calls. Tried to wrap my arms around our financial situation. The banks knew Netherhouse and they knew me. Years of recoveries going back before some of the employees had been born. Surely, they'd look upon us favorably, after all we'd done for them. They told me business didn't really work that way. Treasury had frozen our accounts, it seemed, a hard freeze unable to be thawed by warm relations. And that wasn't all. One of the banks carried the notes on our F-150s, Mak's and mine. Those payments were coming due, frozen assets or no. They'd hate to send someone to repo the repo man. The shame of that image was almost worse than the idea of losing the truck. Almost.

I thought about calling Mak. I brought up her contact on my phone and realized I had nothing to deliver but bad news. I'd already sucker-punched her. She didn't need me to sweep her legs out from under as well.

Sitting there in my dark apartment, I knew what I needed to do. I'd been afraid, of the truth certainly but also of the law. Growing up, I'd believed in the shield of law enforcement. My parents were salt of the earth. Yankees, truth be told. Augments scared them. They'd read about the scarier incidents—Faultline triggering Mount St. Helens, the augmented Russians who'd swept the '80 Olympics—and worried over their place in the world. But they paid their taxes, so they looked to the sheriff and the local cops to keep things safe for normals like us. If you see an Augment, they'd said, find a police officer. And when Treasury assumed control of augment affairs, my parents were right there, nodding their heads. Finally, someone to watch the watchers. To keep the crooked straight. Funny how long I'd clung to that fantasy, even as I'd gotten into the business and seen how many agents were as tempted by power as the Augmented. They were human. Subject to prejudice and anger and greed.

Greed.

I got off my ass and went to see a Treasury agent.

* * *

Despite the Austin address, the inside of Barb's home was Waco chic. She owned a full set of John Wayne DVDs and a scattershot collection of ceramic pigs. There were expansive wood beams bisecting the ceiling and swaths of subway tile in the kitchen. A barn-door coffee table anchored the living room, and throw pillows stitched with random letters accented the furniture. The house offered more styling than I would have expected from Barb. I'd assumed sawdust and spent rounds.

Barb herself was still dressed for business, wearing the navy suit and white button-down I'd watched her stroll in with from the comfort of my truck.

"Help yourself to the Bushmills. It's a twelve-year." Barb unslung her jacket and went to hang it in the hall closet. "She ain't getting any younger."

She didn't seem surprised to see me. Regarded my cat-dragged-in appearance with resignation, as if I was the fate she'd expected all along.

A laptop sat open on the coffee table, a newer model where the screen rotated to become a tablet or a watch or a surfboard. Bold letters promised the content on this screen was restricted to Treasury personnel. I saw active case notes. A con woman pretending to be in repo and making off with augmented backhoes. A known grifter claiming pay protection in fifteen different augmented supergroups. The collected background on the Rita Pham shooting.

"You're on the congresswoman thing?" I asked. "She's a big deal. You're finally moving up in the world."

Barb frowned. She marched over and pushed the laptop shut.

I settled myself into an oversized leather chair and stared at the dark television. A ninety-incher. As thin as my pinkie.

"Quite the place," I said.

"Just me, myself, and I. Leaves me a few extra peanuts."

She finished her Mister Rogers routine. Slipped off her shoes and poured us both half-glasses of whisky and sat across from me on the sofa.

"I saw you in Zilker," I said. "You and Rick Ruiz."

Barb stared at me. The Rock of Gibraltar. The boozer I always saw concealing the hard cop underneath.

"How much is he taking out of your pocket?" I asked. "Blackmail has to be hard on an agent's salary, even a dirty one."

"You didn't see anything." Barb chased her statement with a drink. "You don't know anything."

"Is that an answer or a warning?"

"You're accusing a Treasury agent, hombre. That's dangerous. If we weren't friends—"

"We're friends? That why you chased me to my daughter's chemo? Asked me those questions about Donny? Because you were worried about your friend?"

"Fuck off. You come into my house, insult my integrity. I tell you—you're no better than the rest of them. You don't know me. I have half a mind to throw you out before you finish your drink."

"Mak wants me to go to Elbridge with what we have. To get him off our back."

Her eyes hardened. "Try it."

"You say that, but think. What do I have to lose? He's threatening to close us down. He froze our accounts. I'll lose the business and the money. The money, Barb. You can understand that. I don't know what cash in hand means to you, but for me it means everything. Beds and blankets and drugs I can't pronounce, let alone afford. I need every dollar. My daughter needs every dollar. So, you can tell me what I need to know, or I can call Andrew Elbridge. You know I hate his guts. But I will call."

Barb studied her black socks. One white toe poked through the left foot.

"I told Donny this was too big," she said. "Even back then. Stick to the small stuff. Hoverboards and bulletproof tattoo ink. But he wanted Dimension. Extra grit in Andy's eye, a benefit aside from the payday." She shook her head. "Goddamn greed. It got us both."

"You're Donny's inside man? You whitewash his thefts."

"That's a pretty coat of paint. Most of the time, I just had to turn a blind eye. You steal English-enhancing cues out of some skag's jet-powered Mustang, who's going to notice, so long as they get their car back? The criminal complains, maybe? Who cares? They're not a real person."

Barb's voice halfway between indignation and self-incrimination. I wanted to reach across the distance and slap her. Instead, I took a sip of her whisky. It was good.

"Hank Ruiz fenced the goods?"

"In the beginning. The old redneck had connections. Guys up and down 35 who'd buy augmented stuff, no papers, no questions asked. He kept me and Donny at a distance. Little did we know that peckerwood wrote everything down."

"That's how Rick Ruiz discovered your operation," I said.

"Asshole." Barb seized her glass. "The both of them. Hank goes and dies, leaves that pile of shit to his brother. And that man is a snake. He's dirty, dirty. Not even honor among thieves, for Christ's sake."

"Did you send those two gorillas to beat me up? The Tradens?"

"As if I need help to kick your ass. No, I did not send gorillas to beat you up. You have me confused with Her Highness Ellen Clovis."

"But you did volunteer to scoop me up after DKR? You weren't above chasing me to Jamie's chemo."

Her nostrils flared. "Donny always said you had nothing to do with it, but Donny would claim he saw Bigfoot if there was dollars in it. Elbridge kept saying your name. I had to be sure." She drank. "I wasn't proud of it."

Brown liquid ran down her chin and blotted the collar of her shirt. She didn't seem to care.

"And all the bullshit you sold me in the car? About Ladykiller and the victims? I saw you the other day. The pilgrimage to that woman's house. Was that just theater? Did you know we were following you?"

Her eyes grew curious. "You followed me to Carol's?"

"The old lady with the dog? Yeah. Mak was even in your backseat."

Barb paused. Stared through me as if to take my measure. Then she cackled. "You guys aren't bad, Gayle, not bad. No, I never saw you. I go out there and visit on the regular, her and a few others. A lot of the support groups are too churchy. They serve a good dose of blame with their comfort. I don't do that; I just listen. Makes me easy to be with. Hell, I even drove down to Wimberley with Carol, shopped for tchotchkes and all that touristy stuff. I may be a shit agent, but I'm not an all-bad human being. I feel for the woman. We promised to protect her. Said we'd find the guy. And we failed on both counts. Treasury isn't there to do good. It's a club for social climbers." She dumped half her glass down her throat. "It's every woman for herself."

I didn't have the words. Neither did Barb.

We drank that way for a while. Finished our drinks and Barb refilled. I chipped away at my second whisky in small dollops, but I still felt the alcohol's heat build behind my teeth.

"Who killed Donny?"

Barb swirled the liquid in her glass and didn't answer.

"Is it the buyer?" I asked. "Rick poked a beehive, right? Black-mailed the wrong person, and now they're covering their tracks?"

Barb propped her feet on the table. She balanced her drink in one hand and tilted her head back to stare at the ceiling. "When this is done, you're calling Treasury."

"I said I wouldn't."

"You lied. It makes sense. Whether I confess or not, you have to call. It's your only out. You said it—don't pretend we're friends here."

She contemplated spending her autumnal years in a prison or at the very least unemployed and absent a pension. The image made me wonder how things could have been different. If I'd reached out to Barb back when I started, could we have saved each other from the corruption? Said no to envelopes full of dirty cash?

"You can get in front of it," I said. "Cop a plea or whatever. But you need to tell me who the buyer is."

She kept her eyes on the ceiling and shook her head. "Can't believe Mak was in the goddamn car. She's a fucking Amazon and I didn't even see her."

I'd had too much to drink. I needed to take a piss.

"I'm going to use the facilities," I said. "And when I come back, we're going to figure this out. You're going to tell me about the night at Lady Bird Lake and the bus and who the fuck is phasing people into slag. Sure, you took a cut, but somewhere out there is a crazy person with one of the most powerful augment devices ever created. You cannot let that happen for less than it costs to buy a fucking motorcycle."

I thought about the Manx Norton.

"Most motorcycles," I said.

I stumbled down the hallway before I peed my pants.

CHAPTER TWENTY-FIVE

Barb's bathroom was a tabernacle. It was spotless. A full roll of toilet paper with the end triangled, a candle obscuring unpleasant odors, recent magazines layered in a wicker bin. The mirror was sharper than reality and there wasn't a crusty toothbrush or embarrassing medication to be seen. It was not the neglected disaster I'd expected. Seemed there was a Barb underneath the public image. More than one. The dirty cop. The sympathetic ear. None of us knew the full story.

Out in the living room I heard the television scream to life. Barb cursed and turned down the sound. She was clumsy and loud. But maybe she knew that.

I put my hands on either side of the sink and stared at myself in the mirror. How different were Barb and I, anyway? What mistakes had she made that I hadn't? In twenty years, I might be Barb.

The thought didn't sober me up, but it came close.

The tap water ran cold. I splashed water on my face and took a leak and swung my arms in an effort to force the alcohol from my bloodstream. Augment science had conquered a great many things, but it still hadn't devised a cure for the common hangover.

Drinking had been a mistake. I needed a clear head. Barb had lied to people for years. Friends. Loved ones. Her superiors.

But then, so had I.

I made ready to ferret out the truth. Crack the nut that was Barbara Cahill. That's when I heard the noises.

A low gurgle. Thumping, like a child beating against the wall.

I hauled open the door. Zigzagged down the hallway until I

finally rediscovered the living room. The lights were dimmed and the television—tuned to ESPN Augmented—was muted. Barbara Cahill was sitting on her coffee table with a pair of hands embedded in her chest.

The two hands guttered in and out of existence, thrust into her chest up to the wrists. The wrists were attached to a blur, a smudge on reality I couldn't blink away. On the other end of the blur, Barb was seizing, her face contorted in a rictus of pain, her head snapping back and forth like she'd grabbed a live wire.

I didn't particularly care for Barb. We swapped a bottle of Bushmills at Christmas. I listened to her conspiracy-laden tales of stolen investigations and stymied promotions. I related as much as a man can to a woman's trials. But she was tough company. She was abrasive and tactless. She made mistakes that reminded me of my own failures.

Her face was the color of old meat.

I tackled the blur. Barb sagged and I staggered against something hard, a scarecrow of pointed bone. One flickering hand reached out of Barb's ribcage and swiped at my arm. My fingers went numb and my legs melted. I fell to the ground and bounced off the carpeted floor. It felt like cold steel had severed my arm from my body. I'd been shot before. This was worse.

Somewhere nearby, Barb gargled apologies. She'd fallen backwards over the coffee table and landed in a heap near the couch. The blur couldn't focus—maybe I'd distracted it. Hard edges crystallized and the thing pushed into existence like a snow-buried bike after a spring thaw. The fuzzy cloak melted away and I was confronted with the shape of my attacker.

Baggy jeans. A loose purple polo. A black leather jacket more suited to an offensive tackle than this man, particularly since he'd lost his augmented hammer. Woody Chaikin looked like shit warmed over. He looked like I felt.

He crouched and set his hand on my chest. I blinked as his fingers spread over my heart and I saw a black ring. The underside wrapped in pink yarn to keep the tungsten from sliding off his finger.

"We're not friends," he said, actually managing to sound hurt. "I told you."

My tongue curled back on itself. Pain shot out of my arm and jumped down my torso like electricity. Woody appeared sympathetic.

"Cellular disruption," he said. "Two objects occupying the same space at the same time. Without protection, the effect can be fatal."

He lifted his hand, although I swore I could still feel the weight on my chest. I watched the black circle of the ring rise and arc across my vision like a moon. Doctor Dimension's ring.

Barb didn't move. I couldn't tell if she was dead or alive. The way my arm twitched, I couldn't tell if I was going to live either.

"Why?" I managed.

Woody didn't answer. He wobbled. He frowned and put his hand back on my chest.

"I'm sorry about this," he said. "I am."

I closed my eyes. I couldn't breathe. A little voice in the back of my brain told me to get up. Act now or die on this floor. But my arms wouldn't move. My body didn't listen. I shuddered and bit my tongue until hot blood spilled down my throat and a scream built up in my chest. There wasn't a soul anywhere who could help. There was no hereafter, no great beyond. I'd never believed otherwise, and as the scream neared its escape, I knew that I'd been right. I was going to die.

And then Woody removed his hand.

Water slid down my cheeks. Beyond the tears I could see Woody squatting on his heels, his palms pressed into his sockets, his shoulders shaking.

My body short-circuited. Hot urine spilled down my thighs and drool rolled down my chin. I wanted to ask for help but my tongue hung in my mouth like a wet sock.

"I can't," Woody said, although whether to me or Barb or just himself, I couldn't tell.

He stood. His body stretched like a time-lapse photograph.

Then he walked through the table and the couch and the wall like they weren't even there.

I tried to call Barb's name. Maybe I did.

One breath. And another. Someone would come. Someone would hear.

I closed my eyes and let my heart slow to a complete stop.

CHAPTER TWENTY-SIX

When I woke, the doctor was asking how much deeper he should cut.

The man hovered over me, telescopic eyes blinking huge at my incapacity. My arm was clamped to the table and covered in a thin blue sheet, a square cut where they'd made the incision. Blood welled and poured from the crevasse dug in my arm. Nearby, a metal stand held forceps and surgical scissors and balls of gauze. A glass canister held a floating pinkish-white something that looked like a pork rind.

"Hell if I know what it is." The doctor pulled another string from my arm. "Goddamn cancer tapeworm."

I screamed from the pain, but nobody heard me. My eyes fluttered and I strained my left pinkie toe, but Dr. Tapeworm and his intern chatted like they were on the golf course.

"Ever seen a tumor like this?" The intern rotated the glass canister. Four different monstrosities quivered inside. I wanted to vomit. My eyes swelled and tears pooled helplessly at the corners.

"Hey, wait a minute." Dr. Tapeworm leaned over me, his magnifying glasses scraping my forehead. "There's water on his face."

"I think he's crying." A voice, somewhere else in the room. A nurse maybe.

"He can't be crying." The intern leaned into my arm and I wanted to scream so hard my jaw would unhinge. "Can he?"

"Christ. This guy's waking up." The doctor noticed the intern belly-flopping on my arm. "Get the hell off him. Bradley, push one microgram remifentanil."

"Phase." My mouth was full of sludge. "Damage."

The doctor blinked at me, and then a needle pricked my skin. Numbness invaded my body. I was buried in a sea of cotton balls that smelled like spring. Reality disconnected and I floated away in a cloud of dandelion seeds.

CHAPTER TWENTY-SEVEN

Three days in the hospital, and I was ready to leave. Doctors poked, nurses prodded, and a lawyer from Barb's family hovered with waivers to sign. *Breaking and entering*, she'd said. *You're lucky we don't sue.*

They'd removed five tumors from my body before I spat out the cause. The operating physician immediately injected a payload of healthy dendritic cells. Phase-damage protocol wasn't practiced often, but I was lucky the surgeon fishing in my arm had experience. He'd actually assisted during a procedure performed on one of Dimension's last victims. That guy had died on the table.

Today, they were supposed to release me. I had a full Netherhouse complement on hand to parade me out. Dru, Patrick, and even Mak. My partner present in body if not in spirit.

She leaned against the wall with arms crossed, far enough under the TV she couldn't see *Jeopardy* and close enough to the food tray she could pick at my uneaten applesauce. Dru sat near the bed and touched my arm as she asked how I was. Patrick gnawed at an energy bar and shouted wrong answers at the *Jeopardy* contestants.

I felt stretched and thin. Like Woody had dragged me through the wall after him.

The questions had come. From my team and from the police. And of course, from the pair of blue-and-gold jackets waiting outside, *protecting me*. I'd told them what I'd seen at Barb's. The blur and the hands in her chest and a figure with Dimension's ring. I kept quiet on the blur's identity. I'd share with Mak when the walls lacked ears. Meanwhile, no way I was handing Elbridge Woody's name. Not until

I knew what was going on and how it might trace back to me and mine.

"Barb's in a coma." Mak scooped the last of my applesauce from the container. "Medically induced. She can't breathe on her own and her kidneys and liver are shot. Odds are good she dies before the weekend."

"I tried to help. But there was no fighting it."

"You didn't fight it. You got your ass kicked."

Mak didn't even like Barb. Could be she felt guilty. Had we not fought, she might have been shoulder-to-shoulder with me in Barb's apartment. Woody had the ring, but Mak fought dirty. For her, a kick to the nuts was simply a strong opening move. But if she blamed herself, she hid it well. The way I read her face, she still felt betrayed.

"Bet I can find this blur dude." Patrick ate his energy bar with gusto. "There's a Black guy with an obscuring cloak. Maybe he has the ring. I could ask around."

"You're not asking anyone about Black guys." Mak said. "You're a walking HR violation as it is."

Patrick bristled. "What's that supposed to mean?"

"Nothing."

I stared out the glass slit in the door and imagined myself on the other side. Dru rubbed my arm, like I was some kind of wounded animal. I wished she'd stop. Everything hurt, even my skin.

"How are we doing?" I asked her. "Financially?"

Her eyes avoided mine.

"Dru."

She lifted her chin. "The ambulance ride was a lot."

"How much?" I asked. "Who paid?"

Dru's eyes found Mak leaning against the wall. My partner watching me like a teacher whose struggling student finally grasped a concept.

"Look." She licked her lips. "You know I'd do anything for you, for the business, but if there's no money—"

"Netherhouse is fine."

"It's just there's the wedding. His parents already think we won't make it without help."

"I'm going to fix this, Dru. Don't worry about it."

She smiled hesitantly, then patted my arm. She didn't linger—she had an appointment with Sandoval. She planned to accompany our almost-lawyer to Treasury and cajole them into unfreezing our accounts. The woman was never not looking out for our best interests. What I wouldn't give for half a dozen Drus.

I had no idea how I was going to fix anything.

After Dru departed, Mak drifted to my side. She avoided my gaze, instead fiddling with the bed's remote control. She adjusted the height and angle of my bed. I let her do it.

"The blur." She lowered the bedframe. She kept her voice low. "You saw who it was."

"I did."

"Care to share?"

Jeopardy kept young Patrick riveted. "Your favorite bartender. In violation of his agreement with Treasury."

Mak dropped the foot of the bed. I slid down and my heels hung off the edge. "The Oak Hammer spent the last seven years scratching out an existence running a novelty bar, all the while sitting on the most powerful augment device this side of the Mississippi? PS, he needs investors to even keep the lights on."

"I know all that. I'm only telling you who I saw."

She made a noise. Raised the foot of the bed until I was forced to sit.

"It would explain his hostility the other day. You coming around so soon after he nuked an entire bus, along with your partner."

"You're my partner."

Mak ignored my response. "Barb said Rick Ruiz was the blackmailer?"

"She confirmed it. Makes sense. Rick takes possession of his dead brother's junk farm and uncovers a litany of graft. He figures he's found his golden ticket. He squeezes the three living perpetrators—Donny, Barb, and Woody. Little does Rick know the one-time Oak Hammer is a purebred bastard. Our hero Woody reacts poorly to extortion and goes about the business of tying off loose ends. Exit Donny. Exit Barb. If I'm Rick, I'm looking at vacation homes in the Poconos. Maybe a nice yurt in western Mongolia."

"They were working together."

"What?"

"Barb and Rick. They were working together. I ran those phone numbers I pulled from Barb's phone. Incoming calls from Rick Ruiz, Esquire. They were partners."

"That's not what Barb said."

"The corrupt Treasury agent lied to you? Color me unsurprised. How else do you explain their meeting at the swings?"

"Barb paid Rick. That was the extortion."

Mak shook her head. "All I'm saying. There's more to it."

"Fine. Either way. Woody is cleaning house. He's killed two people so far."

"He spared you."

I could still feel Woody's hand in my arm. Hot tongues of lava curling through flesh and bone. Cooking muscle from the inside out.

"We need to find him," I said. "Treasury's been after him since his Slinger days. We serve him up, they don't look twice at Netherhouse."

Another jerk of the bed. A sudden adjustment that bathed my arm in a river of pain. "We?"

"You and me," I managed.

"What about Patrick?"

As if on cue, our muscle slung his fist into the wall. One of the *Jeopardy* contestants had missed a question.

"He keeps working. Until Dru gets our account unfrozen, we need every dime he can earn." I stared the empty applesauce container. Based on my familiarity with medical accounting, I figured it was probably $200 in mushed fruit. "This hospital trip is going to bankrupt me."

"I paid," Mak said.

"What?"

"I paid for the ambulance. And last night. They wanted to kick you out yesterday."

I stared. Her face gave me nothing. "You can't do that."

"It's done."

"Then you shouldn't have done it."

"Sure. I should have let you die. Buried you in a landfill, then explained to Jamie how you were too expensive to keep alive."

Her face was difficult to read. She was seldom this serious. "I'm sorry, I—"

"Don't. I haven't forgiven you." She tapped the remote against her open palm. "You should thank my mom, though."

"Aroha? Tell me she didn't pay for anything."

"She got this look on her face when I suggested I might be looking for work." Mak left the words there. They sat on my chest like a sack of bowling balls. "I hadn't seen the expression since I'd told her I was going back for my GED. *I told you so.* She'd warned me about you for years. Every morning. A ritual as regular as coffee and toast. The second I said the words, her face lit up and I knew what was coming. Every time one of her predictions comes true, it's license to open the book on my past. Dropping out of school. Joining the army. Getting knocked up. She's so goddamn smug; you have no idea. It's like she made me solely to fix me."

She squeezed the remote so tightly, the plastic creaked. I didn't know what to say. There was nothing to say. Eventually, Mak relaxed her grip.

"I'm not perfect," she said. "But I tell you everything. I screw the pooch—you hear about it. After Digital Divide stole that laptop and locked me in the pisser at Mickey D's, I told you. I got restroom keys left on my desk for a month."

That had been Patrick's idea. My contribution—I'd swiped a key from the adult video store around the corner. The keychain was a bright red high heel shoe.

"I was afraid," I said. "It's not like I let some debtor short my sheets. I took money. I looked the other way."

Mak pursed her lips. "You remember what I did in Iraq?"

I did. Renditions. She'd used her power to extract confessions. I'd gathered the process didn't only involve words.

"When did I tell you?" she asked.

"In the first month." I considered. "No, two weeks in."

"After my first solo job for the firm."

"Martin Dane. He played for the Express. Used that stickum on his glove."

"It was legal."

"He was forty-five thousand in the hole."

"I got him, didn't I?"

A certain sadness framed her face. The banter an echo of what we'd had before.

"I felt confident," she said. "I'd made the right choice in coming to Netherhouse. I felt like I was home, so I told you about Iraq. Because I wanted this job to be clean."

I shifted my arm. Failed to find a position that didn't hurt. "That's all I'm after. To be clean, same as you."

She looked at me as if I was trying to sell her encyclopedias. "You've told me everything?"

"Everything I know."

"And you want to keep at this until what, exactly?"

"Either we have the ring or we have enough evidence to serve Woody to Treasury. In a way that doesn't kill Netherhouse."

She looked down at her hands. She fiddled with the remote. Raised the bed. Dropped the bed.

"You going to let me keep doing this?" she asked.

The bed went up again.

"Probably. Is it helping?"

"A little."

I smiled through the pain. Mak didn't look up but I caught something resembling a smirk.

"We're getting closer," I said. "Just stick with me a little while longer."

The smirk contorted into a frown. "I've been with you the whole time." She dropped the remote on the bedside table. Returned to prowling the edges of the room.

We watched another few minutes of *Jeopardy*. Mak staked out the window and flipped the blinds open and shut. Patrick banged on the rail of my bed. "In-A-Gadda-Da-Vida." It wasn't even one of the Jeopardy answers. With Dru gone the energy drained out of the room.

Just before the show ended, we got word. Treasury Agent Barbara Cahill had died.

CHAPTER TWENTY-EIGHT

Just after noon, the Treasury Secretary slipped into my room, as if he was afraid of waking me. The hospital seemed in no rush to discharge me. Patrick had left, Mak gone to scare up food. When Elbridge saw I was awake, he approached with hands in pockets and an almost-bemused look on his face. As if I was his own screw-up progeny.

"The lengths you'll go to, son. To appear uninvolved."

"For my next trick, I get stabbed in the eye. Further proof of my innocence."

Elbridge grunted. Looked around the room as if Mak might be hiding behind the IV stand.

"You here to arrest me?" I asked.

He drifted closer. I smelled Old Spice and coffee. "Should I?"

"I was the victim."

"That's what they always say."

Silence. Someone moved furniture in the room next door. I imagined the patient and their room full of awkward visitors. They didn't know how good they had it.

Elbridge watched my mind drift. "Investigators say you didn't see a face."

An image. Woody staring at me, his eyes bloodshot. "Just a blur."

"Hard to see a blur, I'll grant you." Elbridge help up his index finger. "How many fingers?"

"It's the middle one, if you're trying to send a message."

"Not your eyes, then. It's good you've got your health. Not everyone is so lucky."

I swallowed. The news only hours old. "I was sorry to hear about Barb."

He studied me as if I might be pulling his leg. Apparently, I passed muster. "She and I got to Austin at the same time. Worked the same cases and pulled the same all-nighters. Used to stuff ourselves on brisket over at Stubb's. Drink one Shiner too many." He curled his lips like he wanted to spit. "Until I moved on and up. And she didn't."

"She was good people." It felt weird, expressing a sentiment I'd never demonstrated. "I'm glad she was finally going to get her shot."

"What's that supposed to mean?"

"That congresswoman thing. Rita Pham. Someone tried to shoot her?"

Elbridge's bonhomie vanished. He fed me a canine stare. "Are you trying to get involved in another investigation?"

"What? No."

"That case went FBI, and if you want to bark up their tree, go ahead. But I'd have thought this whole affair would have taught you a lesson. You have no business involving yourself with augment affairs. Period. You are an unqualified civilian. You will, pardon my French, stay the fuck out of it. Before I decide your friendship with Barb makes you more a suspect in her death than the guy who phased her heart into pudding."

The man loved playing cop more than he did the mourner. Sadly, I was more comfortable with this persona, even if it did mean my ass.

"There was a rumor about Barb," he said. "Water-cooler stuff. She lived well, on an agent's salary. Maybe a bit too well. Nice house in a nice neighborhood. New TV every year."

"This is your friend Barb we're talking about?"

He moved to the edge of the bed. His fingers scraping the sheet near my injured arm. "You were in her place. What do you think?"

"If you're asking me—was one of your agents dirty—I'll remind you I was told to stay the fuck out."

"This is a direct question. From the Treasury Secretary." He studied me lying there in the bed, helpless. "I wouldn't want Barb's name sullied. Unnecessarily."

A cop with a fact was dangerous. You never knew how they were going to use it. "She drank Bushmills. She gave me a bottle every Christmas. I'll bet she did the same with her coworkers, your agents. Short of drinking Old Crow, you'd be hard pressed to find a cheaper whiskey."

He drummed his fingers on the bed. Very close to my arm. He considered my words. "I always gave her Balvenie. They found the bottles in her cabinet. Full."

I held my tongue. Elbridge's eyes tracked up to find mine.

"If you're involved, Hardwood," he said, "I'm going to find out."

He planted a finger in my breastbone. Hard.

"Don't go anywhere," he said.

He walked out.

I left the hospital an hour later.

CHAPTER TWENTY-NINE

The regulars congregated at Big Fight as if everything was normal and the owner hadn't phased his hands through a woman's chest. As the Tradens' Humvee had dismantled the awning, Nick sat on his stool and roasted in the late afternoon sun. He squinted and squirmed, looking almost candy-apple red. It was amusing to watch the devil shade his eyes.

Mak sat behind the wheel of her truck, drinking coffee and watching Nick in her sideview mirror. I ate a chocolate croissant, a reward to myself for not dying. Back at the drive-thru, I'd lurched over Mak's lap to pay the bill. It was the least I could do. I didn't feel like we were remotely even.

"You think Woody's in there?" I asked.

A shrug. Her eyes stayed riveted on the mirror.

"I don't know what he's driving. He used to own that Karmann Ghia, but he had to sell it."

That drew a skeptical side-eye.

"He did look pretty ridiculous in it, yes."

Her eyes returned to the mirror. I sighed and tried to make my arm comfortable.

The layered bandage wrapped my arm from wrist to elbow. Underneath the gauze the suture burned, and I swore something moved under the wound. I remembered the gigantic tapeworm tumor the doctor had yanked from my arm. A corkscrew of corruption, and it had seemed alive. When I touched my arm, I couldn't feel a thing.

"One of us should scout the interior," I said. "He might feel safe enough to man the bar."

"If he thinks you're dead," she said.

Behind us, Nick waved away some normals. He rose from his stool and shouted as they retreated.

"Do you have a grand plan to get us inside?" Mak asked. "The bouncer doesn't seem very accommodating."

"Let me go at him. He'll remember me."

"No doubt."

"I can draw his attention. I'll make a scene and keep him engaged. Then you can sneak around the back. A place like this, the door will be unlocked. You should be able to enter through the service entrance, come up past the kitchen and behind the bar. The office is back there. Woody always liked you, absent me. Tell him you're upset. I'm in the hospital, I might not make it—maybe let loose with some tears, that could really—"

Mak popped open her door and exited the truck. She slammed the door behind her and walked directly at Nick.

"—sell it," I finished, to myself.

Mak crossed the lot as if she'd just conquered Austin and all its people. Nick saw her immediately and braced himself on the stool. But Mak kept a respectful distance and chatted up the devil as if they were old friends. There was an ease about her. Nick didn't relax but he didn't fly off his stool, either.

A black sport utility wheeled into the lot. I tensed, Elbridge's threat fresh in my mind. *Arrest* wasn't a word I'd heard, but I wasn't eager to press the issue. The driver reeked of Treasury voracity. He probably had an arrest quota to meet. His partner stared out the window at Mak and Nick as the car drifted past. I kept my head down and feigned great interest in my croissant.

The SUV rolled close, eventually stopping to idle behind Mak's truck. The cooling fans whined.

Looks like Netherhouse, Frank.

Think you're right, Bob.

They armed and dangerous?

Might as well treat them as such.

They sat behind the truck for a long time. I wondered if I'd feel the sights when trained on the base of my skull.

The SUV moved on. They pulled a U-turn and swung back on the main road.

"Jesus," I whispered.

At the front door, Nick had let his shoulders settle. He had some story on his lips, pontificating with gusto. Mak nodded along, the look on her face suggesting her sympathies lay fully with the tiny red devil. Her attitude only fueled him. He held nothing back.

I was lucky. Lucky the day Mak walked through the door of Netherhouse. Lucky the day she made partner. Lucky she didn't leave my ass in the hospital. I certainly didn't deserve her.

Five minutes later, Nick was back screening customers and Mak was settling into the driver's seat. She sipped her coffee and let me sweat.

"Well?" I said, eventually.

"It's really hot outside." She sipped her coffee. "How was it in here?"

I kept my face flat.

"Do you want to know what he said?" she asked.

"Please."

"First off, he's pissed. Ticked to high heaven, blasphemy aside. He supplied a host of issues fueling his disgruntlement. The Humvee thing. His hours. His pay. I didn't even use my power. He couldn't wait to damn Woody with faint praise."

"And speaking of Woody, did he see the man?"

"Not today, no. But seems the owner left early yesterday. Talking to a lady on the phone."

I frowned. "This is some new power of Nick's? Divining gender via cell tower?"

"Apparently, our man Woody loses his cool when he talks to the fairer sex. His voice hitches up a few registers. *Like a high-pitched little girl*—Nick's words, not mine."

"What did Woody and his lady friend discuss?"

"Nick only paid so much attention. Mostly, he was chapped Woody bailed early while he was stuck outside. But he remembered hearing your name."

A chill. "My name?"

"*I'll take care of Gayle.* Nick said that was an exact quote. Seems the devil listens when your name is spoken." Mak glanced at my arm. "Wonder how he meant to take care of you?"

"I wonder." I rubbed the bandage.

"At any rate, Nick hasn't seen Woody since. He didn't show at open. They had to call the night manager to unlock the doors."

A translucent-skinned couple passed behind the truck, arguing. *You totally slept with her.* The end of their affair looming in those very words. But then, I knew about ruined relationships. The cracks in their union had likely formed long ago. Seemingly small cracks leading to enormous faults.

"I'm wondering about the woman," Mak said. "Who do you think it is? Barb?"

"I can't see Woody and Barb."

"You could see Barb and Donny?"

I watched Nick check IDs and usher another Augment into the bar. Even from the truck, I could see he was frustrated. It wouldn't be the first time an angry employee furthered our goals. Bosses had shit on the help since time immemorial. Often forgetting the help were the only ones capable of operating their privileged little lives. They parked the cars and manned the doors. They controlled the guillotines. "Can we trust Nick? Anger does funny things."

"I didn't get the sense he was lying, but like I said, I didn't check him." She leaned into the steering wheel. "He did mention something else interesting."

"Do tell."

"He said we should ask the monkey what's going on. Apparently, she's in a number of closed-door meetings with the boss."

"Skylark?" I sat back. Promptly came off the seat. "Oh, god. What if she's Woody's woman?"

Mak laughed, the first real laugh I'd heard in a long while. "That might make this whole case worth it."

My partner finished her coffee. Eventually, she kicked on the engine and allowed the air conditioning to cool me down.

"Donny to Barb to Rick to Woody," I said. "And then to Skylark?"

"We know she's visited Big Fight. She whirligigged one of the Tradens over the roof just last week. I don't suppose Ellen offered a reason for that little visit?"

"Not one I'd believe, no."

"Maybe we have to ask Skylark directly."

I shifted in my chair. "She doesn't like me much."

"That's a you problem, not a me problem." Mak checked the time. "I promised Jamie I'd grab Nate early. I can make some phone calls. See what I dig up on Skylark. But if you're hunting her today, you're doing it solo."

"Alone with an Augment like Skylark? I at least need some muscle."

Mak suppressed a sigh. "I'm not your boss. Or your mother."

"I didn't say you were."

The sigh escaped. "Look, I don't want you to get the wrong idea. I'm going to see this Dimension thing through. I owe you that, regardless of the shit you pulled. And I'll do it for Jamie. She doesn't deserve any of this. But after, once the job is done, I don't know where that leaves us. This firm, Netherhouse, I don't know if it can be what it was before. Might be the only way forward is out."

I turned to face her. "What are you saying?"

She kept her eyes aimed out the windshield. "Maybe it's time we liquidate ourselves."

Late-afternoon sun crisped the side of my face. My arm throbbed. Pain made every position uncomfortable, but none as uncomfortable as the position in which I'd put myself.

Eventually, Mak pulled out of the lot and drove me to the office. We didn't talk much.

Some damage, no doctor could heal.

CHAPTER THIRTY

I woke up on a bathroom floor and a brown terrier was licking my face. The inside of my mouth tasted like vomit. The inside of my nose reeked of beer.

"Fuck."

My head was under the toilet bowl, the underside coated in grime and curled hair. The view wasn't great. I pushed the dog aside and rolled into a sitting position. My head throbbed. My heart pounded and fluttered my eyelids.

"You want a beer?" Patrick shouted.

Patrick? I'd gotten drunk and called Patrick? Or vice versa?

I rubbed my stubbled cheeks. I propped against the wall and pushed myself to standing. Nausea swallowed me, then spat me out. A thin film of sweat coated my skin.

"Got eggs and pancakes." A frying pan sizzled. "And Budweiser."

More nausea. I spit into the sink and rinsed the glob down the drain. I staggered into the kitchen. A fresh-faced Patrick fried eggs in a snug kitchen. He'd already prepared me a plate and uncapped a beer. I sat on a barstool at the kitchen counter. Knuckled the beer bottle aside.

"What did we do last night?"

"What didn't we do?" Patrick laughed. Swished a hard-yolked egg from the pan and onto his plate. He peppered the egg with one hand and cracked a new egg into the hot pan with the other.

"I'm serious." I chewed my egg and hesitantly swallowed. It stayed down. "I don't remember."

Patrick shuffled over the tile floor. He wore an oversized silk shirt and brown board shorts. His toes wiggled in his crocs. "Wish I had a story, dude, but we stayed here. You were upset. Would have been a real fucking downer to take you out."

Guarded, I prodded my egg. "What did I say?"

"All my fault. I ruined everything. Netherhouse is going under. Mak hates me." Patrick's eyes flicked to mine. "You were real bad."

Silence. I shoveled in food. Chewed and swallowed. Patrick swished his second egg from the pan and proceeded to eat as he cooked a third.

"You really steal Dimension's ring?" he asked.

My fork scraped the plate. For a moment, I considered blaming the booze for whatever truth Patrick thought he'd gleamed.

"Not directly." Scrape, scrape. "But I looked the other way."

Patrick chewed. Nodded sagely. His dog wandered in from the bathroom and ticked onto the kitchen tile. The dog stared at me with inky black eyes and lolled out a hopeful pink tongue. I stared back, trying to divine the animal's intent. After a few seconds, the dog lost interest and went to find a more promising human.

My host polished off his eggs. Cranked off the burner and stowed the pan in his sink, already full of dishes. "So, where do you want to start?"

I swallowed egg and beer blowback. "Excuse me?"

"You said we're after Woody and Skylark. *Find those two, we find the ring.* You were super pumped, dude. After the drinks."

Apparently, I'd made good on my promise to Mak, albeit fueled by liquid courage. In the cold, sober light of day, I reevaluated my choices. For half a second, I considered the untouched beer.

"You said you liked my enthusiasm." Patrick fiddled with the hot and cold taps, running a trickle of water over the dirty cookware. "Netherhouse is my business, too, you know."

He didn't have one cent invested in the company, but I let it go. Me and Patrick against the world, that was the idea. Against Woody and Skylark, the ring, and an entire government agency. Disaster seemed likely. Me and Mak, that was maybe something. Give me Dru for two hours and I'd find a needle in a haystack on the moon. But me and

Patrick? Patrick of the ill-advised peach-fuzz mustache and steamroller mouth? If it was an arm-wrestling contest, I'd bet on Patrick. A game of poker, you bet, the man's reality-distortion field so powerful, even he couldn't discern a bluff from the nut flush. But anything requiring a delicate touch, anything necessitating patience and finesse? If I hadn't found the bottom of the barrel, I wasn't sure there was a bottom to find.

He looked at me with huge puppy-dog eyes. His face full of hope. He fully believed we could save the day.

I drew vague patterns in the remains of my egg. One tiny adjustment of the fork and I could stab my hand. It was a surprisingly strong urge.

Patrick frowned. I was worrying him.

I was worrying myself.

"You understand this is risky," I said. "Woody is a normal now, but Skylark is augmented. She's in the business. She's a rival. Texas Recovery has the taste for blood. We get caught, it could get messy any number of ways. I don't just mean physically. I mean legally."

"Dude. Not my first time breaking the law."

I winced. "Don't say that to Mak."

"Man, give me some credit. I don't talk to Mak like I talk to you. She's always on my shit. I don't think she likes me."

I let the words sit. He didn't notice.

"I mean—I know I'm a loudmouth," he said. "And I've been inconsistent since the divorce—I'll admit that. But I'm just trying to help. Honestly, bouncing and bartending pay a hell of a lot better. But you've always been good to me, man. Loyal. So, I'm loyal to you."

I squinted out the window. I was afraid he might cry.

The apartment waited for some announcement. The dog. Patrick. Everyone waiting.

I set my fork on the plate. Grabbed the beer off the counter, the neck wet in my hand. I leaned over and handed the bottle to Patrick.

"Put that in the fridge. That's a victory beer."

Patrick raised his eyebrows.

"For when we find them," I said.

CHAPTER THIRTY-ONE

We camped at a burger place a few blocks from Dru's apartment. No sooner had we left Patrick's than a black SUV separated from the curb down the block. Treasury may have released me, but they weren't finished with me. It was bad enough I was involving Dru. I wasn't going to lead Treasury to her doorstep.

Patrick ordered a second breakfast of pancakes and French fries. I settled for two coffees and an ache in my stomach where Patrick's eggs sat. The Treasury vehicle parked across the street. They stayed in the car and played games on their phones. In between coffees, I called Dru. By the tone in her voice I could tell she was hesitant to accept more work. Still, I heard a beep in the background as she powered up her laptop.

"Not that I don't trust you," she said. "But I'm getting paid, right?"

With our accounts still frozen it was a legitimate question. I covered the phone. "Patrick—what happened to the Atomo money?"

"Got it on me. Forty-five hundred, I think."

Ordinarily, I'd ream him for walking around with so much of our cash, but if he'd accepted a check or auto-deposit, Treasury would have frozen that bounty along with everything else.

I uncovered the phone. "How about a grand? That buy me some time?"

The promise of ready cash gave Dru fresh hope. "You know what I make. That's a good couple of hours and then some. I'll keep going until I have what you need."

"Need either one of two. The former Oak Hammer, Woody Chaikin."

"And second?"

"The big gorilla."

She chuckled. I could tell the prospect of tracking Skylark made her excited but also nervous. "A little conflict of interest there, no?"

"You let me worry about that."

"Sure. But aren't we already in trouble with the government?"

One of the agents in the car made eye contact with me. Smirked and drew his finger across his throat.

"Treasury isn't fond of our success," I admitted.

"This is success? We're one step away from the poorhouse."

I watched Patrick consume his pancakes with gusto. Wondered how many more pancake meals we could afford.

Patrick stayed with me out of loyalty. Same for Dru and Mak. But they had little to show for it. And there was the lingering threat of prosecution.

As I finished my coffee, I told Dru about the bribe. All of it, from the night Donny dropped the envelope on my desk to the moment I realized his phased remains coated the turf of Royal Memorial. Nerves kept my hands glued to the paper cup, the caffeine speeding my words like truth serum. At the end of my tale, Dru was quiet. Her usual typing had gone silent.

"You lied," she said. "All these years, you lied."

The coffee and eggs sat heavy in my stomach. Like I'd swallowed tar.

"I could go to jail." Amazement and horror evident in her voice as she absorbed the possibilities. "You realize I could go to jail."

"It would never come to that." The words hollow the moment they left my lips. "I wouldn't let that happen."

Patrick shook his head. I could hear Dru breathing over the line.

"I'll do the two hours," she said finally. "But that's it. Either I find something or I don't."

"That's more than fair—" I began.

Dru hung up.

"She sounded pissed, dude." Patrick rubbed his chest with a meaty hand. "You did kind of fuck us."

I glanced at him. He had syrup smeared on his silk shirt. "Finish your pancakes."

* * *

Dru called back after our third hour driving aimlessly through downtown. With minimal funds and a Treasury tail, our options had been limited.

"This was no easy task," she said. Not bragging so much as reminding me what I had with her skills—or used to have. "Woody lives in an apartment off 183 in Leander. He's current on his bills, but barely. Gets a lot of late notices. He's a quiet neighbor but I got the cops to do a drive-by—don't ask—and he's not home. No one has seen him at Big Fight, either."

The information tracked with what Nick had told us about his boss's absence.

"Skylark lives in a high-rise condo with a secured lobby, but maintenance assures me she isn't home. She isn't at the TR offices. Matter of fact, seems Ellen Clovis doesn't know where Skylark is—she's actively searching for her chauffeur. What I hear, Ellen is driving herself around in her personal BMW."

I savored the thought of Ellen forced to cart herself hither and yon. It was a beautiful image.

"No credit card activity—Skylark must be using cash. She's not answering her phone. Nothing in the way of friends or family, not over here. And pretexting turns up squat. She's very smart, your gorilla."

Typically, skip tracing wasn't this hard. Banks. Public utilities. ADSN tracking services. All the requirements of living a modern life. Everyone was connected. Almost everyone used an augmented device. Simply drawing breath required permission.

"But smart or not, I know where Skylark is," Dru said.

The thrill of discovery ran up my spine. "Bury the lede much?"

There was an aggrieved silence. I buttoned my lip.

"The maintenance man entered her condo," Dru said. "Once sufficiently encouraged. Seems Skylark doesn't believe in screen locks, not inside her own place. She texted an unlisted number about an hour ago. *I'll pay good money for information on the ring. Meet me on Guadalupe across from the University, two hours.*"

The morning's coffee burned a hole in my stomach.

"You'd better get going." Her tone changed. Now that our business was complete, she remembered what I'd done. "You could lose her quick near campus. She'll be difficult to track."

"Thanks," I said. "You're a lifesaver. If we're lucky, this might be—"

The snap as her laptop closed. "Take care of yourself, Gayle."

She hung up.

CHAPTER THIRTY-TWO

Patrick put the car on the highway, agents in tow. I watched our tail nervously as we headed toward the University. Our movement had reinvigorated the pair. It was entirely possible they'd perform well enough to stay pinned to our ass.

"We need to lose the company," I said. "Any ideas?"

Synapses firing, Patrick studied the agents' car in his rearview. "I could pull the spark plugs."

The odds of Patrick successfully stealing spark plugs from a Treasury SUV were slightly larger than the odds I took up ballet, but the difference wasn't measurable.

"Any good ideas?"

"If sabotage is off the table, I'll use my driving skills. You know me behind the wheel, dude. They stand no chance."

I tried to muster a smile.

Patrick slid between lanes, keeping his speed generally in line with traffic. We drove past our exit. Past the exit after that.

"Keep going like this and we'll wind up in Oklahoma," I said.

"Gayle." Patrick appeared insulted. "Please."

Another mile and he found his target. A double trailer, nearly sixty feet of solid truck. After accelerating, he cut off the driver, earning a long blast from the horn. The Treasury SUV sped up, but traffic was thick. Patrick slung his Mini over another lane and dropped back, the semi screening us from the leftmost lanes. The SUV barreled ahead. Patrick took the first exit and U-turned and entered the highway headed south, back toward campus. We checked the mirrors, but no sign of the SUV.

"Boring," Patrick said. "No challenge at all."

I touched the wound on my arm. "Boring is fine."

Traffic was thin but the difference only discernible if you recognized Austin congestion at its worst. Patrick muscled his way into the center lanes and onto the lower deck. He took advantage of a telekinetic illegally lifting a truck to exit at Dean Keaton. We parked in a pay lot just west of Guadalupe, then walked to the main thoroughfare. We strolled the Drag. There was foot traffic, like always, although it was light. We passed an Urban Outfitters. An Einstein Brothers. I bent down to hand a five to a bearded man panhandling in the alcove of a former ice cream shop, the glass papered over. His tattered cardboard sign said MONEY FOR BOOZE. I gave him the money anyway.

"Remember Quackenbush's?" Patrick said. "Tower Records?"

He reminded me how upset locals got when Tower moved into the old Varsity Theater. *Austin is different.* And then the same outcry when Tower closed. Things changed on the surface, but there were still tie-dye shirts and shops selling hemp bags. We approached the intersection at 22nd and found the same Scientology building squatting inscrutably on the corner. A sign in the window said they now offered augmented e-metering. The Drag had changed, like all of Austin. Like those of us who lived in Austin. But we could still choose what kind of people to be.

Ahead I saw a familiar face. I froze and hit Patrick in the chest.

It was the weaselly profile of blackmailer Rick Ruiz.

Rick loitered outside the Scientology building. Today he wore a checkered shirt buttoned up to his neck, straight-leg jeans, and white tennis shoes. His glasses were so thick, they could focus sunlight and melt diamonds. The man worked hard to appear idle. He shuffled uneasily and kept leaning into the street to check the cars. A bad feeling coiled in my stomach.

"Go get the car," I told Patrick.

"But—"

"Go. Get. The. Car."

Patrick jogged back up Guadalupe toward the pay lot. I stared through a shop window and faked interest in Texas Longhorn–branded cologne. I watched Rick from the corner of my eye.

He relaxed. A little smile on his face. For a moment, I thought I'd been made. Then he stepped down from the sidewalk and out into the street.

Toward the black stretch Lincoln Town Car.

"Motherfuck," I said.

The Town Car's side window zipped down. Ruiz leaned into the car and hung his arms over the open sill.

I called Patrick. "He's getting into Ellen's car."

Patrick was huffing. "Is Skylark driving?"

"I don't know. Get over here or we're going to lose him."

Patrick hung up on me. Which was probably the correct move.

The conversation at the Town Car dragged on, to my benefit. I pulled away from the shop window, torn between making a grab for Rick and giving myself away or waiting for Patrick and risk losing our quarry entirely. And when Rick opened the back door and slipped into the Town Car, I figured I'd blown it. But then a horn honked. Patrick's Mini sat in the right lane, angry Austin motorists stacking up behind. I threw myself into the passenger seat just as the Town Car pulled away.

"You see Ellen?"

Like everyone at Netherhouse, Patrick knew Ellen Clovis. She made him nervous. The smartest gut instinct he'd ever exhibited. "I don't know if she's in the car. But follow them. Maybe they're taking him to the TR office."

That notion was quickly dispelled. Ellen's office was downtown, within ass-kissing distance of the capitol. The Town Car swung onto 35 and headed north. Back the way we'd come.

"Going to feel pretty stupid if we wind up at the burger place," Patrick said.

"Ellen wouldn't leave her sunglasses at some college hangout, let alone park her car there."

Sure enough, once we hit 290, the Town Car swung right, not

left. We headed east, traffic clotting, Patrick right on the Town Car's bumper.

"What's out here?" he asked. "East Bumfuck?"

"You're too close; back off." I studied the terrain as we inched along. Identical buildings carpeted the rolling landscape, like a thousand tiny matchboxes. "There's a nature preserve. A flea market. Crapton of suburbs."

"What do you figure TR has cooking? Rick going to sell the buyer's identity?"

"Ellen would never pay."

She might pay. If Ellen got ahold of the ring, she'd not only earn a hefty recovery fee, she'd control the narrative. History as written by the victor. Who knew what Ellen would tell Elbridge, the story all the more palatable when she had the ring in hand.

The Town Car exited. The parade of homes faded away and the land grew lumpy. The road filled with trucks and the sky filled with birds. Patrick cracked the window to smoke but quickly sealed it closed.

"Reeks out there, dude. Like the fucking king of sewers."

I studied the birds. No barn swallows or geese. I saw seagulls and buzzards.

"She's taking him to the dump."

Moments later, we passed the first signs. Austin Community Landfill. Initially, all we saw were grass-covered hills, but soon enough, a mountain range of garbage loomed on the horizon. The putrid smell intensified. Even with the windows closed, the stink oozed into the Mini.

"There's a woman offering augmented recycling out in Bastrop." Patrick marveled at the refuse vista. "The runoff from her operation turned people into frogs."

I stared at him.

"That's just what I heard."

A row of garbage trucks snaked ahead of us, Ellen's Town Car three trucks up. We filed through a gate, blending with the traffic, and entered a large flat area, the ground a greasy grey smear. The trucks split, some off to dump fresh garbage, others to park at nearby administrative buildings. The Town Car slipped down one of many paths.

"Going to be hard not to be spotted," Patrick offered.

"Just hang back." I had my T-shirt up over my nose. "Hopefully, Rick has all their attention."

We wound amongst the refuse. The gulls swarmed, their cries angry, as if they were in danger of exhausting the trash. The mountains of used diapers and swollen garbage bags soared and left us in a narrow valley. We were at the bottom of a waste Grand Canyon.

Up ahead, the Town Car halted. Disgorged a frantic Rick Ruiz from the back seat. He stumbled to his knees then found his feet and ran. Only there was nowhere for him to run. Garbage rose on every side, the only way out the path blocked by the Town Car.

Patrick stopped the Mini.

"You think she'd kill him?"

Ellen Clovis was a lot of things. *Murderer* wasn't a label I would have assigned.

The driver's door of the Town Car opened. Skylark exited. She still wore the suit. She smoothed the lapels before following Rick, her head lowered. She didn't look at Patrick's Mini. Nor did she pause to let anyone out of the back seat.

"Ellen's probably grossed out," Patrick said. "Right?"

I stared at the Town Car's rear window. Tried to imagine Ellen skulking inside with her wine glass and her *New York Times*. The more I considered it, the less likely it seemed Ellen Clovis would allow anyone to bring her to a landfill, recovery fee be damned.

Seems Ellen Clovis doesn't know where Skylark is.

Rick continued to flee. He edged around a pit at the foot of the nearest garbage pile. Skylark pursued with no great urgency. It was clear she was playing a game of minutes, with a known finale.

Ellen I figured I knew. But Skylark—she was another ball of wax. I was sympathetic to her situation, the way she was ogled, judged, and pigeonholed. The abuse must have been terrible. The damage to her psyche unfathomable. What grudges did she harbor? What frustrations did she carry, day after day? When pushed into a corner, there was no telling what most of us would do. Desperate times called for desperate measures. Fifteen years ago, I'd been desperate enough to take a bribe.

Skylark stood tall. A mountain amongst mountains. She moved with great will and with no hesitation.

How desperate was Skylark?

I got out of the car.

CHAPTER THIRTY-THREE

The blackmailer ran out of room. The small ledge Rick had inched along vanished and fell into the pit. I saw flattened packing boxes. Broken glass. Coffee cups and chunks of kitty litter and a grey-green slab of what might have been bacon. Rick turned and put up his hands. "Can we talk about this?"

Skylark undid a button on her expensive custom suit. So she'd have room to move.

I started to run. "Skylark."

The noise of trucks and hungry birds and garbage settling drowned out my voice. Skylark advanced, a quarter-ton of muscle. "Get in the pit."

"I have money." Rick the desperate one, his hands clawing at the hill but coming away covered in a gooey blackness that I prayed was mud. "Not on me, but I can get it."

"Skylark." I was louder this time.

"Get in the pit," Skylark told Rick.

"No." Rick eyed the pit. "No, no, no, no, no."

I stood at Skylark's back. I could strike, if I was suicidal.

"Skylark!" I shouted.

Skylark turned and swung.

Her fist was huge. The flesh grey but amazingly human up close. Wrinkled with life experience, worn from the way she curled her fingers around a steering wheel or hooked a cup of coffee. There was care put into her nails. The cuffs of her sleeves were clean and pressed. But it was still a huge fist.

And then she stopped.

For a moment, me, Skylark, and Rick were rooted to the spot.

The birds wheeled. The landfill's stink hit in waves. I heard the car door open as Patrick exited the Mini and squished onto something soft. After Skylark pulled her punch, she shrugged her shoulders and lowered her arm. I swallowed and listened to the ragged saw of my own breath. Lack of impact aside, I wondered for a moment if I might be dead. Nothing felt real. "You could have broke my neck."

"If it was necessary," Skylark said. "It wasn't." The disappointment in her voice was evident.

Rick's rat eyes studied the changing power dynamics. He calculated the odds he might exit the dump alive.

"What the actual fuck?" Patrick stomped closer. "Take on someone your own size, Skylark."

Skylark's nostrils flared. "Keep your monkey away from me. I mean it."

"Or what?" I signaled at Patrick to hang back. "You going to kill all three of us?"

That measured breathing. More terrifying than if she charged straight at me.

"Rick Ruiz," I shouted. "Nice to meet you in daylight."

"Fuck you." He glanced at Skylark, reconsidered. "Who are you?"

He kept his shaking hands near his pockets. One of the pockets was flat, the other misshapen, as if something was stuffed inside. A phone maybe. Or a knife.

Skylark turned her back on me. "You," she said to Rick. "Get back in the car."

"Where's Ellen?" I asked. "She know you took the car without permission?"

"I don't need her permission. Or yours."

"I don't recall her being this generous in the past."

"The woman doesn't have a generous bone in her body," Skylark snarled. "And butt out."

"I can take the gorilla." Patrick shuffled closer. "Just say the word."

"Shut up, Patrick."

Skylark didn't move. Her muscles rippled like a bag of snakes, but she didn't move.

Why hold back? As she said, it's not like she couldn't tear us limb from limb, if she wanted.

"Where's Woody?" I asked.

She half-turned, frowning. "Why would I know?"

"Big Fight. You weren't there to save my ass. You came to see Woody."

She glanced at Rick as if he might support her confusion. *Do you believe this?* "This has nothing to do with anything."

"Woody had the ring." I held my bandaged arm in the air. "I saw it up close and personal."

The words drew Skylark up short. Rick watched with interest.

"If he has you over a barrel," I said, "we can help."

A quick shake of her head. "You can't help with this."

"I know the man. I may have leverage."

"It's not Woody."

I hesitated. "What do you mean?"

"He's a parasite. He's damaging. I don't associate with him."

"What did he do to you?"

"Not me."

Anger blazed in Skylark's eyes. A deep, burning hurt that went beyond the fee for some augmented recovery.

"Who, Skylark? Who are you protecting?"

She slashed her callused hand through the air. She rose to her full height. "I told you to butt out."

I sensed whatever window we'd had close. There would be no further information squeezed from Skylark.

"I know who."

Rick Ruiz had one finger raised. *Point of order.* Skylark chased his statement with a low growl and made a fist.

I took my chances.

"You need a lift?" I asked Rick.

"Where you headed?"

"Wherever you need to go. You're not a prisoner. That I'm aware."

The little man's eyes tracked a path from him to me. Paused on Skylark. "I don't know that the gorilla agrees."

Only my familiarity with Skylark allowed me to hear the change in her breath. How the cadence sped up.

"I'll go get him." Patrick charged past before I could stop him. "Won't take two seconds."

"Patrick."

But he wasn't to be stopped. He marched himself up to Skylark, who swiveled to face him. I'd always considered Patrick my muscle, but the difference in stature was almost comical. Almost.

"You got something to say?" Patrick asked.

Skylark's eyes narrowed. She shifted slightly, like a sprinter in the starting blocks.

"Patrick," I said, my voice full of warning.

Patrick's breathing had changed too, although his reaction was easier to see than Skylark's. His shirt stuck to his chest. His head went back and forth like he couldn't figure out if he was coming or going. A dizzy bull in a china shop set atop a carousel.

At an impasse, the two stood face-to-face. Then Patrick extended an arm toward Rick and beckoned. The gorilla bristled and raised her arm, enough to throw Patrick off balance. He teetered on the pit's edge but righted himself, without any help from Skylark.

If she threw him in the pit, I'd have to do something. Maybe hit her with the car. I wasn't sure the car would make a dent.

Keeping his eyes on Skylark, Rick inched forward. Skylark turned and followed him with her whole body, puffing out her chest. His path to escape was fraught. The pit on one side, Skylark on the other, and only Patrick and I at the finish line. But Rick screwed up his face and shot the gap. Skylark's anvil eyes tracked him but never fell. Only once Rick passed out of reach did her shifting muscles relax. Her hands hung loosely at her sides.

I let out a breath. Didn't realize I'd been holding it in the entire time.

Rick approached, his body a tuning fork. "I've got a knife," he confirmed, almost immediately.

I shrugged. "Go tell the gorilla about your knife."

His laugh was meager. "Fair enough. No need to get testy."

Patrick backtracked to the car, never breaking his Skylark hate-stare. Skylark couldn't care less. She looked out over the mountains of trash, unreadable.

"The three of us will drive down the road a piece," I said. "And then we'll talk."

Distance from the two heavies allowed Rick to relax. He regained some of the swagger I'd seen at the park. "Any money in it for me?"

"The money you save in hospital bills."

Rick glanced at Skylark. She stopped scanning the horizon long enough to meet his gaze. Her face inscrutable, but her bulk hard to ignore. He put up his hands. "I'll take your drive. At least you're not the gorilla."

I escorted Rick to Patrick's Mini. The relief I felt at having navigated Skylark's bluff replaced by a vague unease.

Skylark was only fronting violence.

What was I prepared to do?

CHAPTER THIRTY-FOUR

The hotel rented by the hour. It was called the Duke, a fleabag we'd used on past jobs to hide Augments, and it made Motel 6 look like the Ritz. Almost always one police car in the parking lot. Loud arguments you could hear from three rooms away. A heavy disinfectant smell. We encouraged Rick to pay for the room, and he reluctantly peeled the bills from under his money clip. He stuffed the clip into the front of his jeans, as if I might pick his pocket.

The room we were assigned was basic, although it did have cable. Brown wallpapered walls and light brown carpet. Small flatscreen on the particle-board dresser. The double bed offered two flat pillows and a spread that felt like fiberglass insulation.

Patrick kicked off his Crocs and flipped on SportsCenter and turned up the volume louder than I would have liked. He sat on the edge of the mattress with the remote hanging limp in his hand. Rick sat in the room's one chair, a high-backed wooden seat better suited for a child. He propped one leg over his knee and bounced his leg up and down.

"Mind if I smoke?" He slipped a pack from his breast pocket. "Augments wind my wires, you know?"

"It's a nonsmoking room."

"What are they going to do? Take my deposit?"

I shrugged. Let him light up.

Patrick leaned in from his position at the corner of the bed. "Can I bum one?"

"Help yourself, buddy."

Rick shook the pack until another cigarette slid out. Patrick snagged it and borrowed a light and took a drag with his eyes closed. Blew out a big dramatic plume like he'd just had sex.

"Introductions seem in order," Rick said. "You guys know me, but I haven't had the pleasure of your acquaintance."

I pointed at the big man. "Patrick." I tapped my chest. "Gayle."

A mildly amused stare. He clearly didn't recognize me from the park.

"I own Netherhouse Liquidation," I clarified.

Rick smiled, recognition dawning. "This is kismet. Fate. I'm familiar with your little mom-and-pop operation." He waved the cigarette between Patrick and me. "Open question who gets to be mom."

He looked pleased with himself, and self-assured. This was fine. A confident man talked more than he should. "You said you knew who has the ring."

"Did I?" Rick shot smoke through his teeth. "It was such a confusing time."

I glanced at Patrick. He rolled over the bed and popped Rick in the knee. Half-hearted but enough so Rick knew he meant business. "Answer the question, dude."

"No need to get violent." Rick shifted so his knee was farther away from Patrick. "You're worse than the gorilla."

"The buyer?" I repeated.

"I know who the gorilla is protecting. I didn't say anything about a buyer."

"You're getting cute. Don't do that. Your brother kept notes. You know about Dimension's ring. You know who was involved in the theft, and who your brother fenced the ring to."

"Look who's so sharp. You know this much, you don't need me."

"Does Woody have the ring?"

"Who's that, now?"

"The bar owner. Woody Chaikin."

"I don't know who that is."

His face guileless. His cheeks slack and his eyes dull. I wasn't a Truther, could no more read his honesty than I could his leathery palm, but I felt he was being straight.

"Fine. If not Woody, then who?"

"I'm not going to just tell you."

I reached over. Took the cigarette from his hand and held it there, just out of reach. He sighed.

"The gorilla threatened to mangle me six ways from Sunday. It's a hell of a lot scarier than you clowns."

The cigarette burned hot under my fingers. I'd only ever smoked one. In college, to impress a girl. I'd figured any more than that might give me cancer.

"Give us the name, man." Patrick kept his eyes glued to the TV. "Give us the name or I start hitting you."

I tried to keep my face neutral. Getting physical needed to be a bluff. I told myself it was a bluff. Rick just smirked.

"Even if you toss me around, those beauty marks would heal. I got bigger problems. She's promising something a bit more permanent. The long nap; know what I'm saying?"

"*She*? You don't mean Skylark, do you?"

Rick opened his mouth. But then he made a point of sealing his lips tight, his lips worm-pale, his smile toothless.

I glanced at my phone. It was going to be a long day. Perhaps an even longer night. With Patrick and Rick.

"This room is on your dime." I returned the cigarette, which he gladly accepted. "The sooner you tell us something interesting, the better."

I took Patrick outside.

"Sit on him for a while," I said. "See if you can buddy up. Do that smokers' bond bullshit."

"There's a faster way, Gayle."

"Do not touch him. We don't work that way."

Patrick shrugged. Agreeing, or disinclined to dispute my statement.

"Where are you going?" he asked.

"Make a phone call. Grab something from the store across the street. You need anything?"

"There's a vending machine outside."

Not nearly far enough away. "I want to stretch my legs."

"Oh. Then an energy drink. Jerky. Pistachios."

Sadly, a fairly normal repo menu. "That I can afford. I'll be right back. And remember what I said. No violence. Talking only."

"You're the boss."

I poked my head inside. Rick smoked with his eyes closed. Like he was at a redneck spa.

"What's your brand?" I asked him.

He opened one eye.

"Marlboro?" I guessed. "Newport?"

A snort. "Fuck Newports."

"Marlboros, then?"

He nodded. Closed his eyes again. The blackmailer the only one among us totally relaxed.

I wished I had his peace.

CHAPTER THIRTY-FIVE

I called my daughter from the dumpster. The dumpster was located out past the wrought-iron gate surrounding the leaf-scummed pool. The spot appealed, as it created space between me and the job. Some days, refuse was cleaner than repo. The smell even seemed quaint after our time at the landfill. I scraped a crushed beer can from the ground and winged it into the rusted green beast as I waited for Jamie to answer.

When she picked up, her mood was vastly improved. A good day, as unchartable as the weather. She was reading about some new cancer treatment, an experimental augment thing up in New England. "It's like they undo the cancer altogether," she said.

"That's great." I was happy to hear her excited. Wary of some new treatment windmill. "I'm sure they'll need to test the process."

"They are testing it. That's what I'm telling you."

I'd read the article she gushed over, news of cancer remedies a scratch I couldn't help but itch. The guy describing the therapy was as snake-oil smooth as they always were. 92.4 percent of the patients experienced regression of their leukemia, as compared to 73.1 percent of those receiving traditional non-augmented treatments. But *Traditional therapy might still work best for those whose cancer exhibits certain characteristics.*

Pay your money. Roll the dice. Realize the advantage is never yours.

"New England, huh?"

"Best place for childhood cancer treatment in the country. That's what everyone says."

Best meant *most expensive*. I couldn't afford a plane ticket to New England, let alone augmented cancer treatment. And thanks to the Dimension fiasco, my financial situation had only deteriorated.

I heard a group of kids near the pool. Teens, one of them sporting a gill necklace. His buddies goaded him into chugging beer. They reasoned he didn't need his mouth to breathe. I was jealous. I'd take their augmented hijinks over the human evil my daughter struggled against.

"We'll have to ask your doctor about it," I said.

Jamie's tone suggested I was the one with leukemia. "What's wrong?"

"Nothing. I'm just tired."

"Bullshit. It's work, isn't it?"

"No. I mean, yes. We're having a bit of trouble with Treasury."

"What kind of trouble?"

The kids laughed. Their easy comradery painful. Carefree.

"Jamie, look—"

She cut me off. "You guys are under investigation?"

"No, not exactly. And how the hell did you find that out?"

"It's the internet, Dad. You're publicly licensed. That's all Freedom of Information."

I pinched the bridge of my nose.

"What did you guys do?" she asked.

"Mak didn't do anything. It was me. It was a long time ago."

"You broke the law?"

"I didn't. I mean." Notions of right and wrong collided in my head. "Donny did a thing. I didn't report it."

Every breath sawed through her windpipe. "Did you steal something?"

"No." I licked my lips. "Donny took an augmented device. And I—" It was hard to lie to Jamie when she sounded this way. But then, it should have been hard to lie to her at all. "I looked the other way."

"Dad—that is stealing."

"You don't understand. Your mother and I— There wasn't a lot of money to go around. You were a toddler; outgrowing clothes every couple of months."

"I don't care." Her voice loud. Despite the toll of the sickness and the increasing toll of the treatment she found energy. "That's wrong."

The objections died in my throat. "I know it was, sweetie. I know."

For a moment, her anger burned hot. I was almost grateful she had the fury to power her. To bring her back to me. But like a fuse, the emotion extinguished once it ran out of fuel. A series of violent coughs wracked her body, fanged malignancies tearing at soft tissue. The effort to endure shattered her anger. After the attack ended, Jamie breathed heavy into to phone.

"Are you okay?"

She snuffled. "Yeah."

"I'm sorry," I said. The words meant to be all-encompassing.

"I guess it's done now. Not like it's going to get any worse."

One chuckle of dubious laughter squeezed through my teeth. I'd flirted with everything from unemployment to prison. Leave it to my daughter to remind me—at least I had my health.

I wanted to squeeze her hand. I wished I'd stayed at the Center and never left her side.

"I love you," I said.

"I love you too, Dad."

I'd called to make Jamie feel better. But who was comforting whom?

We traded goodbyes. *See you soon.* I hung up the phone and let myself savor a rare moment of forgiveness. Maybe even redemption.

And then the vending machine fell from the sky.

CHAPTER THIRTY-SIX

The kids crowded the gate, rubbernecking the twisted steel and ruptured soda cans. The vending machine had landed half inside and half outside the dumpster, crushing the right wall and spraying me with debris. Control boards. LCD fragments. Exploded candy bars. The blowback landed me on my ass, and I blinked away another example of the impossible.

Patrick was muscle of flesh and blood. Rick all mouth. Neither of them possessed the strength to lift a quarter-ton of caffeine and sugar and galvanized steel and chuck it a few dozen yards. But I'd encountered someone who did. As I regained my feet, a sick feeling took hold, a dead certainty. I could only hope I was wrong about the trouble's source.

There were two of them on the landing. They wore camo gear and tightly laced black tactical boots. Gas masks obscured their faces, but I knew who they were. The gas masks were their calling card, not a disguise. The Tradens had found us.

They bigger of the two faced my way, standing near a ragged gap in the railing. His brother tugged on his arm. The big one lifted his chin, giving me a sort of *see you next time* kiss-off. Then he allowed himself to be turned and they slipped around the corner of the second-floor landing and disappeared as if they'd phased into the woodwork. Bystanders ran into the empty street and down the weedy sidewalk. I was the only idiot running toward the action. Pell-mell up the stairs like it was Christmas morning.

On the second floor, there was no sign of the Tradens. A young man hiding by the ice machine might have witnessed their escape, but he'd curled into a ball. I kept moving, not stopping until I reached the room.

Rick lay on his stomach, his head turned to the side. One hand was extended, the other trapped under his body. Blood pooled under his right cheek and soaked into the carpet. Teeth lay scattered around his body like popcorn. A fist-shaped hole was visible in the sheetrock near the bathroom. The bathroom door was closed, the sound of running water audible through the thin wood.

I stepped over Rick. His face was a lumpy mess. His eyes were open, a slight look of surprise forever affixed.

The door wasn't locked. It opened into a small bathroom. Water ran out the sink tap and straight down the drain. Patrick lay jammed in the combination bathtub-shower. His eyes were squeezed shut. He'd pulled his left leg up as far as he could and wrapped his foot in a bath towel. Blood drenched the towel and the floor of the tub.

"Jesus."

"He took my toe, dude." He gritted his teeth. "The fucking big toe."

I called 911. Listened to a TV in the adjacent room. Heard murmurs and quiet laughter. No sirens. I made sure Patrick kept pressure on the wound and told him not to move.

"Not a fucking problem." He looked pale, like he'd sweated out about ten pounds. I returned to the bloody bedroom.

Ruiz hadn't moved, but he was breathing. He blinked, continued to stare at the bed. I knelt into his sightline. Got close enough I could smell his waxed hair, the vague odor of smoke and bubblegum. I followed his gaze and saw a dusty balled sock under the bed.

I looked back at Ruiz. He opened his nearly toothless mouth, and a spit bubble popped between his lips.

"Hang on," I said. "Help is coming."

His mouth and eyes stayed open. He died as I watched.

I sat on the lumpy unmade bed and waited for the police. The kids outside had gone quiet, vanishing before the perpetrators of the law came knocking. I remembered their carefree banter. Their unassailable belief they were each invincible.

I should have kept walking. Once I'd seen the vending machine, I should have kept walking.

I stared at Rick's body as the sirens began their wail.

CHAPTER THIRTY-SEVEN

The EMTs lent the hobbled Patrick a shoulder as he refused to ride the gurney. Rick they wheeled out with a sheet over his face.

The police questioned me relentlessly, like they were sure I'd killed Rick. I avoided the phrase *kidnapping*, instead suggesting Rick was a business acquaintance. When I mentioned the perpetrators were likely Augmented, I received sneers in response. *You civvies think everything is augmented.* When I remained unmoved by their whiplash offers of friendship and prison, the questions ceased. The cops didn't arrest me but made it clear they'd hassle me later.

I leaned against one of the patrol cars, my eyes closed as I tried to find peace. I found the remnants of my hangover. The feeling maybe I should have stayed at the hospital. At least they'd fed me. That's where Mak found me when she rolled up in her truck.

"Dru said you two were flying solo. She was worried." Mak eyed the police presence. The vending machine lying guts-open in the parking lot. When I pointed at the empty passenger seat, she gave me a jerk of the head. *Get in.* I slipped inside and we drove away from the scene.

The tires hummed against the road. We eased onto the highway. We passed through Round Rock and headed toward Dallas. If I stayed quiet long enough, we might make Colorado.

Mak broke the silence. "How's Patrick?"

"The paramedics took his toe. They found it in the parking lot, stuck to the windshield of a strawberry-colored Impala."

She mulled her responses. "Strawberry-colored?"

"That's what the cop told Patrick before they whisked him away. I could hear the big dummy laughing as they closed the doors." I shook my head. "Lost a toe and all he can do is laugh."

She snorted. Maybe, after all we'd been through, she'd found a way to appreciate Patrick.

The sun glowered on the western horizon and cast long shadows over the traffic.

"The woman Woody talked to," I said. "She's the buyer."

"I thought Woody was the buyer. You saw him with the ring."

"Nope. Rick said *she*. He didn't know Woody from Fred Flint-stone."

"You're dating yourself." Mak chewed her lip. "If Woody isn't the buyer, how did he get the ring?"

"Maybe the buyer sold it. Maybe she lost it. Maybe Woody took it from her."

"Goddamn Gollum didn't lose his ring this often." Mak shielded her eyes from the sun. "Wait—Rick Ruiz?"

I told her about Skylark and Rick and our encounter at the landfill. About the Tradens appearing at the hotel just in time to murder Rick and throw a vending machine at me. It said a lot about our history when Mak didn't even blink.

"It's interesting you mention Skylark," she said. "I did some digging. One of my G-2 buddies came back with something. Sensitive but unclassified. One of my favorite phrases."

"You're a repowoman without compare. Please share your wisdom."

"Ellen didn't do shit." Her eyes glowed.

"What do you mean?"

"I mean, she didn't get Skylark out of North Korea."

She was dying to tell me. "Let's hear it."

"Ellen didn't lift so much as one manicured finger, not until Skylark was stateside. She saw a trophy in employing our favorite gorilla—a favor for a friend—but that's as far as it went."

"The friend is who, then?"

"Ever heard of Quan Pham?"

"This is where you tell me I should have?"

"If you didn't live in a cave, yes. He's ostensibly into air conditioning and electrical generators. Parts and service operation. He's one of those self-made minor millionaires. Left Vietnam and never looked back, although he's apparently sensitive to those with similar hardscrabble backgrounds. He got Skylark out, not Ellen."

I chewed a finger. "This makes a certain amount of sense. Ellen didn't know about Skylark's landfill tour. And Skylark got very huffy when I mentioned her boss. Resentful, one might say. Could be Skylark has gone autonomous."

"She's not working with Woody?"

"She hates Woody. No, she's protecting the buyer."

The name Quan Pham rattled around in my head. I squeezed the armrest with my good hand. "I know this guy's name. You're sure he's just in air conditioning?"

"He's not in anything, now. He died a few years back. Maybe you know the daughter? Rita?"

The rattling thoughts finally struck something useful. I about popped out of my seat. "Holy shit. The congresswoman? She was on the radio. Someone took a shot at her."

I pulled out my phone. Ran a search on Rita Pham and got several thousand hits. I missed Dru immensely. But I refined my search and eventually found Rita smiling into the camera and waving, speaking at some rally for minority businesswomen.

"Barb had information on her," I said, staring at the image. "Elbridge said she wasn't working the case, it was federal. But Barb had a laptop with details on Rita's schedule. Route to work, route to home. Information on her security system."

"Barb took the shot?" Mak pushed back her hair. "Jesus, can that be right?"

"She'd need a reason."

"I'm still trying to get from Skylark to Rita Pham to Barb."

"Barb and Donny and Hank Ruiz steal the ring. But they don't sell it to Woody. They don't sell it to Skylark. They sell it to successful businessperson Quan Pham."

"The same Quan Pham who brought Skylark to the good old US of A."

"The same. He buys the ring, for reasons."

"And he never uses it."

I rubbed my head with both hands. "I can't figure that part out, but say we're right. Quan has the ring. He dies. The ring passes to his daughter Rita."

"Then criminal mastermind Hank Ruiz dies. His greaseball brother Rick learns of the sale and puts the squeeze to Donny, Barb, and Rita."

"Rita is a powerful woman. She's not going to be played. She has a life. A career, with the better part of that career ahead of her."

"The scorched-earth strategy. Sure. Leave no one standing who knows the truth. And reach out to close family friend Skylark to tie off loose ends."

"Or throw them in the garbage."

Mak nodded as she digested our theory. "Only, Skylark doesn't have the stomach for murder. She can't kill Rick."

"Allowing Patrick and I him to take him to the Duke."

"Where the Tradens kill him anyway."

"For reasons."

My partner shook her head. "You know, this whole story fits together pretty good. Right up to the part where you see Woody with the ring."

"I can't explain Woody."

"Don't forget the two muscleheads who killed Rick."

"Shit. I can't explain them, either."

Rita's face stared out from my phone.

"Woody had a picture," I said.

"Good for him."

"In the lobby of Big Fight. He hangs pictures of all the famous folks he knows. McConaughey. That band with the augmented fiddle player. And Rita Pham."

"You think Woody is, what, muscle for the Phams? Why, when you've already got Skylark?"

"Maybe Woody does things Skylark won't. Like stick his hands through Treasury agents."

"Maybe." Mak shielded her eyes from the sun boiling on the horizon. "This is pretty thin."

"It does sound desperate."

"You always sound desperate."

The car grew quiet. Without distraction, the pain in my arm began to throb. A line of cars stacked up behind us. Late-evening commuters grabbing sandwiches and coffee. Maybe bringing something home to family and loved ones.

I thought about my empty apartment. How I seemed to drive off anyone who might care. Similar to my late partner.

"Why'd you come?" I asked.

A quizzical look.

"You said we were done."

"I said maybe." She tapped her fingers against the steering wheel. "You told Dru the truth. Me, it sort of spilled out. You were cornered. But you didn't have to tell Dru. Not unless you believed it was the right thing to do." She let out a breath. "That was encouraging."

"I also told Jamie."

"There's no extra credit here."

The miles passed as we drove to nowhere. Or maybe somewhere. Maybe we were getting somewhere.

"There's no point in chasing Skylark again," I said. "And Woody was avoiding us before this shit started. That leaves only one person."

Mak checked the time. "Be dinner soon."

"First dinner. You know we'll eat twice."

"Burgers?"

"I was thinking BBQ."

"God, no. How about Tex-Mex?"

The debate was familiar. And welcome. I smiled and nodded. "Tex-Mex it is. And then we go to Rita Pham's."

CHAPTER THIRTY-EIGHT

The American Dream was a crapshoot. Rita was second-generation elite, but her dad had started at the bottom. He'd scraped out a meager existence in Vietnam and stayed long enough to watch a careless Augment crush his wife and oldest daughter with a building. He escaped with his remaining child in the late eighties as part of Orderly Departure. Worked construction, then air conditioning, then followed a guy who started his own company, then left the service side of heating and cooling to found his business distributing parts. The man had an eye for efficiency. Logistics were his god. He cleared a million in sales within two years. Business ebbed and flowed, but once he'd tasted success, Quan never lived like anything less than a man with wealth at his command, and privilege was all his daughter remembered. She'd married and kept her name and put two kids in private school. Purchased new BMWs every year, one of the current model year sitting unguarded in the driveway. Window boxes birthed flowers despite the heat, and half a dozen men sculpted the lawn and shrubs until they were damn near assembly-line perfect. The nanny had left just after we'd arrived. Considering Quan's impoverished start, perhaps this lifestyle was deserved. Earned, even. But it was hard to watch when your business never cleared more than a couple thousand a year. When your kid didn't want the crusts cut from their bread because they found the taste unpleasant but instead needed a gravity drip of vincristine because otherwise, the cancer would kill them.

Hell, yeah, I was bitter.

We watched the Pham house from down the street, assuming the family might be more watchful after Barb had taken a shot at Rita.

The house was familiar—Barb had inspected it on her trip down serial-killer memory lane. She'd killed two birds with one stone. Or at least plotted how to kill one bird.

"I never figured Barb for murder," I said.

"You're the one who called it. She's a lifelong Treasury agent. She's pulled the trigger before."

"In the line of duty."

"I'm sure it looked that way."

Mak seemed unbothered by the revelation. As if she'd always looked at Barb and seen a killer.

"I keep picturing her with that old lady and the dog. Bringing her coffee." I shook my head. "She didn't seem capable. Not the Barb I knew."

"Maybe you didn't know Barb."

Mak stuffed half a steak-and-cheddar taco in her mouth. I forked through my bowl of carnitas, green peppers, and rice. The inside of the truck reeked of greased meat. The food would sit heavy, but in two hours, we'd convince ourselves we were hungry.

"The records on the house gave me very little." Mak operated her phone with one thumb. "They've got just enough registered tech to avoid suspicion, and the paper is clean. Augmented waste-vaporizing toilets, smart-home AI stuff—that's it. Nothing you wouldn't find reviewed online a thousand times." She swallowed a bite. "The blue BMW there is the husband's. He works at a software company downtown. He leaves at five PM every day to be home with his family."

"I spotted him in the backyard. He grilled burgers and dogs."

"Very dad of him."

"What about Rita?"

"Her people are excruciatingly tight with her schedule. Ordinarily, she's as much about public appearance as bills and laws. I found canned footage of her speaking at an assisted-living facility. Volunteering at a food pantry. However, I was able to confirm she's had no public appearances in the last week. Neighbors say she runs at sunup like clockwork, but no one remembers seeing her in the last few days.

Her car is in a recently rented private garage down on Cesar Chavez. And while her social media is active, it's completely managed."

Mak and I were on hour two. In that time, we'd catalogued only a few visitors. A guy delivering groceries. The in-laws. I'd explored the neighborhood and found only a kid's splashpad and an artificial lake stocked with fish. The place was a bit sterile. I didn't want to live here, but I wanted Jamie to be able to live here if she wanted.

No sign of Rita. No one caught phasing through a pergola.

"She's a ghost," I said.

"I don't think she's a Spectral. But she's definitely hiding."

I drummed my finger on the armrest. "The kids. Even if there's marital trouble, the kids will bring her back to the house."

"We could go after the phone records. She's bound to be calling."

"She could be using an internet service. And Dru did all that stuff. Do you even have a computer?"

"That old Mac the school gave us. Neighbor kid fixes it when it won't boot."

"Not especially encouraging."

Mak stared into the rearview and picked cilantro from her teeth. "We can't sit here another day. Rent wiped us out. Patrick can't do recoveries. Dru won't."

"I can sit on the house. You could pull some repos."

"There's nothing in the hopper. Elbridge put the fear of god into the banks. They won't touch us." She sighed. "I've got to make the payment on the truck. Groceries. Gas. Nate needs an orthodontist and a shitload of hardware in his mouth. I need a plan, Gayle." She raised her eyebrows. "You got a plan?"

I stared down into my dinner bowl. Could think of nothing so much as dog food.

"I'm going to tell him."

Mak frowned. "The pronoun is a bit vague."

"Elbridge. I'm going to tell him everything."

She sat back. "You can't do that."

"I have to. It's the only way the business survives."

"The business doesn't survive the truth. He'll annihilate us."

Her intensity surprised me. "Before, you said I should tell him. You said we should sell."

"You fucked up. I was mad. Did you think I wasn't going to have a reaction? Jesus, why are you always so wrong?"

I fiddled with the bowl. "I can make it conditional. Elbridge only gets me. You and I would work something out with the business. Get Jamie a share. Maybe it goes through Charlie, although Larry doesn't get one fucking dime."

"Stop. We're not doing this."

I sat there with my head bowed. Didn't look up until Mak beaned me with a ball of wadded-up tinfoil.

"Don't check out on me," she said. "I don't have to be here, but I am. I'm invested. Pay me the same fucking courtesy."

I smiled. "No pity party?"

"Goddamn right."

She rested her arms over the steering wheel. Put her chin on her hands. "Let's finish out the night. If we don't have anything by morning, we can talk about a backup plan. Go to the press. Take Treasury to court. Whatever we do, we don't give up."

Engaging the state government in legal action overseen by the state government didn't seem like a promising course of action. But Mak had skin in the game. She had a kid to look out for, same as me. She was my partner.

I nodded. "We don't give up."

We watched the house for another hour, then I got out and walked the nearby streets, checking cars and plates and texting the snapshots to Mak. She could, even on her phone, check the plates against the handful of systems capable of identifying vehicle registration. Maybe Rita had a rental. Maybe Woody was in the area. Maybe—if we were supremely lucky—we'd find another augmented jet-car needing repo. But I failed to find anything out of the ordinary or profitable, and returned to the truck empty-handed.

Just before ten PM, I got a call from Andrew Elbridge. Mak and

I exchanged a look.

"Not one word," she said.

I answered the phone.

"Where are you?" he asked.

"That's a good approach," I said. "Ask the debtors where they are. Then you don't have to spend time tracking them down. Cuts out all the pesky effort and specialized skill. No wonder you guys are so successful."

"Don't give me lip. You want me to pull your paper and pursue you, retroactively, for any unlicensed repo work?"

I didn't say anything.

"Did the line drop?" Elbridge asked. "I didn't hear any shit, so I assume the line dropped."

"I can hear you just fine."

"Outstanding. I'd recommend you exercise your hearing a little more, in the future." Oddly, despite putting me in my place, Elbridge sounded unhappy. "As I was saying, I need to see you."

"Tonight?"

Mak poked me the shoulder. Mouthed *What the fuck?*

"This evening would be better for all involved."

I glanced at my partner. She offered an obscene hand gesture. The suggested activity was one I was unlikely to pursue with Elbridge. "I'm not sure I'm up for that."

"Your situation can do nothing but improve."

Mak watched me, expectant. Salsa stained her shirt and curlicues of cheese speckled her lap. The both of us a hot mess. The firm on the verge of extinction and no plan for making rent or buying the next meal. Yet Mak hadn't left my side. She was my partner and my best friend. She was willing to do whatever it took. Like always.

"Let me come to you," I said.

"I never intended anything but."

Elbridge texted me the address. He told me to come alone. Then he hung up.

CHAPTER THIRTY-NINE

Mount Bonnell slouched. Peaking at just under one thousand feet, it was more mound than mountain. Nevertheless, in the dark, it took me half an hour to reach the top. Limestone steps scaled the rise from the trailhead, a handrail running down the middle like a rickety metal spine. The grey-green sky turned to ash. A handful of tourists and stoners came down the steps as I ascended, warning me of the men at the top. *Fucking cops*. At the top of the stairs, blocking the way, I found Elbridge and his escort of four agents, waiting.

Elbridge looked tired. The dark adding gravity to his face. He clothes smelled like yesterday's laundry. "You carrying a phone?"

"Alexander Graham Bell went through all the trouble of inventing it."

He held his palm out and gestured. *Give*. Reluctantly, I handed it over. My phone went into a zippered pouch held by one of his groupies. Then he turned and led the way to the top.

Vegetation choked the summit, nearly swallowing the park's attempts to carve out civilization. Picnic tables, trash barrels, and concrete slabs all drowned in a morass of aggressive Texas shrubbery. Metal fencing and shin-high twisted cabling kept us from falling off the cliff, but we had amazing views of the hills and the bright cluster of downtown. Below us, the city was scattered like discarded jewels on a sea of black velvet. Boats cruised down the fat artery of Lake Austin, marine lights twinkling in the inky darkness. Crickets chirped and dogs barked and the faint voices of children reached up to remind us some people still lived normal lives. A beautiful place at night, and peaceful.

Elbridge's agents spread out. They'd already cleared the mountain-top. We were alone.

I shuffled toward the cliff. Toed the crumbling shale. Crushed cans and gum wrappers littered the dirt near my feet, but past the stone columns, nature ruled supreme. The drop wasn't sheer, but walking to the river wasn't an option. I stopped at the fencing and peered over the edge. Tall grass waved above a jumble of sharp rocks.

Elbridge stayed close. "Quite the brouhaha at Big Fight the other day."

"You brought me out here to ask about a bar? You know you can read the reviews on the internet."

"Don't give me your usual. I'm serious. Those Traden morons almost killed you. First the bar, then the hotel. Why?"

I saw Ruiz's body. Twisted and broken on the floor.

"Same as you," I said. "They think I have something I don't."

"Huh." He put his hands on his hips. "Wonder how Woody figures in."

I was surprised to hear the name pass Elbridge's lips. "Excuse me?"

"Woody Chaikin. The Tradens and he go way back. I got paper on them a mile long. Back from the Hammer's League of Six days. Well, his wannabe days." He chuckled. "League turned him down. Bet that stuck in his craw."

This information felt valuable, but I wasn't sure how. It was a stereogram I couldn't connect or decouple.

An agent stood nearby. They all had buzz cuts. This one had an eye in the back of his head. A literal third eye, with a steel lid. The lid was closed.

"You going to tell me what this is all about?" I asked.

Elbridge grew serious. He stuffed his hands in his pockets and stared across the lake. "What I'm about to describe is a limited-time offer. Considering our history, you'll understand how it pains me to even extend the proposal. If asked, I'll deny this conversation ever occurred."

The agent's augmented eye opened. It was all pupil. Totally black.

"Doctor Dimension would like to see you," Elbridge said.

He could have pushed me over the edge and disturbed me less.

"That's—"

Not possible.

"He's dead," I managed.

"Doctor Dimension was injured, but he was very much alive and kicking when the Treasury Department apprehended him on the shore of Lady Bird Lake. He was taken into federal custody and, considering his reputation, remanded to the most secure augment-holding facility the United States government has to offer."

Ellen Clovis in my head. Cackling.

"Bonnell Prison doesn't exist," I said.

"You're not entirely wrong. For purposes of this conversation, let's say it exists enough to hold Dimension. He's been imprisoned in Bonnell since that day by the lake. Without saying one word about what happened to the ring, by the way."

Numb, I stared at my hands. They were remarkably still. The traitorous hands that had taken Donny's envelope stuffed with cash.

"Why does he want to see me?"

"I wondered that myself," Elbridge said. "He's playing a game, for sure. He's no less clever for having been locked up all these years. What he says, what he tells me, is he hates Netherhouse Liquidation. Donny, in the specific. Somehow, even in another time and space, he's heard Donny met his maker. He doesn't believe it. He wants to meet with you and ask if Donny is well and truly dead. He wants to see your face. Read your eyes. All sounds like bullshit to me. I think he wants to fuck with you. Frankly, I'm fine with that. If he gets me what I want, I don't care. And then you—well, you're off the hook."

I looked at him. Even in the dark, I could see his face was lemon-juice sour. "I'll regret asking this, but I'm trying to understand why you would even entertain such a batshit idea."

Elbridge worked his jaw. "He says he can find the ring."

A laugh forced its way through my teeth. Followed swiftly by a flush of cold panic. "Bull."

The shrug was slight. "I've always suspected Dimension could feel the damn thing. That he knew where it was, on some level. Hard to tell for sure inside Bonnell. The place…does something to you." He cleared his throat. "Regardless. We bring you in. You talk to Dimension. You tell us everything afterwards, and I mean every word, gesture, belch, every steely stare you will relate to us in full. And, in exchange, I am prepared to believe you had nothing to do with the shenanigans at Lady Bird Lake. The Treasury investigation into Netherhouse will end."

We thought we knew the buyer's identity. We thought. She was tantalizingly close. She was also as tangible as drunken inspiration written on the back of a napkin.

Our business. Our livelihood, Mak's and mine. Life for the people that depended on us.

"I don't believe you."

"Hardwood." Deliberately mispronouncing my name for the umpteenth time. "I don't want to be here. I already had my boot on your throat. Do you really want me to push down and snap your neck?"

I watched one of the boats churn down the river. Jamie loved boats when she was little, especially the double-decked paddle-wheelers. *Silly boats.* When she'd see one of the tours cruising the lake's breadth, she'd point and grin so big her eyes disappeared into her chubby little face.

"Okay," I said. "Take me to prison."

He snorted. He turned away from the edge and walked back to the main pavilion, and I trailed along behind. The other agents remained at their posts. Elbridge stopped at a marker placed directly in front of the main viewing area. The roughhewn stone monument was shaped like a thumbnail and came up to his waist. He stood behind the marker and waited.

"I don't get it," I said.

Elbridge's smile was trite. "Read the inscription."

In the dark, I was hard-pressed to read the faded lettering. I knelt and put my hands on the stone and leaned in close. One corner of the monument had been sheared off. Some of the words were incomplete.

"Bonnell," I read. "A park by Covert Sr. Travis County. 1936." I squeezed the rock under my fingertips. "This is just a dedication. What is the point?"

"This is the only part I'm going to enjoy."

"What part?" I said, looking up.

Elbridge was pointing a gun at my head.

He shot me.

CHAPTER FORTY

A star-spotted expanse. Spinning sky, a bowling ball soaked in midnight.

Pain. The bullet slowing as it spread skin and pierced bone. Slamming into brain meat and shredding vital connections.

Blood bloomed. Sound died.

Color. Purple and magenta and maroon amidst the black. Agony. My body hauled through a wall of lava. Nails of fire shot into my eyes, mouth, and ears.

Hands reaching. Elbridge? Scythe? God?

Falling.

The ground.

Fast. Rushing.

A bright light.

Final.

Death.

Everything went black.

CHAPTER FORTY-ONE

Antoinette wore armadillo-skin boots—beat to hell just like mine—and a faded azure skirt. A brooch rested above her left breast, a yin-yang symbol anchored in the center. When she lifted her chin and looked over the end of her nose, I was convinced she could smell my every weakness.

I was in a cell, the walls pitted rock on three sides, solid Plexiglas on the fourth. An old drive-in movie-theater speaker hung from the rock above the synthetic glass, and Antoinette's voice piped through it.

I wasn't dead.

"You know where you are? Who I am?"

I was lying on the ground. Not a cot or metal bench to be seen, nothing but cold, crusted rock. I was alone. The back of my skull felt like I'd drunk a liter of Jameson.

"Sorry about the headache," she said. "Side effect of ionization."

Antoinette didn't sound sorry. I knew her name was Antoinette because she wore a lanyard with her name printed in large block letters on the card. There was no title.

I pushed into a sitting position. Last thing I remembered was Elbridge's cold stare and a bullet that by rights should have killed me. Previous events blurred, like hands phased into Barb's chest.

Antoinette sat on a folding chair on the opposite side of the glass, one leg crossed over the other. She stared out from under ash-colored locks that she swept aside with the back of her hand. Smile lines creased her face, but she'd set her lips in a grim line.

"This is a violation of my civil rights," I said.

She smirked. "Call a cop."

"I might," I said. "Where is Elbridge? Is he here too?"

"Where do you think *here* is?"

She enjoyed having all the answers. I stopped asking questions. My back ached from lying on the cold floor, so I stood and stretched, like I was coming out of a long nap. I craned my neck to check the ceiling. The surface was rough like the walls. A small browned-over light bulb provided light through a tiny metal cage. There were pinpricks in the rock, like cooled lava shot through with air pockets.

"You haven't Mirandized me."

"No."

Her eyes were grey agates and ageless. She could play forever. She gave two shits for me, if that.

When I pushed a toe against the rock, it passed through about a quarter of an inch before encountering resistance.

"Nice brooch." My foot probed a few other spots along the wall, with similar results. "Does the jewelry make the illusion, or is that you?"

"Neither. And you're starting to irritate me."

The walls flickered and went out, replaced by utilitarian grey steel. Overhead, the pitted ceiling vanished, replaced with a bank of fluorescents that spilled light throughout the cell. A pull-down bed with a mattress and two pillows hung from the far wall. A toilet anchored the corner, a stainless-steel throne with an empty toilet paper roll and no water. The old-timey speaker and Plexiglas remained the same.

"What are you doing in my prison?" Antoinette asked.

A fair question. Entry via bullet to the head certainly cut down on the number of accidental visitors.

"Lady, I was invited."

"Not by me."

I kept silent. If we were playing some game, I needed to understand the stakes. And how Elbridge factored in.

Antoinette continued.

"We've got you on camera, Gayle Harwood. Climbing two

hundred yards of rock and scrub. Wandering all over hell and gone. Almost as if you were searching for this place."

She rattled off my name to prove she knew everything. To show she held all the cards.

"Is that a crime?"

The smirk took over both sides of her mouth. "Damnedest thing—turns out it is."

"If you have me on camera, you know who I was with." I looked around the cell. "Where is good old Andy? Did he get his own room? He did shoot me, after all."

Antoinette's expression shifted back to neutral. "I'm not at liberty to discuss prisoners. Or staff."

Coy. No threats or denials.

"I did some research," she continued. "Seems you're famous. *Infamous* perhaps the more appropriate description. An augment repoman. The sort of jackal I'm surprised society allows to exist. Small-time, typically, and yet I see you tangled with a big-league augment criminal. Treasury was involved. All three networks covered the dust-up, four if you count the crazy one. Your name ruled the internet for fifteen whole minutes. You preempted a special on the pope's disappearance."

"John Paul died."

"Of course he did. My mistake."

Antoinette kicked her heel while she talked, clearly enjoying herself. One finger stroked the brooch on her chest.

"What do you have to say for yourself?" she asked.

"Every story is a mix of truth and fiction," I said. "Kind of like this prison."

"This prison is quite real. You may have the rest of your life to find that out."

At this point, I imagined most people shit their drawers and spilled everything in the hope the lady would let them go. I made myself take a breath.

"Like I said before, I was brought to this prison, by a federal official, no less. And that stunt with the fake surroundings—the Augment

Registration Act doesn't allow it. No deception in the course of an augment investigation. You're way outside the lines here. When I call my lawyer, he'll blow the lid off this place."

"The ARA protects the Augmented," Antoinette said. "Which you are not. Besides, who said you're getting a phone call?"

Her voice pierced the Plexiglas without the assistance of the speaker. As I studied her, she became uncomfortable and stood. She shook out her skirt and pushed the hair back from her face.

"I'll be more direct." She stared right at me. "What are you doing here?"

I made a show of investigating my cell. Walked to the bed and sat down.

"You can play dumb," she said. "But until you tell me why you're here, you'll stay in this cell. No phone call, no lawyer, no dumb white males to play dumb-white-male games with."

She turned her back on me. I didn't wait for her to pretend to leave.

"Doctor Dimension."

She paused. "What of him?"

"Is he here?"

"Are we negotiating now? Remind me what you have to offer."

I hesitated. All the lies from my past crowded around to see what I'd say.

"Dimension asked to speak with me." No movement. "There was an incident on the outside. There were deaths. He might be connected." Still nothing. "If he knows something, I might be able to make him talk."

Finally, a calculated shrug. "You'd need a séance. The man's been dead for years."

"I read that. Nevertheless."

Antoinette turned and slid closer to the glass. At that distance I could perceive new details. She wasn't as timeless as she'd appeared. Crow's feet sculpted age into her features, but she wasn't decrepit. She was attractive. Fifties, maybe.

"I know you're holding him," I said.

"Would you like a cookie?"

"Prison cookies? Sounds wonderful. And to think I just came for the view."

Her smile showed a few teeth. "Imagine I entertained the idea. Dimension alive. You seeing him. What would you say? What would such a man care to hear from you? Someone so intimately involved in his imprisonment?"

I wondered if this was the plan. Elbridge luring me to Bonnell only to shoot me in the face. Wake me in an otherworldly cell where this woman would pick me apart with questions and coerce me into admitting my role in the vanishing of Dimension's ring. There were many punches to duck. One was bound to clip me in the ear and send me staggering.

Only, Antoinette seemed to know nothing about my arrangement with Elbridge. And I didn't see the Secretary at all.

Maybe something had gone wrong. Maybe I was never getting out.

I approached the glass. "How do I know you won't leave me in the cell?"

"I might leave you in the cell regardless. Your odds of release improve if you tell me what Dimension wants to know."

Our staring contest dragged. I had no hope I would win.

"I'd need a guarantee," I said. "Something in writing."

"You can read? I'm surprised."

"I went to school. Accredited and everything."

Antoinette winked. "I do like an educated man."

She flirted like we'd just met in some bar. Confused and embarrassed, I looked down at my boots. I looked at her boots. Hers hovered half an inch above the floor.

"How are you doing that?"

She frowned, and quickly the gap between her boots and the floor closed.

"You're her." I should have figured it out sooner. "Antoinette's

Leap—the woman who jumped to her death to escape the Indians. You're *the* Antoinette. You're a Spectral."

She snarled and turned to mist, the walls behind her becoming fully visible through the cloud of her figure. Her eyes swirled and knotted like black holes. "I'm Tonkawa, you idiot. A Spaniard forced me off that cliff, not a so-called Indian."

Again she hovered, the outline of her profile fraying like tattered cloth.

"There was no man, no lover, only me. This mountain was thick with Mexicans and Spaniards. There were hardly any white men on the mountain when I died. Your people were the least of my worries. Then."

The lights behind her flickered. I realized I was out of my depth.

"And since you know so much about me, let's talk about you. Gayle Harwood."

She extended spectral fingers that penetrated the glass. I backed up.

"Repo man. Partner in Netherhouse Liquidation. Ex-husband. Liar."

Her ghost fingers brushed the tip of my nose. I felt a feather. A tickle.

She paused. Pulled her hand back through the glass. The mist she'd become coalesced and she was again a passable human being. The anger in her eyes faded, replaced with something different. Uncertainty. A touch of concern.

"You're a father."

The lights blazed behind her, and an amplified twang crackled through the overhead speaker. "Christ on a crutch, what is going on? Get him out of there."

At that moment, for the first time ever, I felt relief at the sound of the man's voice.

Andrew Elbridge had saved me.

CHAPTER FORTY-TWO

We marched down a narrow hallway with tall walls that disappeared into gloom. The ceiling must have capped out at over fifty feet, if the ceiling existed at all. Floors and walls and stairs abutted each other awkwardly, as if assembled piecemeal. A warren of narrow walkways and cubbies snaked away in all cardinal directions and beyond. Rumor had it Bonnell was a slapdash job performed by the Army Corps of Engineers back in 1943, during the dark days of World War II. The prison originally constructed in N Space as an internment camp for Naturals and device Augments of foreign birth. The place lacked the Army's usual military precision, and the layout seemed devoid of any rhyme or reason. I'd lost track of the twists and turns we'd taken since leaving the cell. Were I to escape, I didn't know where I'd run. Not that escape was possible. Antoinette led the way and guards followed ahead and behind. My legs were shackled and my arms were loosely cuffed in front of me. I shuffled more than walked.

Ahead, a single door blocked the end of the hall. A leaded-glass door with blue etching that read ANTOINETTE-WARDEN.

The warden walked like she owned the place. Hovered.

We passed through the door and entered a small office. Inside, the sterile prison decor gave way to textured ceilings and painted walls, a mélange of white, yellow, and red. Antoinette glided behind a wooden desk covered in books and spindled paper. She sat in a brown leather chair and managed to look rather comfortable. She might bang out the great American novel from this very spot.

A guard guided me to a stool and unlocked my chains and forced me to sit. Then he joined his comrade outside, the pair positioning themselves on either side of Antoinette's door. Last to enter was Elbridge.

The Secretary was disheveled. He looked like he'd entered the prison via tumbleweed. He ignored me and went right at Antoinette. He pointed his finger like it might shoot lasers. "I don't appreciate you interrogating people I send through."

Antoinette seemed unconcerned. She tented her fingers and kept her attention on me. She was hard to read, either because she was dead or because she was experienced at being cagey. "He's no worse for wear."

"That's not the point. I need him in one piece."

The guards loomed. I wondered if they worked for Antoinette or for Elbridge. The air dwindled and I felt like I was sucking the last few oxygen molecules into my lungs.

"I thought he might tell me what he wouldn't tell you," Antoinette said. "Without involving any third parties."

The words stopped Elbridge short. "What did he say?"

"He's right here," I said, raising my hand.

A smile quirked Antoinette's lips. One more evocative of sadness than humor. "He's worried. About a great many things."

"He ought to be. Considering where he's headed."

The words stirred thunderstorms in Antoinette's eyes. "He implied as much. You're not serious?"

Elbridge loosened his tie. I swore I heard the starch crack. "As death and taxes."

"That doesn't mean a lot to me, as you well know."

My irritation grew as they continued to discuss and simultaneously ignore me. But their conflict might prove beneficial. I played the good son and let them argue.

"I've counseled against this kind of thing before." Antoinette folded her arms. "Why now?"

"The man asked. And Netherhouse excels at question-and-answer." Elbridge squinted at me, uncomfortable with the idea of delivering compliments. "Squeezing blood from reluctant stones."

The warden wasn't happy. She sighed and rubbed a spot between her eyebrows in a move I recognized. Frustration.

This was almost funny. I was rooting for Elbridge.

"He's playing you." Antoinette raised her eyes. "Alton's playing you, Andrew. You realize that?"

Elbridge frowned. "Excuse me?"

"It's a shell game."

"I wasn't born yesterday." Still, a vein throbbed at Elbridge's temple. "He better not be."

"What did he want? Five minutes with this man?" She looked at me and *tsk*ed. "A glorified car thief? Of all the people he could have seen? And once you produced him, then what? What could Alton possibly offer to make this charade worthwhile?"

Elbridge didn't answer. He merely looked guilty. Unfortunately, this was the rare time I needed him to be more authoritative.

"Who is Alton?" I asked.

Antoinette shifted in her chair and let her eyes settle on me. "Alton Zimmer is Doctor Dimension."

"Never heard him use that name."

"Alton is his birth name. We deny the prisoners augment affectations like costumes and pseudonyms. Inside, they're ordinary criminals."

"What name does he prefer?"

"He'll answer to either. Why?"

"If I'm going to talk to him, I'd like to get the name correct."

"Alton Zimmer killed two of my guards." Antoinette went a little smoky. "He's also suspected in the murders of Raymond Cart and Paige Butcher. Raymond took a library book Alton had on reserve. Paige swiped one of his cigarettes."

Cognition and the Butcher Baroness. A Telekinetic and an Invulnerable.

"You get any closer to him than this," Antionette said, "and he may kill you."

I didn't have an answer. Elbridge tried to bluster his way through the situation. His posture got very John Wayne. "This is going to happen, Nette. You need to get your mind right."

Antoinette ignored him and focused on me. "Why does Alton want to talk to you?"

"I'm not sure. He has a grudge."

"Understandable. Considering you arranged for him to be here."

"That was more my partner than me."

"Alton has mentioned Donny Spielman before. In an unflattering light."

"Well, Donny is dead now. Maybe that fact will be of some comfort."

"Again, I'm interested in why you, or the Treasury Secretary, would offer Alton any comfort."

"That's state business." Elbridge touched his cufflinks. "Not your purview."

"Nevertheless." Antoinette glowered, and the temperature in the room dipped ten degrees. I'd dealt with a few Spectrals, and the more powerful could adjust the elements. "I want an answer, or he can go back to the cell."

Ordinarily, I'd have responded with something smart. Pushed Antoinette's buttons like a kid in an elevator. But between her and Elbridge, they held my fate in their hands. And despite promising a deal, Elbridge seemed unbothered by the prospect of me in chains for all eternity.

"Dimension knows where the ring is," I said.

"Horseshit." The Secretary was not happy with my revelation, but Antoinette seemed unperturbed by his flush of anger. "Alton Zimmer has been in this prison for fifteen years. He'd be the last person to know the ring's whereabouts."

"Nevertheless."

"Dimension knows where the ring is? Right now? How?"

"I don't know. But he does."

Antoinette hooded her eyes. "Why are you doing this?"

I eyed Elbridge, who still looked steamed. I looked at my hands.

Hands that guided Jamie across busy Austin streets and pulled her from the froth of Barton Springs Pool. Hands that were useless on the other side of steel bars or trapped a universe away.

When I looked up, Antoinette's face was stone.

"You said I was worried." I kept my voice neutral. "You weren't wrong."

A flicker of emotion. A pulse in her throat which said, dead or otherwise, Antoinette felt something.

"Say I believe any part of this. How would you even get Alton to speak? He's notoriously tight-lipped."

"I know people," I said. "I have connections in the augment community, and normals play nice with me. People on the bottom, especially. A class of people without cufflinks and monograms."

Despite himself, Elbridge checked his shirt.

"Throughout his career, no matter what his *success*, Dimension spent his time with ordinary people. He trusts the working class. I know them. I *am* them. You think I haven't done this before? My whole livelihood is built on convincing everyday people to hand over a piece of themselves, this augmented miracle they've built their life on. They say they can't do it. They say they won't do it. They say they'll die without it. But after I talk to them, they hand over what I want anyway."

"That's your argument? You're a professional liar and thief?"

"Sometimes," I admitted. "But mostly it's about convincing a man what's important. An augmented device is just a thing. Things come and go. All I do is remind people once they've handed over their device, life will go on. They have husbands and wives. Children and brothers and sisters. Family—that's what's important. And most of the time—these desperate souls—they listen. Because everyone cares about something, no matter how much they've lost."

A bunch of bullshit, like Donny at his best. But I saw a glimmer in Antoinette's eyes and knew I'd hit close to the mark. She'd lost something in her past. She'd let me in for those reasons, if nothing else.

Elbridge wasn't moved. He looked down his nose over the glasses he wasn't wearing. "I don't give two shits about Dimension's soul. Harwood goes in because I said he goes in."

The pulse in Antoinette's neck flared like it might erupt. For a moment, I thought she'd kill every living one of us. But her eyes stayed placid as they met Elbridge's stare. "We're going to revisit the capacity question. There are too many inmates in this facility. It stops."

That *aw shucks* cowboy evasion. "Nette—"

"I mean it. If you want this to happen, figure something out."

Elbridge lifted his chin. He didn't say anything. Finally, he waved his hand dismissively to prove he didn't care. "Fine."

His largesse did me no favors. Antoinette's hair stirred in a Spectral wind as she shifted her attention back to me.

"Half an hour. In. Out. A full report afterwards, to both Andrew and myself. And when you leave, not one word to another living soul."

If I could put the Dimension fiasco behind me, I had no intention of discussing the incident. Ever. I nodded in agreement.

The temperature plummeted again. Veins of frost lanced across the windows and the glass in the door. Antoinette reached across the desk and grabbed my wrist, a move that wasn't possible while maintaining solid form. About half an inch of her chest sank into the burled hardwood. Her eyes floated like grains of sand in water.

"And you better be telling me the truth. Or I will find you, no matter where you are."

Whatever sympathy she held in her heart for me and my daughter had evaporated. Her breath was the summit of Mount Everest. Where she touched me, I felt the most painful, bone-deep cold.

Elbridge looked at me. His smile just as frigid.

"Let's go ask *Alton* what he knows."

CHAPTER FORTY-THREE

We walked through the belly of the most secretive augment prison facility in the world. Elbridge and I stumbled along in our cowboy boots. Antoinette levitated above the hard cement as if she was untouchable.

"We don't need guard towers," she said. "Although the Pillars of Hercules aren't far. Bonnell sits astride a fault line, a rift between our universe and N Space. Lightly displaced from reality."

We'd moved from the chaotic emptiness of Bonnell's offices to the more traditional olive-painted cinder-block hallways of a government facility. The guards again trailed, their expressions drawing tighter as we descended. My boots echoed against the prison's hard surfaces. I wondered how much of what I saw was an illusion.

"The Pillars of Hercules," I said. "Isn't that the Rock of Gibraltar?"

"Gibraltar is one of the two pillars, yes. Bonnell touches many places back home. And none of them. All at the same time."

Solid flesh had replaced Antoinette's ethereal form. Her face and eyes were once again guarded. She acted as if this field trip was her idea. A guided tour she'd gladly conduct any day of the week.

"Pain in the ass, walking this far," Elbridge interrupted. "Should have brought Dimension to us."

"Alton is not to leave his cell, Andrew. My prison. My rules."

"You lease the prison from the United States government. Dead folks don't own property."

Antoinette floated, ignoring him. The dynamics between them were complicated, and I felt lost trying to navigate the transient alliances. Mak and her talent for getting people to open their mouths would have been particularly useful.

We reached the end of the hallway. A polished steel door blocked the way, looking freshly minted. Checkered beams of yellow light escaped the door's wire-mesh viewscreen. The passage appeared impenetrable. Given the prison's occupants, *impenetrable* was probably the idea.

Off to one side, a guard worked the door from behind the safety of a Plexiglas screen. He pushed out a metal drawer and the guards dropped their guns inside. I was asked if I had any rings or keys, pocketknives, or bottle openers. The booth guard asked Elbridge the same questions. He didn't ask the warden a thing.

The door swung back. We passed through. And then my life changed.

Flash. I was delivering packages wrapped in butcher-block paper. I'd been doing it for a couple of months and the payout was an easy couple grand. Working my way up the organizational ladder had taken time and a disregard for breaking the law, something I'd sworn I wouldn't do in the beginning and had undertaken with a cold detachment only just last month. But today was different. Today, the client had told me to leave quickly after my delivery, as if hanging around might be a bad idea. The package felt heavy. I told myself it contained money. I told myself it contained drugs. But the package had contained an explosive device and had nearly killed a man. After I received my payment, over five thousand dollars in cash, I asked if there were any more deliveries. I didn't care how much the package weighed.

Flash. I was holding the phone bill in my hand and I knew Charlie had been cheating on me. The house was a mess and I'd been working more hours than I should. I felt like I'd swallowed the grief of death and divorce all rolled into one. The unknowing of the person closest to me. The thought of what I'd be like on my own, without her, was too much. I stuffed the folded paper back in the envelope. I would pretend I never saw it.

Flash. The envelope was in my hand, the one Donny handed me.

He was standing on the other side of my desk. He wasn't grinning, but he wanted to. The envelope weighed a thousand pounds. I thought of all the things the money could pay for. Marriage counseling. Augmented treatments for Jamie's cancer. Maybe even a hotel and a drive down to the Gulf. But none of those things was a fix. I handed the envelope back to Donny and told him to figure things out. Return the ring, or I was gone.

Flash.

I was back in the prison. Of all people, Elbridge was holding me up. He'd propped me against a handrail and was snapping his fingers in front of my eyes. The look on his face was unfamiliar. I think he was concerned.

"You back with us?" he asked.

When I attempted to speak, my stomach tried to fall out. I tasted bile. A harsh burn in my throat. I closed my mouth and shook my head.

Elbridge looked at Antoinette slantways. She hovered just behind us. "Least you could have done was warn him."

"Everybody has to experience it. He wanted in, he's in. Let him live with his choices."

Elbridge grunted. Took a deep breath and let me go. He looked like a slab of pork shoulder left out in the sun. "Easy for you to say. Your choices have already been made."

"They were taken from me."

"If you two are done." I blinked and stood straight, reminding myself that Donny was dead and Charlene gone. None of the events I'd witnessed had happened—at least not the way I'd seen. "What was that?"

"Lost choices," Antoinette said. "When the prisoners are let out, for their one legally mandated hour of exercise, we put them here. And they get their exercise. Along with every choice they made, every path not chosen, everything they gave up or destroyed along the way."

Antoinette pushed past me. Part of her shoulder ripped through my chest. It was unpleasant.

"This isn't a halfway house. I'm not rehabilitating them. This place is about punishment and reflection. Believe me when I say you will leave here having considered your life."

Elbridge shook his head, and that left me wondering. If Antoinette was the bad guy, what the hell did that make Elbridge?

We moved on.

The prison's central chamber was the first location I'd seen all day that met expectations. A windowed monitoring station towered above us, yellow-painted handrails and walkways forking from the base. Lights blazed overhead and the walls were pockmarked with tiny barred closets stacked five levels high. Nobody moved. No faces appeared in the cells. The prison was little different than Hollywood would have me believe.

Flash.

I saw Charlie in my mind's eye. The hollowed-out look on her face as the truth about her affair came tumbling out. The guilt transferring from her to me.

Flash.

Keep walking. If Elbridge can do it, so can you.

Next to me, the Treasury Secretary walked like his shoes pinched. A pained expression cracked his usually smooth veneer, and I was willing to bet his monogrammed dress shirt was soaked through with sweat. The knowledge he was fighting his own missed opportunities gave me pause. The fear I'd crack first kept me going.

Above the monitoring station, the ceiling rose a hundred feet. From inside the tower a guard watched me, his hands hidden below the lip of the window. He wore a navy dress shirt and a blood-red tie and looked like a banker. He had dead eyes.

Antoinette floated along. She'd seen all this before.

"Each cell is a different pocket universe." She'd gone transparent, her hair floating along behind her although there was no breeze. "A closed loop. Over two hundred and fifty realities, connected to N Space and thus Bonnell by the gates you see."

"That's impossible," I said.

"You're an augment repoman. You should know better. This is the gateway, or was. The point of entry for over seventy percent of the world's augmented devices. A stable reality nexus, until the government capped the well in 1919."

"The Treaty of Paris. The end of the First World War. That was about Bonnell?"

"Everything is about Augments. Or didn't you know?"

Elbridge leaned against the railing. "Is all this really necessary?"

"You let him in here to judge me, I'm going to tell him the whole truth. I've been *leasing* here for over one hundred years. How about you, Andrew?"

He swallowed any remaining objections.

"Take a good look." Antoinette swept an arm around the vast hive of imprisoned Augments. "There are beings who have been incarcerated here since the beginning. A few born in the shadow of Napoleon. And not just the device-powered. We have Naturals as well. Your history books suggest mutation from asteroid or earthquake. Call it instead a dimensional rift—they were granted power by what fell through this space, and that power bled out of this hole for years."

I stared at her. Dumbfounded.

"That's a certain justice to the situation," Antoinette said. "Augments derived their power from the Bonnell nexus. Now we trap them in the same conduit."

"You've had people imprisoned here for over one hundred years?" There was horror in my voice. Judgement, even.

Antoinette paused at the foot of a zigzag staircase. "How long are the dead dead? One hundred years? Two hundred? The souls these people have taken are never coming back to life. I promise you—we punish the prisoners not one second longer than it takes to undo their crimes."

Maybe I was wrong. Maybe I'd never seen pity in Antoinette's eyes.

She drifted up the stairs, drawing the pair of us along with her.

"As for the Naturals," she said, "Bonnell is resistant to its offspring.

N Space lies between folds in reality, where augmentation holds less meaning. Other than within the facility itself, the recognized laws of physics don't apply." She pointed at a cell on her left. "Electricida can't kill you if she has no conducting medium."

"Even Naturals are powerless?" I asked.

"Even Naturals are powerless."

I tilted my head back, gawked at a dome larger than any football stadium. When I looked down, Antoinette stared back at me, the cells behind visible through her transparent eyes.

"But you exist," I said. "Bonnell hasn't ended you."

"She exists only because of Bonnell." Elbridge waggled one bony finger at Antoinette. "This is what she avoids."

The Spectral woman shrugged, the bright light spilling through her, casting no shadow.

"It just kills her—no pun intended—for you to think she chose this line of work. She's trapped here, same as any prisoner. Died on the cusp of N Space. She's doomed to live forever, unless Bonnell unthreads itself and the universes spin apart."

Flash. Mak and I sitting at Woody's bar. I notice her beer is only a quarter full and order another on the sly. She discovers my clumsy subterfuge and smiles. I'd told her about the Dimension bribe months ago. I'd just offered her a full partnership in Netherhouse. She'd only worked at the firm for two years.

Flash. The image was gone.

Charlie. Donny. Mak. Were all the roads not taken better choices?

Antoinette had paused on the stairs. She watched me with a doctor's insight. "You're ready to talk to Alton."

We climbed. Antoinette went through the motions of lifting and dropping her legs. She'd probably spent decades pretending to be something she wasn't. Normal. Alive. Was she Bonnell's warden because she believed in the punishment or because she had nowhere else to go?

Elbridge took the stairs one at a time, his hands concealed in his pockets, his neck twisted and bent. He looked like a sunbaked rooster.

For the first time that I could remember, Andrew Elbridge looked old.

We didn't stop until we scraped the ceiling, walking the penthouse level of the prison. Elbridge had obviously been there before. He walked straight to Dimension's cell without any guidance. He stopped in front of the thick horizontal bars. Behind the bars—a gaping maw. Nothingness.

Elbridge tried to smile. "It's not as bad as it looks."

I slowed, the reality of my situation settling in. Suddenly sure Elbridge had no intention of honoring our arrangement. I'd be lucky to leave Bonnell alive. "Don't pretend you give a damn."

The half-smile dropped from his face. "Open the cell."

Antoinette circled a finger in the air. Obscured weights and pulleys ground and clanked. A buzzer sounded and a light above Dimension's cell flared an angry red. Whether she directly controlled the prison's gears or her hidden minions spun the wheels, I couldn't say, but the yellow bars swung back.

"He won't be restrained," Antoinette said. "Watch yourself."

"And just because he can't get out," Elbridge added, "doesn't mean he won't kill you."

The entire situation was nuts. Lunacy of the first order.

"Great," I said. "Thanks for the pep talk."

For Patrick and Dru. For Mak and Nate. For Charlie and Jamie and anyone who depended on me and Netherhouse.

Because I'd disappointed them all.

I stepped through.

CHAPTER FORTY-FOUR

The cell was nicer than my apartment.

Inside, there were no bars, no metal toilet, no mock-up of Alcatraz or Devil's Island. There was green. There was the smell of cut grass. Sunlight streamed from a downy sky and bounced yellow and gold off the casement windows of the cottage. A tiny green English cottage with a brown door set smack-dab in the middle of a vibrant garden.

I walked closer. Damp soil ground quietly under my boots. A wasp droned past my ear. A cluster of fuzzy ageratums brushed my legs as I reached the foot of the stairs leading to the door. I didn't know a ton about flowers, but my mother had planted ageratums every year, watching them bake and burn in the Texas sun. And then she'd plant them all over again. A hardy soul, my mother. Up until the cancer ate her from the inside out.

It would have been easy to think about Jamie. Instead, I circled the garden.

More plants. Ivy climbing the house and trees hugging the stairs and flowers exploding in a riot of color. A tarnished sundial kept time on the perimeter. A pile of mossy stones threatened to topple over but didn't. The whole place bordered on chaos but was obviously well kept. Somewhere, a gardener kept nature organized.

I found him on his hands and knees. The greatest villain of all time, clad in tan work pants, a floppy-brimmed crusher hat, and foam kneepads. He dug in the earth with a trowel. He looked like he'd been pulled from a plumber's armpit.

He'd killed Treasury agents. Armed guards and fellow prisoners. If

I turned around now, I could escape. Assuming I could find the door.

Alton Zimmer looked up and spotted me. Squinted. He sighed and set aside his trowel and got to his feet. He worked barehanded.

"Are you another lawyer?" He put a hand to the small of his back and pushed out his belly. "I told them to stop. I don't need more lawyers. They are slimy."

He was a slight man, weighing a hundred and fifty pounds soaking wet, if that. Salt-and-pepper hair cut close on the sides and grown long on top. Fuzzy mustache with even more grey. An older Groucho Marx, had the man kept his hair.

"I'm not a public defender." I stood my ground. "I'm Gayle Harwood."

He stared, nonplussed.

"I work for Netherhouse Liquidation."

"No. You don't." He flavored his voice with an accent, something Eastern European.

"I'm afraid I do. I'm a partner in the business."

"Donny runs Netherhouse. I've met him. He is an asshole."

Alton, and I thought of him as Alton now, pronounced Donny like *Doonie*, adding a certain exotic flair in death my ex-partner had lacked in life. The asshole part was spot on.

"He's no longer with the company. You want to see Netherhouse, that's me. I'm in charge now."

"If you're standing in my garden, I don't think you're in charge of anything." He stared at me. "But I did ask for Netherhouse, and if you are it, you'll have to do." He glanced down at the furrowed earth. "You're interrupting me, but come inside. You can have espresso."

I hated espresso, but Alton didn't wait around for an answer. He marched inside the cottage, leaving me alone with the bees and harsh sunlight. I followed him.

Inside, the cottage was well decorated. A scuffed hardwood floor covered with throw rugs. A coffee table littered with scrawled papers. High-backed chairs scattered here and there as if I'd interrupted a dinner party. And books. Every wall a bookcase stuffed with books, from floor to ceiling. Small-paned windows bled light into the room and gave everything a warm glow.

Nicer than my apartment.

Alton stood at a slipcovered white couch situated behind the coffee table. He bent and selected one of the scribbled sheets and looked down his nose at the contents. "They tell me I need trifocals. Do you know what those are?"

On the other side of the living room was a kitchen. A closed door perhaps led to a bedroom.

"Helps you read. See close. See far."

The paper sagged in his hands. "They are signs of age."

"Okay. It's not my area of expertise. I failed biology."

"I wouldn't brag about that."

He tossed aside the paper and discarded his hat. Wandered into the kitchen and grabbed a tall pot. He disappeared around the corner but I heard water running. He didn't invite me in. "They won't give me a real machine, so I have to make do with the stove. I don't mind. I did it on the outside. There's satisfaction in creation, you understand?"

A dig, perhaps. I let it slide. "Sure. If you say so."

He leaned back so I could see him. He held a stainless-steel filter full of dark powder, the granules tiny like brown couscous. "I remember someone, an assistant of Donny's. You're the boy?"

Forty-two years old. Been a long time since anyone had called me *boy*. "I worked for Donny, yes."

"And how is he? Your boss."

He stood there, cocksure. He knew the answer. "He's dead."

The information left him unimpressed. "I've heard this. It seems unlike him."

"Unlike him?" I laughed. "Sure. Definitely poor form for old Donny to expire."

"I've seen him escape tight spots before. Wiggle free of circumstances that should have left him incapacitated at best."

"He did have a knack. Somewhat famous for it, actually. But this time—" I searched for the words. "He's dead."

A grunt. Alton ducked back into the kitchen. Clicks and then a pop as he ignited the stove.

"You were there. When Netherhouse stole my ring."

My stomach flip-flopped. "Funny you should mention the ring. I hear someone found it."

Metal clattered. Alton reappeared, wiping his hands with a white towel. "Someone besides Donny? This means he lost it. That's amusing."

The urge to defend Donny stampeded through me. Even after all this time. "There's no proof Donny had anything to do with the ring's disappearance."

"I'm not surprised there's no proof. He's an accomplished thief. Or he was."

"And you're a murderer."

I'd clenched my jaw tight. Dangerous words I might regret. But Alton expressed no visible emotion at my statement.

"I've killed men." He held the towel loosely between his fingers. "But only with reason."

My silence expressed doubt. He lifted his chin.

"This is a specific claim?"

"The mafia guy. You killed him. And several FBI agents."

He frowned. "Who told you this story? Treasury? This story is nonsense." He paused. "The one gentleman—he came at me with his gun drawn. I was young. It was my first such assignment and I was scared. I stuck out my hand and it went into his chest. I pulled back, but it was too late. He died of a heart attack. Myocardial infarction, they said. He was dead before his body hit the floor."

Alton wiped dirt from his naked hands.

"Sometimes, you make bad choices," he said.

Then Alton Zimmer got angry.

"This business with the brains. That I stuck my hand into the heads of those poor boys. Ghoulish. More Treasury fabrication. Have you heard the one about the fingers?"

I shook my head.

"Supposedly, I have a trick," he said. "A thing I do when I'm questioning a law enforcement officer. I shove my finger into the pinkie and then unphase my hand. The victim's fingertip pops. The pain is excruciating, and I do this thing while he—or she—is still alive. Slowly. One finger at a time."

He looked at me. Weighed my silence.

"This is sick," he said.

"I agree."

He nodded. Half-turned toward the kitchen.

"What about those agents down at Lady Bird Lake?" I asked.

He stopped.

"I was there," I said. "There were three of them. They all died."

Alton glanced at me from the corner of his eye. "There were many bad choices that day."

He threw the towel into a wicker basket. It was full of other towels, all of them stained dark brown. The color of dried blood.

I heard water run in the kitchen. A quiet punctuated by the squeak of Alton's shoes on tile. Eventually, he reappeared and led me back to the couch and high-backed chairs.

"This talk of what we do for money is interesting," he said. "For example, how much did Donny pay you to look the other way?"

I had to remind myself of the endgame. Get Netherhouse reinstated. Pay for Jamie's treatment. Everything in between was sticks and stones.

"You don't remember the size of your bribe?" Alton sniffed. "It disappoints me I was sold out for so little."

"You made your choices. Don't put them on me."

The words failed to ruffle Alton. He sat in one of the high-backed chairs and indicated I should park it on the couch. I stood, a small act of defiance.

"Donny didn't have the ring?" he asked.

"No."

"But you know where it is."

I looked up at the low roof, the surface spider-webbed with cracks.

My finger reached out and pressed against the plaster almost of its own accord. As if I couldn't believe the place was real.

"Elbridge told me you could find the ring," I said.

A slow smile appeared. "He thinks we are in cahoots, you and I. That you were holding the ring for my eventual return. Only I was betrayed, and you sold it for profit."

The revelation chilled me. Elbridge had suggested I was no longer a suspect. To realize he still harbored suspicions and had managed to remove me literally from the face of the earth...

Alton seemed to know what I was thinking. He watched me with a psychiatrist's scrutiny.

"You know that's not true," I said.

He made a noise. "I have been held prisoner a long time. Anything is possible."

"Oh? So, you don't know where the ring is?"

"It entertains me for the Secretary to chase his own tail. For Netherhouse to be the subject of his pursuits would also be pleasing."

There was no indication Alton was being anything less than truthful. But he was an excellent poker player. I could read him as easily as I could Sanskrit. I wasn't entirely faking when I caved under the pressure and sat on the couch.

"Is this why you brought me here? To gloat?"

"I wonder why you came here at all. This is a prison. The prison. The only one who visits voluntarily is the Secretary."

"Treasury regulates my industry. I did it because he asked."

"As a favor? For the man that could put you out of business?"

"Does it really matter?"

Alton pursed his lips. "Calm yourself. I'm simply curious. It is interesting to know who else he has under his thumb."

"He doesn't control me, if that's what you're saying."

"You're angry. I understand."

"Fuck off."

He shrugged. "Take that tack, if you wish. But I will not sit here and be insulted. I have a garden to attend to."

"You have your whole life to attend to that garden, as I understand it."

He played it cool. "True."

Silence. A wasp banged against the glass window. Again I reminded myself I only needed to keep him talking. He'd promised Elbridge the ring. I just had to stay out of the way.

Assuming Alton kept his side of the bargain.

"Can you really find the ring?" I asked.

He shrugged. "I could disabuse Treasury of the notion you and I ever worked together."

"You could. But why would you?"

"The game. As you say, I have my whole life to attend to my garden. I have my whole life to attend to anything in the universe. In this universe, and this alone. I will never leave. I must find joy where I can."

Alton's espresso percolated in the next room. I focused on this completely normal sound. It reminded me Alton was just a man. He drank coffee. He fretted over his garden. He puffed out his chest and blustered when he lied.

"Bullshit," I said. "You wouldn't give up on your property. Not that easily."

"My property?" Alton smiled a little. "Andy would dispute such claims of ownership."

Andy, not Andrew or Mr. Elbridge. My return grin was genuine. "He most certainly would."

I wasn't sure if the moment was real or fake. But Alton seemed at ease. He kept his hands loose in his lap. Occasionally tapped his toes.

"Can I ask you a question?"

He spread his hands. *If it pleases you.*

"Woody Chaikin."

Immediately, the man looked pained. His eyes fluttered. "There is a torture unlike any other."

"Not a Woody fan?"

"He is a hangnail. That never heals."

"But he was in the League of Six."

"He was in no such thing. He had aspirations. Delusions of grandeur. He appeared with that gaudy mallet and plans for secret hideouts as if we accepted any Augment off the street. He was better suited for a comedy club. The Velveeta Room, perhaps. He would kill there."

"So, you never worked with him."

"Comedy is not my forte." He pressed his fingers to his temples. "*Under the airport*, he said. *We could dig tunnels*, he said." He shook his head. "Idiot."

I could only imagine Alton's reaction to hearing Woody wielded his precious ring. But he changed the subject.

"How long did our friend Andy give you?"

"It's not him, actually. Antoinette gave me thirty minutes of chitchat. You may have requested me, but she permitted me, on her timetable."

Antoinette's name triggered him. He narrowed his eyes. In the silence, I could hear his breathing. Steady, like a panther's.

"If you have a card," I said, "you should play it."

The man had been in prison for fifteen years. They'd caged him more securely than almost any other. Even without his ring, they were terrified of him. And I sat here with him, playing word games. Poking him. Inciting him.

Some days, I wondered if I wasn't as self-destructive as my critics claimed.

"The air here," Alton said. "It isn't right. I can grow vegetables and herbs, but the cilantro…it tastes like soap. The strawberries come up with mold." He gestured toward the window. "I don't know if she does it to me on purpose, or if this universe is not ripe yet. The plants die. Tomorrow, I will walk into the garden and the forget-me-nots will have withered. I'll find the pansies stunted in their bed. Even the garden gnomes. There are three now, the fourth is…failing. Was it vandalized? Or did it fall apart because this place is unnatural? This— this is the answer to your question."

I frowned. "I don't understand."

He moved to sit next to me on the couch.

"If we were outside, I could find one." Tension leaked out of his face as he closed his eyes. "At my home, I had a beautiful garden. Likely the property has been sold, but someone would have the gnomes. And I could find them."

He thrust out a finger. Turned like he was divining water.

"She does something to me, in this place. I cannot be sure anymore. But on the outside." His finger stopped. It pointed somewhere over my shoulder. "There, perhaps. Or it was and now has been moved?"

The look on his face. Mak's father had Alzheimer's, before he passed. The anguished uncertainty was the same.

He opened his eyes.

"On the outside," Alton said. "I could be sure."

Silence. Had I imagined birdsong when I'd arrived? The hum of bees? Were insects and squirrels allowed in the bubble universe? As it was, I heard nothing.

Alton waited until I had no choice but to ask.

"And the ring?" I said. "Do you know where that is?"

"It's close," he said. "Northwest of here, maybe twenty miles, give or take. From inside the prison, I can't be more precise."

I stared at him. I didn't know what to say.

"He thinks I will trick you into revealing the location of my ring." A cold fury gripped Alton's face. "What he doesn't realize is I already know. Whenever the ring is used, I can feel it. It is a part of me. I could no more lose it than my hand. He says too much, our Treasury Secretary. When he visits, his base appetites are clear. His political ambitions. His hatred of me. Of you. I will use it all against him. He will get ash. I will watch him flail like a beetle on its back, and all his posturing will be for nothing. He will be embarrassed. Humiliated. When I am done with him, he will be lucky to retain his badge. And most importantly, he will know that I fucked him, even from inside the inescapable prison."

He looked at me. He narrowed his eyes. "The espresso is ready."

"What?"

He popped to his feet and shuffled into the kitchen. "No more rain. It means the espresso is finished."

Crazy. The man was certifiable. "No more rain?"

"The popping sound. It reminds me of rain." He swung into view with the pot in his hand. "I haven't heard the sound in many years. In my cell, it's always a sunny day. A perpetual spring. They have to bring me water for the plants."

It made sense Donny enjoyed battling Alton all those years ago. Donny loved to talk, to confuse people with non sequiturs and go-nowhere stories. Alton Zimmer was his kind of criminal.

"Rain?"

"Yes. Listen."

Feeling like an idiot, I cocked my head. And although I heard a faint popping as the pot in Alton's hand cooled, I didn't hear the gurgling of coffee as it bubbled up. I heard a new noise.

Thunk.

The cottage's frame rattled. The light outside died and the smell of cut grass faded.

I began to stand but Alton moved faster. He held up a hand, set down his pot, and darted toward the cottage entrance. On the threshold of the doorway he paused, then frowned and checked the windows. The sun had gone out, consumed by a thunderous sky. Angry black clouds boiled and surged toward the cottage.

Alton flew back and forth across the room. Jumped on the furniture and flailed at the open windows. He didn't bother with the locks, instead trying to close as many windows as possible before the darkness burst in. The faint espresso smell still hung in the air, but another odor was powering through. Harsh and thick. Tainted with the lingering smell of garlic.

"What's going on?" I asked.

Alton stood on a bookcase with his grip on the last window, leaning into the room like he could ride the vapors. His eyes widened. "Kolokol-3."

Blank look. I'd never heard of it.

"A modified opioid. We'll be knocked out for five or six hours. Unless the gas kills us."

Hoarfrost spilled through the kitchen doorway and blossomed toward the interior.

I backtracked, fear powering my legs. Alton jumped from the bookcase and stumbled. Scrambled to stay on his feet.

Albino fingers multiplied and a great billow of frosted wind exploded into the room, advancing like a dozen spectral Antoinettes. The coffee table froze solid, cracked, then split in half. One of the high-backed chairs twisted under the intense cold. Not only was the cloud an opioid, it carried an arctic deadliness.

I stuffed myself into the corner. Alton wedged in beside me.

The ceiling groaned and turned to ice. Bitter cold shattered windows and curled the fibers of the throw rugs. The advancing cloud howled at us. We faced a wall of winter.

Alton pressed his mouth to my ear. "He will never let you leave."

The wind exploded into me like a Mack truck. Nails of ice raked my hands, chest, and face. I dropped to my knees, my muscles seizing. When I opened my mouth to scream, I swallowed a glacier. My eyelids froze open, and I could see icicles forming in my lashes. The wind howled in my ears. My heart slowed and my blood stopped pumping. I felt so cold, I thought my bones might crack.

So many people I'd wanted to apologize to. The chance now lost.

Alton moaned and fell over.

It's entirely possible my bones did crack, my skeleton flash-freezing and shattering into a thousand pieces. Pain magnified a thousandfold. But I never felt it. I blacked out and let the entire miserable experience pass me by.

CHAPTER FORTY-FIVE

I woke with one hand speed-cuffed to a hospital gurney. It hurt.

Afterimages pulled apart and reassembled. Alton Zimmer with frost in his mustache. The blood in my veins freezing under my crackling skin. The gas had numbed me, but the impression of my heart freezing solid still lingered. For a moment, I thought I was still dying, and grabbed at my chest. I felt gauze and metal. A lead ran from my breastbone to a monitor next to the bed, and an echocardiogram blipped twice to remind me of my tenuous lease on life.

I turned my head and inspected the cuff. Through blurry vision I recognized the rigid grip and tight ratchet. The keyhole reachable only if I rolled over.

An orderly appeared. She was petite. Her black hair yanked back in a ponytail. Black eye shadow. Blunt nails. "You need to lie still."

I rolled over anyway. She grabbed my shoulder and pressed her thumb against the walkie-talkie at her waist. An alarm chimed. Another orderly appeared over her shoulder.

"Do that again," she said, "and I'll have you sedated."

Her words made a lot of sense. I stopped moving.

I was in a large open room divided by freestanding partitions. Beds had been placed haphazardly—gurneys, most of them empty. Signs on the wall explained how to treat heart attack and choking. Every sign carried a stern reminder not to remove the prisoner's handcuffs. One patient shared my space with me. A woman with purple skin. She stared at the ceiling, glassy-eyed. Her attendant treated a large incision that ran vertically up her arm, and she stared at me as if daring me to speak. I faked a smile and turned away.

There were no clocks in the room. I could have been out for hours or days. While I was unconscious, someone had changed my clothes. I wore a white T-shirt and orange prison pants. Like I belonged in Bonnell.

Alton's last words.

He'll never let you leave.

I waited impatiently for a few hours. The orderlies came and went. The adhesive leads were ripped from my skin. I asked for a deck of cards and was again reminded to stay quiet. I felt helpless. Powerless. Like any debtor we'd ever pursued. By the time Elbridge arrived, I was tired and frustrated and bored.

He looked down his nose at me. This time, he was actually wearing his reading glasses. "You're lucky Treasury has all these rules for handling prisoners." He pushed the glasses up his nose. "Less-scrupulous parties might have left you to freeze."

"When am I getting out of here? You promised me."

He hunted for a chair and found one by the door. Dragged it over to sit bedside. He almost managed to look concerned.

Antoinette was nowhere to be seen.

"What was it like?" Elbridge asked. "The Kolokol?"

"Ever seen one of those nature shows where a waterfall freezes solid? I was the waterfall."

He reached behind him to a small wheeled table, handed me a plastic cup full of chipped ice. I poured a couple of slivers on my tongue. I chewed slowly. Elbridge let me take my time.

"You heard him, didn't you?" I asked. "When Alton said he could track his gnomes? That's why you gassed us."

"Surveillance is standard in every cell, his included. And don't get righteous with me—Nette pulled the trigger. If anything, I'm the only reason you're still alive."

Owing Elbridge my life wasn't a concept I wanted to consider. And the prospect of Antoinette shutting off the life support when I thought she might secretly be on my side—that was a bitter pill to swallow.

"Don't take it so hard," Elbridge said. "There's a reason we put her in charge. You think we'd take any old ghost and hand them the keys to two hundred and fifty criminal Augments?" Elbridge patted me on the arm, the same one sutured with tiny wasps of pain. "She jumped off that cliff. She wasn't pushed and she didn't slip. She turned into the clear blue sky and voluntarily left terra firma. A fact we commemorate every time we enter the prison. Antoinette's way is the only way. You want to enter Bonnell, you die. Thus the nine-millimeter headache." He mimed a finger-gun barrel to his temple. "If it makes you feel any better, I had to eat one too."

"Marginally."

A grim smile crossed his face. "The experience should tell you something. Antoinette committed suicide rather than bend a knee to the Spanish or the Comanche or whomever the hell she claims elbowed her aside. And then she came back, crossed the hard line between death and life. Came back and asked to run this prison, which she's run for damn near one hundred years. Think on that. Consider the force of will."

I shrugged his hand off my arm. "Where is she, then?"

"Preparing the prisoner for release. She doesn't like it, and a hundred years is great and all, but the United States government is almost two hundred and fifty years old. We have seniority."

I'd hoped to create opportunity from chaos, but this was more chaos than I'd had in mind.

"You're letting Alton out? Why would you do that?"

"Don't sell yourself short, Hardwood. You made this possible. Performed far beyond my expectations, getting him to admit his affinity for the ring. He didn't like being bamboozled, but once I made it clear his accommodations could be improved, he became agreeable. He understands he's never getting out of Bonnell, but *never* can be a long time. Might as well take the option with espresso machines and gardens that don't die. Make things easy on himself. All it required was a little cooperation with the department."

"This is what he wants. You said it yourself—he's dangerous.

You're being an idiot."

Any pretense of Elbridge and me as fishing buddies drained away. "The only reason I'm here at all is to remind you about the terms of our deal. The investigation of Netherhouse's involvement in the incident at Lady Bird Lake will end. But that's no get-out-of-jail-free card. I can still nail you on fraud charges. I have complaints from Augments, respectable ones, going years back. I can leave you unable to practice repo anywhere in the great state of Texas."

"You can't make anything stick," I said, with a confidence I did not feel. "Once I'm out of here, I'll make your life hell."

When he grinned, I expected to see a wolf's yellowed teeth, but all I saw were pearly whites. "Once you're released, you very well might."

He hooked a finger in my restraint and rattled the cuff against the rail.

He turned toward the door.

"Wait." I raised my cuffed arm as far as I could. "You can't leave me here."

"Oh, I don't have the keys. You'll have to ask Nette for those."

Elbridge's lips peeled back to flash those teeth. He was a wolf, a lean old dog watching another pretender accept the fact he was beaten.

Whistling, Elbridge walked away down the hall.

CHAPTER FORTY-SIX

Bonnell's quiet was unnatural. A silence laced with missed opportunities. Inhuman shrieks echoed down the hallways and then cut off. I thought I heard a child singing, her weak voice echoing through the ducts. Footsteps paced the hall, but when I called out, they faded away. Had I been shunted into a pocket universe? Jamie would never know what had happened to me. Mak and Dru would mourn but then move on.

I talked to myself. Said I wasn't going crazy.

"The pocket universes keep them sane."

Antoinette stood in the room, fully realized.

"Bonnell Prison is no place for the living," she said. "There's a reason life doesn't take hold in the seams. The spirit bleeds here, the last drop of existence around the drain. The screams. The noises. They are souls too weak to escape. They are trapped here alone, denied the paradise of friends and family, forever."

Eyes of topaz stared back at me. I wondered if this was the face she wore when she'd gassed me.

"Something bothering you?" she asked.

"Like you said. Bonnell is a creepy place."

Antoinette looked like she wanted to say more. Instead, she closed her mouth and shrugged. "If it makes you feel any better, I was against releasing Alton. We put him in here for a reason."

Her words reminded me of Ellen ensconced in her limousine, talking about what was best for the augment community.

"He'll find the ring, you know," I said. "Alton Zimmer."

"Calling him by his real name now, are we?"

She drifted closer, watching me.

"That was a neat trick. What Alton did with his finger." She closed her eyes and spun like a weathervane. Opened her eyes and smiled. "Andrew certainly gobbled up the entertainment, like a child at his mother's knee. So well orchestrated. Was that your intention?"

My thawed face ached. I tried to rub out the pain. "If you're against releasing Alton, why is he getting out? I thought Bonnell was your prison."

She smiled, but in a fake way. Like I'd told her she was pretty. "You do that a lot."

"What?"

"Ignore uncomfortable questions. Flip things around. I imagine the tactic works pretty well. With most people."

On the outside, I would hire Antoinette in a second. She and Mak together would kill me, but death would be worth it. "I don't always get what I want by asking nicely. Repo isn't all two-martini lunches. Most of the time not even lunch."

The purple woman with the slit wrist refused to turn our way. She feigned sleep. She was afraid of the warden.

"Why did you do it?" I asked. "Gas Alton and me? We could have died."

"You didn't."

"Semantics. When you pushed the button or raised an eyebrow or whatever, you could have killed us. Why do it?"

"Alton Zimmer killed two of my guards. Killed countless more on the outside. He is dangerous, he is a criminal, and I am the warden. This is my prison. I don't have to explain myself to you."

She dealt me a frosted look, and I recalled the feeling of my trachea filling with ice.

Her anger passed. She moved closer, fluctuating between translucent and opaque. "So, what will you do when you leave here? Return to scavenging powerful trinkets?"

I was afraid to ask if I would, indeed, be released. "Your friend Andrew claims he'll reinstate my firm. I imagine I'll return to work. I need the money."

She sat on the edge of the bed and touched my arm as Elbridge had. The good arm this time.

"It's not so much the money, though, is it?" she said. "I had several business operations in flux at the time of my demise, but I don't think of those opportunities in my darkest moments. I think of my sister. She was only thirteen. Naudah had a cleft lip—she had trouble even asking for water, and so few understood the finger language."

She squeezed my arm a little tighter. Stared into my eyes.

"The loss of loved ones," she said. "That's what kills me."

The way she looked at me. Appraising. That reminded me of Elbridge too.

Antoinette turned and rose from the gurney. "But enough third-degree. I'm to prepare a guard detail for Andrew. Seems I can't decide whether Alton stays or goes, but I can provide men when commandeered."

She paused, looked over her ghostly shoulder. "Mr. Elbridge will want more men than I can provide."

A raised eyebrow. The speed cuff released and clattered to the ground.

"The men I encounter are all the same," she said. "Dangerous fools who believe nothing is more important than their own wants and desires. I hope you are different."

My mouth hung open as—one last time—she went transparent. She was every inch the Spectral force rumor and legend suggested.

"Get out of my prison," she said.

And off she floated.

CHAPTER FORTY-SEVEN

The open door was a dead giveaway. One door propped in an otherwise seamless hallway. The interior was jammed full of printing paper and batteries and manila folders. It was a supply closet and not a place I'd find anything useful. Other than the guard's uniform hanging from one of the shelves.

I shrugged it on. It was my size.

This section of the prison was sterile, a maze of white-tiled floors and green-painted walls. My footfalls echoed throughout empty hallways. At the first intersection, a ceiling-mounted speaker growled static at me. At the next intersection, the same thing. Not a soul to be found. Literally.

I carried on, following the signs. Dark hallways meant I was walking the wrong direction. I followed the lights.

It was possible my escape was some elaborate trick. A long con arranged by Elbridge and Antoinette, the bad cop and the good cop or vice versa. They planned to feed me enough rope to run loose around the prison until I crossed some arbitrary threshold, then accuse me of escaping the prison to which I'd been so nicely invited. Maybe they'd crack open a nearby bubble universe and throw me in for all eternity. But why bother with such an elaborate contrivance? I'd already been chained to the bed. Trapped in an otherworldly cell. It wasn't as if I was on the cusp of escaping in the day's laundry.

The hallway ended at a pair of mag-locked doors. Red letters warned me to stay out, to proceed only if I felt I was authorized personnel. There was no fire alarm override. Just a door with a warning and the probability of a very loud alarm. I pushed it open anyway, and warnings failed to sound. When I passed through, I heard doors shut and the lock seal like a slide being racked.

Get out of my prison.

Ahead waited a line of bored guards. They sighed and huffed and acted as if they'd been there since the dawn of time. I attached myself to the end of the queue and nobody cared. They complained about overtime and low pay. Shuffled forward when the opportunity presented. Eventually, we inched around the corner and into a vast open chamber. Only then could I see where we were headed. I saw something I couldn't unsee.

"Hate this part." The guard nearest me rolled his neck until the tendons popped. He looked like a bullmastiff. "Not so much the going back as seeing myself from the outside."

The space was immense, a giant intestine with a gaping maw archway that we all entered through. This part of the prison was less manufactured and more primal in nature. The floor and walls a porous stone, pink and marbled like a cut of steak. The rock glowed with pulsing phosphorescence. A trough ran parallel to the guards, and I squinted in the dark to make out the contents. The stink was like an outhouse baked in the Texas sun. It was a brick-lined trench funneling piss and shit from the prison above. Funneling waste out ahead of us, over a ledge, and through a ribbon of space.

Bullmastiff insisted on talking to me.

"Biggest garbage dump in the universe," he said. "I keep telling them—a day will come when someone shows up to block the drain."

"Who?" The guard in front of Bullmastiff dipped his head at the shit stream. He was older and spoke with an accent. Polish, with hard eyes of arctic ice. "Nobody lives in N Space."

"We're living here. What makes us so special?"

"Quiet." Elbridge appeared behind us, startling me so much I almost stared right at him. "You'll give the prisoner ideas."

The guards stopped talking. Elbridge walked on, and Bullmastiff waited until he was out of earshot to resume his bitching.

"Where does he get off?" he said. "What ideas? Does he think

Dimension is going to ride out on a river of shit?"

Polish snorted. I kept my eyes on his knees. He swung forward without asking any questions.

More guards spilled from the archway. They walked Alton Zimmer out with his hands front-stacked, one hand cuffed over the other. He looked frazzled. His hair was jacked like Skylark had given him a scalp massage. As he passed, I caught of whiff of body odor, heard him muttering in a language I didn't understand. Alton was afraid. I didn't think it was a game.

Alton's escorts shuffled him to the front of the line. A good half dozen guards surrounded him, as if he might sprout extra arms or soar into the heavens or just explode. The system still saw Alton Zimmer as Doctor Dimension, ring or no.

Elbridge hung off to the side. He seemed nervous too. "Open it up."

The lights blazed. The ribbon of space flared purple and blue-black. And the wall of space changed.

The guards shuffled back from the edge. I didn't blame them.

Where the river of piss and shit waterfalled off the cliff, a shimmering wave ran end to end, stretching the width of the platform. A blurred mélange of blue and black. In another place, the undulating curtain would have struck me as marvelous, but a freak-show parade marred the surface. Bodies, dozens of them. They cycled by like a rack of cheap watches, each more grotesque than the last. Worst part was, I recognized them. They were us. We were them.

Our bodies. Trapped in blue sap.

"Fuckin hate this part," Bullmastiff repeated. "Somebody tell me this is just a drill."

I wanted to, but I was fresh out of lies.

Elbridge barked at us to get moving, and the first pair of guards stepped up to the wave. Each trapped body was caught in a tortured pose, mouth gaping wide, eyes frozen open, hands made claws and wrapped backwards as if to rend flesh from bone. A nightmare made real and all the worse because the bodies were ours.

All my cohorts seemed shaken, and past experience had prepped them. I'd walked in cold.

I promised myself—once back on the outside—things would be different. I'd be a better person. Go to church. Mend fences with Charlie. Hell, I'd even make small talk with Larry. Whatever it took to stay out of places like this.

One of the guards at the head of the line—an entirely too young brown-haired woman who seemed capable of bench-pressing my body weight—tensed. She watched a dark form buried in the wave. The form drew closer as the wave undulated right to left. It came into focus. Mouth stretched wide. Eyes sweating. The spine arched to an inhuman degree. And, just visible in the smear of humanity, matted locks of brown hair.

A horror you'd never approach. For the guard, home sweet home.

She stepped forward as her body came around. There was no magic gate, no wormhole that gave way in a magnificent flash. Instead, she fought her way through a sucking mudhole, a consuming bog. For a moment, she resisted, pulling back an arm that came away coated in black oatmeal. Her torso bent unnaturally, yanked in by the ribs, and she reared back, gasping. The rest of us stood stock-still.

"Hell of a thing." Polish had shifted to stand at my elbow. "Coming back to life is a bitch."

The guard screamed.

Flash. Woody with his arms buried in Cahill's chest.

Flash. Jamie on a chemo drip.

I closed my eyes.

The smear sucked the woman in slowly, her head disappearing last. She screamed the entire time. Only when her dirty brown hair slurped through the wall did the scream fade.

Her soul and body disappeared.

"Next," Elbridge yelled.

The process continued. Twenty minutes, me watching each guard scout out their lost body and reentering with a mix of gusto and dread, like rats scoping electrified cheese. Not a single guard cracked a smile or let loose with a joke.

They took special care with Alton, tugging on his cuffs to ensure they were secure. He stiffened as his body appeared. His Adam's apple swelled as if he'd snapped his own neck. One of the guards chuckled uneasily. The rest of us stood in silence.

Alton Zimmer reentered his body and seized as if hit with ten thousand volts. The last we saw of him, his leg was still twitching.

My two buddies—Bullmastiff and Polish—got real quiet before their bodies appeared. Bullmastiff was crying when he disappeared. Polish spewed expletives in his mother tongue and vomited as he went under.

The wave rolled around. It was my turn.

Up close, this slice of Hell revealed details I couldn't spot from the back. A pitted surface. Grey and green streaks, tapeworms in the seam of reality. An entire ecosystem living inside the wall, creatures shaped like tongues stabbed with thorns, a cockroach with human eyes, a severed limb I couldn't attach to a species. And then the slow revolution of bodies. Every employee of Bonnell Prison except Antoinette. She was the only one to enter the prison through another door.

I saw my body appear out of the darkness. My eyes were haggard and deep wrinkles carved ruts in my face. Old men wore their years on the surface, and I carried a lot of miles. It was a rough thing, seeing yourself from the outside.

Nearby, Elbridge paced the platform, his mouth set in a grim line. He watched the stragglers and inspected them for perceived weakness. He walked toward me with suspicion in his eye.

Behind me, someone made a joke, an off-color remark about Antoinette's abilities *in the sack*. Elbridge zeroed in on the offender.

My time was now.

I lurched forward.

Fire raked my skin. Angry swaths of heat crawled up my arms. As my face entered the wall, I opened my mouth to scream and swallowed a freight train of blue Vaseline. My lungs compressed. My vision burned away, the wave pulverizing my eyes and leaving a searing residue of ground Jalapenos. I couldn't breathe and I couldn't move and I sank further into an unstoppable wall of mud. In the end, I wanted to die.

But instead, I was alive. The ground smacked me in the face, a heavyweight's rocky punch to the cheekbone. I choked, gagged, and threw up. Hands reached down to grab me and pull me out of the way, as the next guard landed in my spot. He reached the ground with more grace. Until he slipped in my vomit.

"What the hell is wrong with you?" Bullmastiff pounded dust from my back. "Next time keep your mouth closed."

The moon was still up. Either no time had passed or I'd lost a whole day. Crickets sang and the passing river lapped at the shore. We'd arrived at Lake Austin. One of the last sights I'd seen before Elbridge blew my brains out.

Alton Zimmer sat in chains on a large rock. He looked ready for the parole board. His hair was plastered to his skull and his prison jumpsuit was freshly pressed. He'd slipped on his old body like a suit just returned from the cleaners. The guards avoided him. Ignored him as if he wasn't there.

Elbridge appeared. He landed on his back and didn't say a word to the rest of us.

We were on a narrow strip of land between the foot of Bonnell and the river, the peak and park benches hidden high above, behind the shoulder of the mountain. The facilities on the bottom weren't nearly as nice as the facilities on the top. A few boulders crowded the gravel, and stubborn weeds forced their way into the seams. The remains of a campfire littered the ground near my feet. I smelled mildew and wet bird shit. The place wasn't inviting.

Quiet fell over the group. Even Elbridge managed only a somber "We leave in five" before wandering down riverside.

I managed to look busy. Kept my head down. Kept moving. No one seemed to notice I wasn't producing anything. Almost no one.

Alton Zimmer sized me up from his perch on the rock. Out here, he looked rejuvenated. Reborn. A force to be reckoned with. Antoinette was right. He should never have been released.

A pair of focused spotlights lit up the night a hundred yards out on the river, painting the rough chop a gas-lamp yellow. Elbridge stepped into the light and waved his arms. Alton was hustled off his rock and made to stand at my back.

"Law enforcement officers." Alton chewed a stick of gum, likely supplied by one of the guards. "Austin police. I wouldn't tell them where we're from."

"Quiet." Elbridge frowned into the approaching lights. "We're working a Treasury matter. The uniforms don't need to know spit. That's an order."

Despite how Elbridge framed the words, he still appeared to be taking orders from Alton.

The boat pulled up along the shore. Dual outboard motors cut off and the boat drifted through the surf. One of the guards secured the boat while the rest of us clambered aboard. When I helped Alton climb over the rail, his hands still bound, the man smiled.

Elbridge hopped aboard last, leaving it to the cops to cast us loose. The boat's engines fired up, quieter than I would have thought, and we swung out in a wide loop before heading south.

Spray peppered our faces. We grabbed hold of metal guardrails and braced ourselves against the boat's surge. One of the cops bragged how they'd seized the boat from a drug dealer operating near Balcones Canyonlands. He made it sound like a big deal.

Alton lay on the boat's floor where the Bonnell guards had tossed him. As if allowing him to stand was too dangerous.

After ten minutes, Elbridge left the driver's side to kneel by Alton. He leaned over and put his mouth to Alton's ear. The wind tore their words from me, but I saw Elbridge point further south, and I saw Alton nod. Elbridge returned to his post inside the cabin. As he passed, I caught a look of smug self-satisfaction.

Were we headed toward Rita Pham? Woody Chaikin? Could I trust Elbridge to seize the ring and leave us alone, or would I need more insurance?

Eventually, we cut toward shore and approached a low, flat area.

A series of awnings covered merchandise racks—suntan lotion, sunglasses, *Keep Austin Augmented* T-shirts. Next to a rack of kayaks I spotted a couple of Austin's finest, their flashlights snapping back and forth to signal us in.

Lady Bird Lake, where all the Dimension trouble originally went down.

Elbridge was busy mumbling into his radio, so Polish took over. He ordered four of us ashore, then had another pair lift Alton from the floor of the boat. They passed him over like heated nitroglycerin. Again Alton smiled as I touched his arm.

All this law and order rankled. I wanted to punch Alton right in the face.

Elbridge signed off his radio and exited the boat. He shouted at the pilot to hang tight without so much as a *please* or *thank you*. Once on the ground he oriented himself, spinning like a wind-blown weathervane. He made us wait while he hiked the trail to the street. I wound up shouldered next to Alton while the other guards broke into cliques. Nobody wandered far.

"You planned this all along." I slipped the words out the corner of my mouth. "They'll never let you out of their sight."

"Situations change. I see you managed to escape, for example."

He looked very calm for a man under such heavy guard. But then, he'd been exiled from his body for over fifteen years. Things were looking up.

"Fuck you. You're playing games."

"Donny played games." He sounded angry. "What we are talking about is my welfare. My life."

I'd been through enough. I'd come clean. Been to almost literal Hell and back. "You're not the only one who knows where the ring is."

He eyed me with renewed interest. "This other person is you?"

"I've been free and clear and on the outside. Finding things is what I do for a living. My life."

He scratched his chin with a cuffed hand. "You would not have entered the prison if you could secure my ring. No."

"Elbridge shot me in the head. It wasn't much of a conversation."

A guard looked over at us from the glow of his cigarette. He tipped his head back and blew a plume of smoke into the sky. Nothing like being able to poison your real body.

"My issue was with Donny," Alton said. "You have served your purpose. You do not have to be an obstacle."

"An obstacle? You're in custody. Where is it you think you're going?"

"Do not get in my way."

The threat simmered in the evening heat.

"I need this over and done with," I said. "I have nonnegotiable reasons."

"What in my history makes you think I will care?"

He stared into me as if he were Antoinette. Taking measure of my soul.

Elbridge gingerly sidestepped his way back down the hill, a dozen Treasury agents stumbling in his wake. He'd summoned a sufficient number to replace all of the remaining Bonnell guards.

"Escape if you have to," I growled in Alton's ear. "But stay away from the ring."

Alton smiled, and then it was too late.

Elbridge appeared, his face in mine so fast, I didn't have time to turn away. Only darkness kept me from discovery. "Appreciate all you boys have done for the Treasury Department," he said. "We'll take it from here. Tell your boss I'll have Doctor Dimension back in her hot little hands tomorrow."

He yanked Alton away from me and spun him around sharply. He jerked on the cuffs to make sure they were tight. Thus comforted, he passed the prisoner to his men and gestured up the hill. "Get a hood on this guy. Before he's prime time on Fox."

One of Elbridge's proteges roughly pulled a hood over Alton's head. I saw a twinkle in his eyes, then his visage was masked by black nylon.

"Enjoy the return trip, boys," Elbridge said. "Try not to flinch."

I could still hear him cackling as he passed out of sight.

North. South. They could have been headed to Canada or Mexico or any point in between. Alton was as lost to me as the ring.

The guards gathered around. Polish slid into Elbridge's spot with ease, barking orders like he'd been genetically cleaved from the Treasury Secretary's ass. Most of the guards fell in line, either readying the boat for cast-off or climbing into the back for the return trip. The pair of cops who had greeted us at the shore snuffed their flashlights and moved upriver.

If I didn't leave soon, I could look forward to discovery and interrogation. A possible bullet ride back to Bonnell. The end of everything.

I stepped away from my supposed comrades. Melted into the tree line and held my breath. None of the guards noticed my absence. They piled into the boat and motored from shore, joking and laughing to take their minds off what was to come. Only once they were well clear did I run for the trail. I scaled the hill and crossed the sidewalk and stood at the street's edge. It was another typical night of Austin traffic. Cars and trucks and buses growling and grinding through the narrow streets. No Elbridge. No Alton. No money in my pocket and phone to call for help. No one to cajole or blackmail. I was left only with a fading parade of taillights that might be the escort for the criminal formerly known as Doctor Dimension.

A car rolled up while I stood there. White Ford Escort, the front bumper punched in and one window covered in packing tape. The vehicle jerked to a stop right in front of me.

One of Elbridge's men, come to haul me back to Bonnell? Rita Pham, out to permanently tie off another loose end?

"You need a lift, boss? You look miserable."

Dru Sessions. Summer smile, caffeinated 24-7, lost without her laptop Dru Sessions.

I hopped into the passenger seat and let slip with words I'd never uttered, in almost twenty years of repo work.

"Follow that car."

CHAPTER FORTY-EIGHT

The lights ahead swung right, over the Lamar Street Bridge. Dru followed, keeping three cars between us and the last of the government-issue sedans.

"We've been looking for you since you disappeared at Bonnell. You're going to owe me back pay."

I didn't deserve her. "Mak's here?"

"No, she's down in Lockhart. But she's been looking. Patrick too. Matter of fact, Patrick's the one who led us here. Well, a friend of his." She shook her head. "He had a buddy watch Elbridge. He did a stakeout on a Treasury agent's house. Can you believe it? Guy did it on a dare." She whistled low. "The things you boys do."

"I don't understand."

"Elbridge's truck is up ahead, the white F-150." She lifted her chin, and I realized the vehicle at the front was actually part of the escort. "Patrick's guy said two government types drove the truck from Elbridge's house down here, middle of the night and everything. Mak has been on you and Elbridge since Bonnell. She knew neither of you came down from the mountain." Dru hesitated. "Were you really in the prison?"

I danced around my promise. More worried about what Antoinette might do than Elbridge. "They're turning."

The Treasury convoy jagged left onto Riverside. We kept our distance but Dru snuck up a car. The road was narrow, and they could lose us in traffic.

"How did you find me?" I asked.

"Patrick called Mak. Mak called me. I relieved Patrick's guy. I couldn't have waited more than thirty minutes when Elbridge showed up. No big thing. I couldn't very well leave business in the hands of someone outside Netherhouse, could I?"

"You're back?"

"No." Dru wasting no time correcting me. "I took a PI job. It's steady. It's predictable work with less Treasury involvement. Smaller likelihood we'll be shut down." She cleared her throat. "This is a one-time thing. For Mak."

I swallowed. "That's fair."

"I know."

Silence ruled the car. I fumbled for something to break the tension.

"Mak's in Lockhart? What is she doing there?"

"Working. The banks are sending Netherhouse business again. That's what tipped Mak to be on the lookout. *I know that asshole did something*, she said." Dru side-eyed me. "You were the asshole."

"I gathered."

We snaked along Riverside, hugging the angry taillights in front of us. We beat a red light and kept Alton's escorts close. The convoy cut into the left lane and accelerated to merge onto 35.

"Who are we following, by the way?"

Visions of an eternity imprisoned away from the ones I loved. Yet what were the lies buying me?

"Alton Zimmer."

Her face was blank.

"Doctor Dimension," I added.

"That's not possible. He's dead."

"A premature diagnosis, it seems."

Credit to Dru—she processed the information with little fuss. "Where is he going?"

"He says he can find the ring."

"Interesting. I thought Rita Pham had the ring."

"Alton doesn't know that. At least, I don't think he knows. At any rate, we couldn't find Rita. Mak and I bird-dogged her and got nothing."

"I could have found her. If you hadn't fucked things up."

It was unusual for her to curse. "I am sorry."

"I know you are. It just doesn't change anything."

We quit the highway early. Exited at Ben White and blazed a trail east.

"Do we even care?" she asked. "Treasury backed off the banks. You and Mak are free to work cases again. Isn't that what you wanted?"

She wasn't all wrong. Mak was already out earning. I could join her. We'd have a hell of a time replacing Dru—who was I kidding; we'd never replace her—but we could rebuild. Slam-dunk a few repos, stash some money in the bank, and hold the line. Keep the bill collector at bay and live to fight another day.

Only, Rita would still be out there. Between her and Woody, they'd killed three people.

"I need Jamie to be safe," I said. "I can't stop until she's safe."

Dru didn't say anything as she changed lanes. She stuck with the Treasury vehicles as they passed the airport hotels. We entered familiar territory.

"This can't be a coincidence," I said.

We spied the parking lot but didn't pull in. Just after two in the morning and the place was still open, although the lot was sparsely populated. The sign blazed brightly overhead, a beacon for the lost and lonely, or just plain tired. Giant letters, visible from the highway.

BIG FIGHT, the letters said.

* * *

We left the bar behind and went down the road to a utility station. The three government vehicles plus Elbridge's F-150 pulled into a gravel lot and rolled to a halt. Dru stopped outside the property and parked on the street.

The cars ejected agents, and Andrew Elbridge soon followed. After a moment's conference with Elbridge, two agents pulled Alton from the rear of the middle sedan. They jerked free his hood and frisked him. They sandwiched him and marched him toward the utility building. Elbridge walked off to the side—apart, even among his own men.

One of the agents went to shoot the padlock off the door. Elbridge batted him away and directed the man back to his car. He popped the trunk and retrieved a set of bolt cutters. Elbridge cracked the lock himself. He tossed the bolt cutters back to his lackey as if he'd just belted one out of Fenway.

We watched Elbridge and Alton and the agents disappear into the structure. The door closed behind them, leaving four agents at street level. They were armed with radios and phones and badges, not to mention the guns. Assaulting a federal agent wasn't a charge currently leveled against me, and I wasn't eager to changes that fact.

"That's an electrical substation," Dru said. "Why is Dimension taking Elbridge there?"

The ring and electricity. Did Alton recharge? Did the ring? Could he trace the ring through the utility wires?

None of it made sense.

"Most of these substations aren't even active anymore," Dru said. "It's just miles and miles of empty tunnel and abandoned infrastructure."

Empty tunnel.

Under the airport.

"Jesus Christ," I said. "Woody actually built a fucking lair."

Dru looked at me. I shared Alton's tale of Woody's failed bid for the League of Six. His boast of a secret hideout. The storyteller's identity shook her more than anything.

"You had coffee with Doctor Dimension?"

"Espresso. He made it on the stove. I've had worse."

She fumbled for words she never found.

"The underground tunnels are old," I said. "They were constructed in the 1930s." I pointed at the abandoned substation. "The city built the telecommunications, electrical, and sewage infrastructure, but they co-opted the existing steam tunnels where they overlapped. I've heard stories about those tunnels. They run under most of the city. The University. The Governor's Mansion. The highways. Out toward the airport and under every business along the way."

I watched one of the guards throw us a look. Dru ignored him and instead stared at me.

"You're going to Big Fight," she said.

"Yes." I never took my eyes off the guard. "But not through the front door."

* * *

Dru called a friend in UT Utilities. He lacked utility-station access but knew of several steam-tunnel entrances throughout the city. Dru drove to the closest one, a manhole cover located at the end of a deserted cul-de-sac. It was welded shut, and I lacked Elbridge's sexy bolt cutters or the more brute-force approach of an acetylene torch. We shrugged off the failure and found the next closest access point. This time, we encountered a padlocked grate, and Dru had her lockpicks in the glovebox. I attempted to pick the lock myself, but Dru snatched her tools from my hands. I felt a little like her old man, protecting her when I should simply step aside. She popped the lock in under a minute. Together we heaved the grate from its resting place and uncovered a long, narrow ladder plunging away into darkness.

"I'm not going with you," Dru said.

My foot paused above the ladder's first rung. "Isn't that my line? Sounds like a man kind of thing to say."

"It's nothing. I'm just not a big fan of dark tunnels."

She kept her eyes away from me. Dru of the sunshine smile and relentless honesty.

"I understand." I dropped down another couple of rungs. "I owe you one for the ride."

Dru handed me her lockpicks. "You owe me more than one."

I accepted the gift. "True enough."

We stood there in silence. Dru squirmed uncomfortably. "Gayle, I—"

I cut her off. "Take care of yourself, Dru."

And down I went, one foot after the other. My pulse hammered the vein in my neck, and the walls pressed closer. When Dru shoved the grate back into place and the metal slammed home, all I could think of was the doors on the cells of Bonnell Prison.

CHAPTER FORTY-NINE

I stood on a brightly lit concrete landing, the platform edged by a four-foot-high metal railing. Steps led down to the tunnel proper and steel piping ran overhead, the rounded surfaces covered with faded valves and washed-out dials. When I leaned over the rail, I could see more blocky corridors implanted with elbows of piping. A faint hum charged the air. The tunnels seemed like the kind of place a serial killer would lurk.

I took the stairs down to the floor. The tunnel ran off in either direction and was scaffolded with pipe. I oriented myself in the direction of Big Fight—Elbridge and Alton would be headed there from the electrical substation. I kept an eye out for sensors and security cameras. Maybe there wasn't any surveillance, state budgets being what they were. Unless the monitoring equipment was too small to spot with the naked eye.

The ground changed as I progressed. Poured concrete to gravel to sand. The lights changed too. Bruised fluorescents to naked halogen bulbs. I passed shelves stocked with what looked like old car engines, and a gated area filled with reel-to-reel tape and chairs with straps on the arms.

Conspiracy theorists believed there was a time before Bonnell. Before the government knew what to do with Augments.

I kept walking.

The tunnels dragged on, the sections joined together like Frankenstein's monster. One segment all cinder-block halls, another where the tunnels seemed carved with a spoon. Some the size of whales and others barely wide enough around to crawl on hands and knees. I entered a section where red and green pipes crisscrossed overhead. Passed under one labeled ACID WASTE.

I'd never considered myself claustrophobic, but I felt like I was in an MRI tube with no panic button.

I could just scream. What would be the harm?

Footsteps.

I paused. I was in a brightly lit section; for once the fluorescents all working, blazing like a newborn sun. The ceiling hung low, and the walls were bristling with clusters of rusty pipes. There was nowhere to hide.

Shoes scuffed around the corner. I backtracked. Searched for a weapon and found only burnt-out fluorescent bulbs. I grabbed one and held it at the ready. A desperate man. A Star Wars fan after too many drinks.

A head appeared around the corner. I brought the bulb down toward his neck. He whipped around and snatched the bulb out of midair. He stepped into me and hit me in the chest. Knocked me backwards to the ground. My head bounced off hard concrete, and amoebas of the dark unknown swam in my vision.

If I lost consciousness again, by god.

The man above me extended a hand.

Alton Zimmer.

"You are an idiot," he said. "They should have left you in Bonnell."

* * *

Alton walked and talked.

"How do you think I got away from Andrew?"

He led the way down the tunnel. The walls changed color. Painted green to painted yellow to naked concrete. Copper tubing branched alongside. I didn't want to follow him, but he knew where the ring was, and I didn't.

"I don't know how you got away. That's why I asked."

"I have no weapons. They'd cuffed my hands. What does that leave?"

We reached a four-way intersection. Alton didn't hesitate. He turned right.

"Magic?" I said.

He frowned. "Again. You are an idiot."

I absorbed this in silence. He sighed and went on.

"The League of Six used these passages to move about the city. Back then, the police didn't have the tricks they have today—it was impossible for law enforcement to monitor the miles of tunnels. No grand citadels or fortresses were necessary. We shunned such trappings, as they served only as tombs in the end. Instead, we laid low, beneath the city. We fortified certain pockets, gave ourselves hidden gates and trapdoors to avoid capture, should the tunnels ever be infiltrated. You would have enjoyed the look on Andrew's face when I pulled the floor out from under him. Right about now, he's lying in a pit of tar and wondering where it all went wrong."

Alton reached out and ran his hand along the wall.

"I saw his saloon. Your friend Woody Chaikin."

"He's not my friend."

The man ignored me. "We gave him his audition down here. He was a warm body. A possible substitute for the Queen. They arrested her on tax evasion, of all things. Had the woman never read a history book?" He chuckled dryly. "I suspect even then, Woody imagined himself in my shoes. Strolling about my hideout. Wielding my ring." He cocked an eyebrow at me. "The Hammer has my property, doesn't he?"

I was prepared to let him think Woody held the ring. Although I'd seen Woody use the device with my own two eyes, I wasn't convinced he currently wore it on his finger.

"Another in the League recommended Woody," Alton said. "So, I gave him an audition. Slinger, he called himself. Ridiculous. The League of Six was powerful. Effective. There was nothing we couldn't do. And all Woody wanted to do with this unique creation, this well-oiled machine, was rob banks."

Alton spit at my feet without breaking stride.

"Normal people can rob banks. We were the League. We changed the weather over Moscow for eight weeks." Alton huffed. "I had Woody ejected within an hour."

We passed graffiti. *P—Forgive me.* Alton smiled when he saw it.

"What is your plan?" I asked. "Just walk up to Woody and take the ring? *Give it back, it's mine?*"

"Something like that. I know men like Woody. They are all talk. He will make big promises, and when I challenge him, he will turn tail. He is a terrier. I am the bulldog."

I saw Barb's dead-fish expression with Woody's hands shoved into her chest up to the wrists. I said nothing.

Eventually, we reached a ladder with yellow-and-black taped rungs, leading up. Guarding the bottom were two augmented heavies, watchmen of a sort. The Traden brothers kept vigil, having reached the somewhat-inevitable end of their long road. The big one sat with his back against the wall, his head tilted oddly to one side. When I went to check his pulse, I discovered why his pose struck me as unnatural—his gas mask was full of liquid. Equal parts bone, brain, and blood. A bit of fluid leaked out when I nudged the body, and I quickly looked away. His brother had fared better, if being dead could be graded. His body appeared intact, but ragged camo exposed his arms and chest. He lay on his back, staring glassy-eyed at the ceiling. Through his shredded clothing I saw red lesions. Phase damage. He'd played a game of cancer tag and lost.

Alton said nothing. He ignored the bodies and eyed the ladder where it disappeared into an access tube. He put a foot on the bottom rung.

"Hands where I can see them."

I'd found a pistol in the small one's waist. I'd never shot anyone before, only blasted away at targets on the range. I wasn't particularly accurate, but those paper men had been farther away than Alton. I held the gun aimed at his chest.

"You're going to shoot a defenseless man?" He held his position. "After all your outrage at my behavior?"

"We are not the same."

"True. I only defended myself. This would be murder."

He watched me hold the gun. As I looked down the barrel, I could see a tremble in the sight.

He turned around.

"Don't do that," I said.

"Now you'll shoot me in the back?"

"I don't want to."

"Then don't."

He scaled the ladder.

I glanced at the Traden brothers. Then stared up the tube. The ladder ascended, but I felt like it led straight to the mouth of Hell.

I let the gun fall to my side. Then set it on the floor.

I could only imagine the look Mak would have given me. She'd have stood back and swept her arm up the ladder.

After you, genius.

Up I went.

CHAPTER FIFTY

Topside was empty. We crawled out of the floor into an enclosed space—a closet, really, just four brick walls and a door made from chain-link. An old hardline phone hung on the wall. A cot and a blanket were pushed in the corner. Overhead, a naked bulb protruded from a plastic cone. The place smelled of dust and motor oil.

Alton knocked dirt and spiderwebs from his pants. He cast a wary eye over the surroundings. "Another prison," he said.

I stayed on the ladder. Maybe it wasn't too late to leave.

Through the chain-link door we saw dim lighting and heard glasses clink. Tap water ran and plates clattered. A woman chattered in a thick stream of Spanish.

Alton approached the phone. He lifted the receiver from its cradle and tapped the plastic hook. Tapped it a few more times and put the phone back in place. *Dead*, he mouthed.

The phone rang.

We froze. Alton's hand hung over the receiver, only a finger's length away.

The phone rang again.

Alton and I stared at each other as echoes rattled off the walls, an eternity passing while we waited for something to happen. And then we realized. It wasn't the phone in our room. The ringing came from outside, from a phone in the kitchen.

A woman answered the phone in accented English. She didn't say much. We heard a lot of *yes, sir* and *no, sir*. Then she hung up the phone and shut off the tap. She barked orders at someone else in the room, again in Spanish. More plates clattered and then the shadows fell away and the voices faded.

Quiet reigned. We might have been safe in the brick room, but I wasn't waiting around to find out. I got down on one knee and retrieved Dru's lockpicks.

The chain-link door was secured with a gold-plated steel padlock, the hardened alloy looped through a hook bolted to the brick wall. The shackle was as wide around as my index finger, and the lock's heavy steel body sat in my palm like a giant's filling. Even Skylark would have had trouble ripping the lock free.

Dru's picks lay nestled in their pouches. I extracted an aluminum shim and went to work.

The creased metal rested lightly in the palm of my hand. I unfolded the wings and pushed a bump into the middle of the aluminum strip. Once modified, the shim was ready for business. I slid the shim against the lock and pressed down, slipping the fragile metal into the space between the shackle and the body. It could have taken a few minutes to pop the lock. Apparently, karma thought I was due. The lock opened right away.

Alton patted me on the back like I was his pride and joy. To my disgust, I actually felt a little warmth in my chest.

The former prisoner moved into the hall. He paused for a moment, then pointed a finger at the ceiling.

There, he whispered.

The ring was directly overhead.

We advanced down the hallway and found display cabinets filled with newspaper clippings. I saw a picture of Woody, the man wearing khakis and a vest and his best bolo tie. Behind him sat a tiny building with a narrow doorway and a plastic sign, the place a kernel of what it was today. BIG FIGHT.

I squinted closer. Woody seemed happy. Almost carefree. A man who thought he'd achieved everything he'd ever wanted. His eyes drifted to the woman next to him, a woman of Asian descent. She seemed satisfied, almost smug. She leaned against Woody with arms crossed, comfortable but not intimate. She was there to support someone she'd known a long time. She'd been there all along.

An iron stairwell wound from the basement to the ground floor. The railing thumped in tune with the faint rumble of the bar's soundtrack, some sort of electronica bullshit Woody played for the younger crowd. The music seemed louder than usual. A good way to obscure conversation. Could be Rita was upstairs, drinking the house red. Could be a welcoming committee waited with bone disrupters and ocular grenades. This was why Netherhouse didn't repo when the debtors were home. Occupants meant confrontation. Confrontation meant violence.

We climbed.

At the top of the stairs, Alton and I faced another locked door. Again, I used the picks to disengage the lock. Once cracked, the door swung open under its own power, and my hair stood on end. Well-oiled hinges or invisible bodyguards? Everything felt dangerous. Staff. Busboys. Customers. No one in sight, and only my imagination to fill in the gaps.

Alton shoved past me. He walked the ground floor like he wasn't afraid of man or beast. I followed, the still-sensitive wound on my arm tingling, as if aware of the ring.

What would happen when Alton got within sight of his prize? He made a mean cup of espresso, but whatever his barista skills, he'd killed men. I'd seen him murder those agents down at Lady Bird Lake. He wouldn't be denied when confronted with a badge. What made me think I could stop him?

We kept moving. We found them waiting in the bar proper. Woody sorting receipts. Rita Pham sipping from a bottle of amber-colored beer, watching me like I was the last inning in a ball game she'd bet against.

My path reversed. Feet backtracking without my brain supplying the instructions. It didn't matter. I hit a wall. A hard primate wall.

Skylark lurked behind me, maybe following us the whole time, maybe taking a shit in the bathroom. She folded her arms and blocked my escape like the Hoover Dam. I waited for her to crush me, but she didn't do anything. Simply swung back and forth behind me like a wrecking ball. When I gave her my attention, she grinned, all gums.

"It's nice to meet you, Gayle Harwood." Rita Pham toasted me. "Why don't you take a seat?"

The gorilla took my arm. Grabbed Alton with her free hand and steered the both of us to the bar near Woody. He didn't look up when we were thumped against the rail. He continued to stack scraps of paper.

"How are your atoms doing?" My voice came out not nearly as confident as I wanted. "The ring put five cancer worms in my arm."

Woody kept his eyes down. "You're lucky that's all it was."

Rita looked tired. Bagged eyes studied me from under greying bobbed hair. She wore a wrinkled cream blouse buttoned at the wrists and a pair of rumpled blue jeans. Very much not the politician's garb.

I looked at her hand. The tungsten ring pulled at me like an envelope full of dirty money.

"You tripped five different alarms in the steam tunnels." Rita eyed her bartender. "There's no paranoid like an experienced paranoid."

Woody raised his head in response and smiled. The look in his eyes when he stared at Rita—it was the same as in the photo. I'd had that look when I'd still pined for Charlie. It explained a lot about his motivation. But I didn't see the same look in Rita's eyes. Whatever their relationship, it wasn't what Woody thought.

"You made this challenging." Rita rotated her beer bottle with one hand. "I had no issue with you."

"Your boyfriend had issues. Seemed that way when he scrambled my arm."

"Boyfriend? Is that what you think he is?"

"I should have killed you then." Woody mashed a receipt onto a pile. "Just to shut your mouth."

"Don't let him get to you, Woody," Rita said. "He thinks he's solving a mystery. We don't have to humor him."

"He's not your boyfriend, then?" I said. "Does he know that?"

Rita made a gesture, and suddenly Skylark was pushing me toward the table where she was sitting. She nodded at the high-backed chair in front of me. Skylark made me sit.

She was a small person, up close. Five foot two. Maybe wearing kid's shoes. A firecracker, the old-timers would say, to their peril. I was willing to be she wouldn't take to the label.

"What am I supposed to do with you?" she said. "You gave me no choice."

"Don't blame me. Treasury thought I used that ring on your finger to kill Donny. They weren't taking my word for it when I proclaimed innocence."

"You could have hired a lawyer. Wouldn't that have been easier?"

I remembered Rita's house and her cars and her nanny. "Sure. Only I'd just bought the Gulfstream, so money was a little tight."

Her eyes flicked up to meet Skylark's, who promptly cuffed me on the back of the head. My brain sloshed against the front of my skull. A balloon of pain inflated behind my eyes.

"Don't make me do that again, Gayle," Skylark said.

She was matter-of-fact, this employee of Ellen Clovis. Or of Rita Pham.

"You were at my house," Rita said. "Why?"

I blinked away tears. "I knew Skylark was involved after that shit-show at the dump. She clearly wasn't on Texas Recovery business." I was careful, knowing the subject of my sentence had little concern with thumping my skull. "Your dad got her out of North Korea, yes?"

"I owe them everything." Skylark answered for herself. "You have no idea what they did for me."

"Murder seems like expensive payback, is all."

"Skylark didn't kill anyone." Rita looked over my head at the gorilla, her face washed in regret. "It was my mistake to ask her to."

"Why ask her to do anything? Why keep the ring at all instead of chucking it into Lady Bird Lake? Your dad never even used it."

"Dad wasn't a fan of augmented devices. He thought they were dangerous and wanted them off the streets. The city wouldn't do any-thing. *Keep Austin Augmented*, all that PR crap. So, he took action.

He used his wealth for the greater good and acquired a number of notorious items."

I squinted at her. "Quan was a black-market collector?"

She didn't like that phrase. "He spent his own money to take weapons off the street. Do you know how many people die because of these things?" She made a fist and brandished the ring. "It was a public service."

I laughed. "Sure. He paid a dirty repoman, a corrupt cop, and a fence as part of a social crusade. Big Quan, cleaning up the streets."

Skylark whacked me on the head again. This time, the pain didn't fade entirely. Instead, it clamped onto my temples like a strong vise.

"If you break his neck, you won't learn what he knows." Alton looked casual, drumming his fingers on the bar. "And hello, Woody, it has been a while. I see you finally built your hideout." He scrutinized the bar. "It really is something."

Woody turned away and stuffed a wad of receipts into a vinyl bag. He wouldn't look Alton in the eye. "Fuck off."

Alton pursed his lips, as if he would take it under advisement.

"How did you get him out?" Rita pointed at Alton. "And why? You talk about murder. He's known to have killed dozens with this ring. It's not disputed."

"I dispute it," Alton said, his good humor gone. He stared at Rita, who didn't look away. I watched her hand where it wrapped around the smooth glass. Her fingers shook.

"I cut a deal," I said.

Rita glanced at me.

"You asked how I got Dimension out of Bonnell? I cut a deal. I promised I could find the ring and broker its safe return."

My captor waited.

"He can track the ring," I said. "Didn't you know that?"

Again Rita's eyes found Alton's. He smiled like a cop.

"Once I find the ring, I give the signal and Treasury swoops in," I said. "All charges against Netherhouse will be dropped. Things will go back to normal for me. Relatively."

"Bullshit." Scorn laced Woody's voice. "He's lying."

"Is this true?" Rita lifted her hand and spread her fingers so the ring was exposed. "You can track this?"

For a moment, I thought Alton was going to deny me. He turned back to the bar and leaned over the counter and fished a longneck from a cooler. He seemed unconcerned with me or the bartender or the hulking gorilla. But after he unscrewed the cap and let it fall to the floor, he did answer.

"I can," he said.

Swig of beer.

One side of Rita's face tightened. Like she was having a stroke. "How many powers do you have?"

Alton winked. Enjoyed his beer.

"If your story is true," I said, "and this was an altruistic play of your father's, then why get involved? Once he died, you could have returned the ring to Treasury. You didn't steal it."

"Return the ring to Treasury? So they could assign it to a police officer? Next time some kid from the wrong neighborhood runs a stop sign and talks back to a cop, he gets his brains jelloed? Is that the outcome you're after? No way. I believe in Dad's work. I would never jeopardize the good he did."

"You believe in your political career. Which would have been over once the story broke."

The words hung there like a cartoon word balloon. Rita picked up her drink and took a sip. The beer steadied her. "Woody said you were a talker."

The statement had an air of finality to it. Like being a talker would be my legacy.

Dead men had legacies.

I stared at the ring. "Why are you wearing it?" I asked.

She blinked. Her eyes followed mine. "I'd never used the ring before. Never used anything augmented, not even Woody's hammer. I didn't know." She trailed off. "I have to protect myself. I was being blackmailed. I didn't start this."

"But you're finishing it? Barb and Rick. The Tradens downstairs. How many bodies will make you safe, exactly?"

"I didn't kill all those people."

"Sure. You had Woody handle Barb. The Tradens handle Ruiz. But someone had to handle the Tradens. Someone with the ring."

"They did not look good," Alton volunteered.

"Do you really want to do that again?" I asked. "Take a human life? On purpose?"

Rita breathed like she carried the entire bar on her back.

"You're in charge here," I said. "Skylark and Woody are loyal to you. You say the word, and it stops. No one else has to die."

Behind me, Skylark shuffled closer. Either threatened by my words or interested.

Across the table, Rita studied me. Her ring beat out a tune on the tabletop, a number only she could hear.

"If I gave you the ring," she said, "what would I be left with? Prison? Shame? Ruin?"

"You'd be left with your soul. You'd have your family."

Her eyes narrowed. "I should kill you for being within eyesight of my house."

She cupped the beer bottle.

"I'm not worried about me," she said. "It's my husband. My beautiful children. I have people that mean more to me than you can ever understand. Skylark, for example. You think Ellen Clovis would exercise one little finger to save an augmented child halfway around the world? One who looks like a gorilla? South Korean or North Korean or Vietnamese? Ellen didn't look any farther than the front of her limousine. She needed an employee, so she hired a driver. She didn't risk anything. She didn't help anyone."

Skylark set her fingers on the back of my chair. Lightly, like a child. "Rita."

"You talk about family?" Rita's eyes lifted above my head. "Skylark is family. And family is everything."

"What about Woody?" I asked.

My former friend slammed his hands against the bar. "Keep my name out of your mouth."

"He killed Barb. He hired the Tradens. That's going to set him up nicely, isn't it?"

"Shut up," Woody said.

Interestingly, neither Rita nor Skylark said a word.

"The worst you take," I said, "is the business with the bus. That's tough, but with your lawyers, I'll bet you get that talked down to involuntary manslaughter. You do seven years. Maybe five. You're out before your kids go to college."

Rita set her beer on the table. She looked at her friend Woody.

"What is he to you? He thinks you're the bee's knees, but I'm thinking you're in this for something more practical. Why else the investment in the bar? An augment bar, no less. Daddy wouldn't be happy."

"Woody understands," she said. "He's been helpful to the cause."

It was all I could do not to laugh. "Wow." I looked over my shoulder at the world's most hypocritical bartender. "*I don't talk about my customers.*" I faced Rita. "He gives you information on the Augmented."

"On the *criminal* Augmented. Like I said, he believes in the cause."

"When that cause is himself, sure. You think he won't flip? What state was this bar in when he asked you for the loan? How close to broke was he? I'll bet he was about to lose Big Fight. Without this place, he'd be nothing. The great Oak Hammer looking for jobs as a barback. That would rock a man to his core. Make him desperate. I've seen Woody at the end of his rope—he'd say anything to save his ass. Back in the day, he begged Donny and me to keep him out of jail."

"I kept him out of jail," Rita said softly.

I fell silent.

"Dad wanted to let Woody rot, but I pleaded with him. He didn't understand. Woody made me laugh. He got me. He was there and has been since he was fourteen. I thought he'd change. *He'll give up the augment life; you'll see.*" Her voice was almost a whisper. "Dad used his influence, but we had to keep that quiet. We let Netherhouse take the credit."

Woody was right. Everything in our relationship was a lie.

A shadow fell over me. Skylark loomed. Ready to follow her savior into hell, if necessary.

"Skylark," I said. "What do you think? You think Woody wouldn't feed Secretary Elbridge Rita's name in exchange for immunity? I mean, best friends or not, Woody is staring at three murders, even if he only committed the one."

From behind I heard the measured breathing. Felt the floorboards underneath my chair groan as Skylark shifted her weight from one foot to the other. She squeezed the back of my chair.

"No," she said. "I don't trust him."

Woody muttered. He didn't dare cross Skylark openly.

"Not that I trust you, Gayle." Skylark came around the table, stood between me and her boss. "But Slinger's motives have always been questionable."

The reference to Woody's criminal moniker must have stung.

"Maybe we do like he says, Rita." In Skylark's eyes, those reddish almost-human eyes, I saw concern. "Hand over the ring. Navigate the fallout. Once the worst of it is over, we relocate. Move to Little Rock, like you've been talking about. Make a run at that congressional seat."

Credit Rita. Even when pressured and cajoled, she held to her course. She didn't blink. She took two seconds to consider Skylark's offer, if that.

"Woody." Rita closed her eyes. "Bring the shotgun."

And then the front door to Big Fight opened. And in through the fancy curtains walked Nick Holiday.

He wore a look on his face. One I'd seen before. Frazzled and cranky, like he'd forgotten his smokes. He wandered in, mumbling to himself and punctuating unheard phrases with strong hand gestures.

All the time I put in, I heard him say.

Rita watched him as if she couldn't quite believe he was real.

Working night and day for fucking peanuts, I heard him say.

He marched past me and headed for the bathrooms.

"Hey." Woody leaned into the bar. "You're supposed to be watching the door."

Nick barely looked at him. "I'm not inclined right now, Woodrow. I got better things to do."

The bartender glowered. But before he could speak, someone at the front door interrupted him.

"Yeah, Woodrow. Maybe he's better than playing second fiddle to a has-been."

Finally, after a hell of a day, I got what I wanted. Nothing I deserved but something I so desperately needed.

My partner.

CHAPTER FIFTY-ONE

"What a bunch of fucking amateurs."

Mak slow-clapped. Long and loud. She approached the five of us with a smirk on her face.

"Lined up all in one place like a set of bowling pins. You make the dumbass Augments I typically chase look like a bunch of fucking wizards. Lord Dopamine drove into a utility pole after I repoed his pills, but even he knew better than to hide in a bar with a giant blinking sign."

Mak observed the gathering with a soldier's amusement. Humor in the face of long odds. I had no idea what she was thinking, if she was thinking at all.

Rita had turned around. She fiddled with the ring like she was warming it up for action. "You're Makareta Black. I've heard of you."

"Great?" Mak strolled past our table, keeping an eye on the hulking presence of Skylark. She bellied up to the bar alongside Alton, giving him a critical once-over.

"This is the great Doctor Dimension?" she said. "He looks like my dad."

Nonplussed, Alton said nothing.

Mak banged a hand on the bar. "Barkeep. You serve any good scotch around here or just that hoppy bullshit your boss is drinking?"

It galled Woody, but he looked across the bar to check with Rita. Time passed so slow, I could see individual oxygen molecules floating in midair.

Rita bit her lip and nodded.

A bottle of Oban came out from behind the bar, and Woody

dropped a small splash into an empty mason jar. He passed over the jar with a curt smile, ever the polite bartender. Mak sipped at the glass like she was sampling mouthwash, swishing the warm liquid over her gums. Typically, she favored near-beer and only drank scotch on special occasions. Christmas. Her dad's funeral.

"You've saved me some trouble," Rita said. "After we finished with your partner, you'd have been next."

Mak grunted. "He is still my partner. Believe me, I've tried to divest myself of Mr. Gayle Harwood. The trouble is, it never sticks. He's too damn charming."

I smiled tightly. My stomach was in knots.

"Rita." Skylark looked earnestly at her friend. "We don't have to do this."

Mak squinted at the gorilla. "I don't understand you, Skylark. You're always putting your fate in the hands of some Napoleon."

The remark turned Skylark around. She left Rita's side and shuffled to the bar and dealt Mak a hard stare. She demanded a beer, and Woody tossed her a Shiner without comment. Skylark flipped the cap off with her thumb. She drank and glowered at my partner. But Mak just leaned into the bar, her back to Woody, letting Skylark huff and puff off to starboard. She reminded me of the young lady who had walked into Netherhouse all those years ago and demanded a partnership in the firm.

"You should listen to the gorilla," Mak said. "You don't have to do this. A scene is what that fucker Elbridge wants. I can read the headline now. *Legendary Lawman Takes Down Corrupt Congresswoman.* You voluntarily surrender, you make them look inept. Out chasing their tails while you do the right thing."

Rita stretched out her legs and took her beer in hand. "Are you using your power on me right now? Trying to make me talk?"

The accusation rubbed Mak wrong. "Sister, I wouldn't break so much as a sweat on you."

The bottle paused at Rita's lips. She dropped her head, and her eyes lost focus. I saw defeat, for a moment. My words and Skylark's and Mak's piled on until they about broke her spine. But then the passion that had driven her all the way to Congress set fire to her eyes. The moment felt explosive, as if the right word could tip the conversation either way. A true word. A false word. It wouldn't matter so long as the word was right. I opened my mouth to say I didn't even know what. And then Rita phased her beer bottle into my right hand.

The bottle passed through skin and vein and bone as if it wasn't there. A shark slipping below the water. A gorilla passing through the mist. I didn't feel one lick of pain.

Then Rita released the bottle.

Atoms snapped back into place, or tried. Encountered foreign matter and scattered, like fleshy buckshot.

The glass disrupted molecular bonds. Exploded cells and shattered tissue. The connective bonds in my hand snapped, the veins burst open, and the glass bottle chewed into my hand like I'd stuck the appendage in a garbage disposal. Bits of flesh flew off and hit me in the cheek. The pain was unimaginable.

I screamed and tipped over backwards in my chair.

Pandemonium had its day.

Alton hopped the bar, planting a hand on the polished wood and vaulting the thing like an Olympian.

Skylark grabbed Mak by the jersey and yanked her off her feet. My partner was drinking her scotch. She was completely unprepared.

Woody's oak hammer had been sanctioned by the government long ago, but like any good bartender, he had a shotgun behind the bar. A Browning, from the look of it.

Hard to say if the action went down in the order I thought. I lay on the ground, the last two fingers on my right hand reduced to ground round, the others twitching like I'd jammed them into an electrical socket. I tried to make a fist. The chewed nub of my ring finger screamed; my pinkie finger felt absent entirely. Events passed me by. The pain was so bad—god help me—I wanted out of my body and back in Bonnell.

Woody trained his shotgun on Mak's legs, either a bad shot or intending to wound. He got nowhere, as Alton checked him into the bar, knocking the Browning from his hand. The gun clattered to the floor and disappeared from sight.

I rolled over, my jeans painted in blood. My blood.

Mak wrenched herself free. She slid between Skylark's legs and popped up behind her. She scaled Skylark's back and hooked an arm around the gorilla's giant windpipe. But Skylark was no lumbering behemoth to be choked out by a nimbler opponent. She ripped Mak from her back and with two hands threw my partner into the far wall. Mak hit the ground with her eyes already rolled back in her head. When she landed, she didn't move.

Rita stood in the eye of the storm. A shredded finger's length from me.

Skylark kept moving. She bulldozed toward Alton, jumping over the bar without touching the surface. Woody regained his feet just in time to be bowled over, annihilated by half a ton of augmented human gorilla. Alton scrambled out of the way, spry but no gymnast, catching the back of Skylark's arm as he climbed over the bar. He spun off the slick wood as if he'd been thrown. However, to my great surprise, he bounced back to his feet and charged straight at Rita. She ducked out of the way but not nearly fast enough. Alton slammed into her, and they both went down.

I tried to push myself to my feet, but an ocean of black nausea rose in my gut. Vomit tickled the back of my throat and burned my esophagus. Reality blurred.

Blink.

Jamie lay in her bed at the Center. She'd lost all her hair but looked beautiful. Like when she first came out of her mother. I wanted to teach her everything all over again.

Blink.

Charlie told me our daughter had cancer. Our daughter was seven. Our bank account was empty.

Blink.

Donny stood at the door. I held nothing close to a million dollars in my hand, but more than enough to change my life. *Buy yourself something nice*, he said.

Blink.

The past receded and reality unhitched. My old partner vanished and Mak swam into view, her body lifeless on the floor. Club music blared. Something ubiquitous and forgettable.

This was how I would die. It seemed unfair.

Skylark climbed over the bar. She approached Alton and planted a size-fifteen leather boot on the back of his neck. She didn't beat her chest or bare a tooth. She prepared to kill Alton like any other ordinary human. Cold-blooded.

Then Doctor Dimension turned over. He slapped a hand against Skylark's calf. This giant—this creature I'd seen tackle a cyclops and a radioactive dragon and even argue with Ellen Clovis—she screamed.

Dimension removed his hand from her calf. The ring glowed like something out of a story.

And Skylark fell over.

I didn't know whether to laugh or to cry. Fingers of unreality bled into my vision. The tunnel was closing. I was going to pass out.

But not Skylark. She had fought her way clear of a family that hated her. A country that exploited her. Made a name for herself in a world hostile to her in every way. She lumbered to her feet and swung her arm around so fast, I thought it fell from space. She hit Dimension like a freight train. Or would have, had he been any more solid than his jailer of the past fifteen years.

Using the ring must have been like riding a bike. Fifteen years off the pedals, and the man still remembered. He phased out as Skylark's arm swung around and phased back after it passed.

Dimension was inside her reach.

A quick punch to the mouth, again phasing in and out so as to shatter her front teeth. Skylark's mouth bled like she'd faced Ali or Tyson.

Zip. Dimension stepped through Skylark and turned around, peppering her kidneys with short, sharp punches.

Poof. Gone again but not for long, Dimension reappeared at Skylark's side. He lifted his foot and struck. The full force of his blow landing on her phase-damaged calf.

Skylark toppled. She hit the floor with a grunt and stirred like there was fight left in her. Her hand twitched, then went limp.

I forced myself to my feet. Stared at the jagged half-bottle I gripped in my good hand. At the mangled remains of the other. I staggered into the fray completely unprepared, as if I could make the slightest difference.

Just in time to watch Rita Pham shoot Doctor Dimension.

Maybe, if he'd seen the shot coming, he could have phased before the load hit him. No telling how fast the ring worked, what chain of commands triggered the unspooling of so many connected atoms. In his prime, maybe Dimension could have done it. But he was turned away from the blast, and he was fifteen years removed from walking through walls. From dodging bullets.

He whirled around, defiant. Blood bloomed across his prison jumpsuit, an ugly brown butterfly spreading lopsided wings. I don't think he realized he'd been shot. With surprising dexterity, he backpedaled, thrust an arm out, and phased through the bar. As he unphased, the color drained from his face. Pain exploded like a firecracker. He fell against the back wall, sending bottles of vodka and gin crashing to the floor.

Rita held Woody's shotgun like someone intimate with firearms. Steady hand on the grip. Pad of the right index finger resting on the trigger. Her next shot wouldn't miss. Not with Alton slid down on his ass, his body limp as if he'd been deboned.

Would it be so bad if she made the shot? One bad guy killed by another bad guy? Happened every day in the augment community, same as it did with the normals. So many witnesses now, it hardly mattered where the ring landed. Mak and I just needed to escape with our limbs intact, with the ability to draw breath. Rita was distracted, her eyes focused on Dimension and the ring he'd restored to his hand. Me and my partner could bug out, and I doubt she'd try hard to follow. If

I turned state's evidence, Elbridge might even let Mak go.

But I couldn't be sure. Not with someone like Rita running around. Fifteen years after the crime and she'd still returned to tie up loose ends. She was a completionist. She wouldn't forget.

I snuck up behind Rita. Reached out with my empty, bloodied hand to seize the shotgun.

Under my foot a glass fragment snapped.

Rita reacted instantly. Spun around with her shotgun at the ready.

Neurons pushed instructions down my arm, but the bad hand didn't move fast enough. Rita smashed the shotgun into my right arm, sending fresh sparks of pain up my side. The remaining fingers on my hand curled. Went numb.

Pain. Fire. Anger. I swung at her with my left arm. But she snapped the barrel around. Then up. My left arm went with it.

I lurched forward. Used my weight to throw her off balance. Rita pushed back and tottered into me. And my left hand—the hand holding the jagged top of the beer bottle—plunged into Rita's bare neck.

Surprise.

Thick blood gushed, like I'd uncorked Niagara Falls. Rita dropped right away, no bravado or inhuman feat of strength left in her. The volume was amazing, the ocean of vivid red-black that poured from her throat. Her blood sluiced through my fingers, even as I dropped the bottle and backed away.

Rita gurgled, tried to staunch the flow of blood. Her feet kicked. A disconnected part of my brain told me to move, but my feet didn't listen. I just stood there, blood dripping from my hand. My blood. Her blood.

She flailed, then went silent. Swallowed great, wet swallows. Around me, people moved, but no one approached. I was impregnable. Untouchable. Alone at ground zero.

Eventually, time caught up. The sounds of agony and frustration returned. And somewhere in there, underneath the club music and the pain, Rita Pham died.

CHAPTER FIFTY-TWO

Time vanished, sucked up and spit out somewhere outside the bar. People talked but I didn't track the conversation, and no one seemed to need my answers. Good thing, too. Answers were among the many things I didn't have.

A feather-light touch on my arm. Mak stood at my side, her right arm pinned against her ribcage like she'd nailed it there. She looked at me as if she'd never seen me before this very moment.

"Can you hear me?" she asked.

"Of course I can hear you." My voice sounded like it came from behind a brick wall. "You're standing right there."

"I said your name five times. You didn't answer."

I looked around the bar. Blood splashed everywhere. Motionless bodies lying face down. A giant gorilla hunched over the bar.

"What time is it?" I asked.

"What?"

"Is it day? Night? I need to know what time it is."

Mak reached out and touched me again. "You sure you're all right?"

"I never said I was all right."

She pulled away. I felt guilty but not enough to apologize. I looked down at Rita's body and tried not to think about her husband or her kids.

Family is everything.

"I need to sit down," I said.

Mak dragged over a chair. I sat. Skylark hung at the bar and Woody stayed flat out on the floor and Rita Pham was still dead.

When I looked around, there wasn't a single sign of Doctor Dimension.

CHAPTER FIFTY-THREE

A sharp-suited man with silver hair and jet-black eyebrows swooped in from legal heaven to ferry Skylark away from the bloodbath. I recognized him—Benjamin Gott, the augment defense attorney who'd nearly bankrupted Kentucky. The lead Treasury agent shook Gott's hand. Gott mentioned the agent's children by name. Skylark was out in under an hour.

Mak endured a few questions, but her hands were clean. Woody had a lot to explain, and local law enforcement never really forgot his time as Slinger. He was taken into police custody.

I was a different story.

One of the cops approached me. A normal, no augmented strength or weapons grafted to his hands. He had sincere eyes. He looked at the glass phased into my hand and the body lying on the floor.

"We're going to need you to come with us," he said.

* * *

The emergency room sobered me up. Moments took shape as boredom seized hold and shock receded. Once again, I was chained to a gurney, pseudo-arrested until a doctor finished suturing my decimated hand. I waited five hours before someone became available. The doctor eyed my police escort as he worked.

In between winces, I nodded at the surgical needle. "Mind leaving that?" I glanced at the guards. "These guys don't look so friendly."

He flashed me a humorless smile and kept stitching. I stopped cracking jokes. My hand already resembled a homemade football. I didn't want to see how much worse things could get.

Things did get worse. They took me to jail.

They sat me on a narrow bench bolted to the wall. My hands were cuffed behind me, even the injured one. A cop with a camera embedded in her chest grabbed my mug shot, her eyes blinking each time she snapped a picture.

"You know that's not useable in court," I told her.

"There's a socket behind my left ear they use for downloads when I'm on the stand," she said. "It's as good as eyewitness testimony. Better, even."

She stepped closer.

"Now strip."

I received a change of clothes and a full-body search. The search was done the old-fashioned way, the state unwilling to splurge on augment technology when humiliation and discomfort were options. I gritted my teeth and thought of Elbridge trapped in a pit of tar. It was easy to conjure the image. The cops processed me under the watchful eye of my friends at Treasury. Two blow-dried carbon copies of Elbridge without all the mileage.

"Got anything smart to say now, Harwood?"

The lead agent. He had a dimple and a sneer. I kept my mouth shut.

"Thought you might like to hear the charges," he said. "Since you've got nothing to say."

He read them from memory.

"Obstruction of justice. Interfering with a Treasury investigation. Augment device fraud. Aiding and abetting the escape of an augmented prisoner."

He paused.

"Manslaughter," he said.

I met his stare for an instant. Looked away.

"I want a lawyer," I said.

Before they stuck me in a cell, I was allowed to wash up. I had to keep the bandage out of the water, only the fingertips of my wounded hand catching the lingering drops. For the first time since the clusterfuck at Woody's bar, the damage to my hand hit me. It was a pain monster with gnashing teeth. It hurt like hell.

The dude they got to stuff me in the cell was huge. He walked slow and dragged me along by the arm like I was a piece of luggage.

"When am I being arraigned?" I asked.

The guard squeezed my bicep. He stopped and turned to face me. He had one dark green eye and one dark black.

"I can see your astral self," he said. "You're covered in lies."

I couldn't tell if he was augmented or just plain crazy. I let him speak his peace.

"I hope you burn," he said. "For what you've done."

We walked the rest of the way in silence.

My cell was a cozy affair. I was roommates with six other dudes in a space meant for five. They looked at me squinty and made sure I didn't have room to sit. I leaned against the bars at the front of the cell and wished—for the first time—that I wore Dimension's ring. I could have charged through the bars like a linebacker through wet tissue paper. The thought made me smile.

Time passed. Twenty hours of boredom spiked with moments of sheer terror. The wheels of justice moved like a car with four flat tires. Then Ellen Clovis came to see me.

The guards fetched me and took me to one of the communal visitation rooms. No video feed or Plexiglas arrangement—in this case, I was allowed a face-to-face visit. Long pine tables ran the length of the space, benches attached to the tables like church pews. Ellen sat at the table farthest from the prisoner door. Otherwise, the room was empty.

The guard shoved me down opposite Ellen. She looked dressed for a funeral.

"They took my purse," she said. "It's a Marc Jacobs."

The guard went to stand back by the door. He was too far away to hear our conversation or intervene quickly were Ellen to shiv me in the eye.

"That your doing?" I tried to stick a thumb over my shoulder to point at the guard. My cuffed hands got in the way. "Usually, they're up your butt like a randy dog."

"Pleasant. You've been in jail too long already, I see."

"It's not my first time. Apropos of our earlier conversation, I can now speak definitively to the state of our augmented correctional facilities."

She shifted in her chair. She hadn't known about my visit to Bonnell.

"So," I said. "You come to bust me loose?"

"I could. Shall I?"

Again I looked over my shoulder. Our guard was studying the ceiling tiles. Intently.

"That's a pretty low bar. I could probably walk out of here."

"If you still had the ring, I imagine you could, yes."

I laughed, the sound thin. A three-day-old balloon with the last of the helium escaping. "Can't trust the feds to keep anything a secret. They're like my gram's knitting circle."

"Is your grandmother relevant to our conversation?"

"She could help you with your technical operations. Last time we talked, she'd just logged on to *the Instagram*."

"I have over two million followers. Your grandmother is welcome to join them."

The conversation had been more fun when Ellen had her wine and I could leave any time I wanted. I smelled her perfume, something like dead lilies, and quietly gagged.

"Why are you here?" I asked.

Ellen placed her hands on the table. Interlaced the fingers. "There was some unpleasantness at the Oak Hammer's watering hole."

Blood on the walls. The glass as much a part of my hand as my fingers. Rita's dying eyes. "Woody's place? Yeah. That was a little out of control."

Ellen watched me sort my emotions. "I'm sorry to hear you were caught up in the unpleasantness."

The act bugged me. Her false concern. "You ought to be. You know your pal Skylark played no small part."

Ellen's hand twitched. Ten bucks she was reaching for a nonexistent glass of wine.

"That particular Augment no longer works for me," she said.

"That's been true for a while."

"Apparently." Ellen tried to mask her irritation. "I don't understand it. I spared no expense on that woman. Went to every length to ensure she was treated as any other employee."

Dear sweet Jesus. She really did ask for it. "Employee?"

"Yes."

"You know you screwed up, right? Skylark wasn't looking for a boss. She had plenty of bosses in Korea. Ownership and authority defined her."

"I was not her keeper. I was her employer, and a good one. I gave her a place at Texas Recovery. She was so very outspoken. I did her a favor. Even establishments hiring Naturals wouldn't have tolerated her relentless contrarian attitude."

I thought about Mak. Brash. Argumentative. A Natural Augment. Reasons both for and against making her a partner, but in the end, I'd made her my equal.

Mak. Walking into a bar full of dangerous Augments just to save my ass, and smiling at me. Like it was no big thing.

She'd always been my equal.

"Skylark was looking for friendship," I said. "And a little loyalty."

Ellen shifted on her bench. The hard pine didn't coddle like the back seat of her stretch. "All of my employees are loyal. They are well paid."

"Lady, for someone who claims to understand Augments—you don't know shit."

Ellen Clovis wasn't used to people talking to her like she was at the DMV. There was a weird sound in the air, like squirrels burrowing through the overhead ducts, and I realized it was the sound of Ellen grinding her teeth.

She changed the subject.

"You will be formally charged in the morning. The manslaughter charge will not hold—video from Big Fight's security cameras and Skylark's testimony are likely to support your self-defense claim. Treasury obtained a warrant for the Pham residence. It's early, but the evidence, thus far, circumstantially indicts Rita. Certainly, the debate continues to rage in official circles, but most paint Woody Chaikin as the mastermind of the whole affair."

On some level, it was amusing. Donny would have hated Woody getting all that credit.

Ellen sat back, her irritation giving way to a mystified acceptance. "And, believe it or not, the Treasury Department isn't particularly interested in seeing you painted as a killer. Although Andrew bears you no love, not after spending several hours trapped in the steam tunnels."

I couldn't keep the relief off my face, a fact Ellen reacted to with a quick, cold smile.

"Don't pop the champagne. The evidence cuts both ways." She held up two fingers, brought them together like a pair of scissors. "Treasury also visited Ruiz Salvage. Hank Ruiz's documentation was still intact. There's mention of Netherhouse quite explicitly."

I thought about how reckless Donny had been. And how after I was in charge, nothing had changed.

"The assumption is that Netherhouse as a whole is guilty," Ellen said. "This, combined with a handful of other infractions, will amount to at least three felony charges. Charges likely to become convictions. Two more than the state needs to shut you down forever."

Ellen let the words echo in my ears. A dose of color returned to her hands, and her eyes regained their usual imperial sparkle. She waited for me to speak. My throat closed up and I had to talk around a bowling ball of pride.

"Unless I do what?"

"It's very simple. You convince Makareta to take the motorcycle."

The bottom dropped out of my stomach. I couldn't feel my hands, and I breathed through twenty pounds of sand.

"You understand what I'm saying?" Ellen asked. "She takes it.

Strings attached."

My mouth went dry. "Mak wouldn't ever choose to work for you."

"She has a child. She abrogated her right to choice long ago."

I licked my lips. Considered. "We're partners. I can't decide for her. I can't make her sign."

"Please. She followed you into Big Fight even after learning of your deception. She engaged Skylark in fisticuffs. What wouldn't she do, for Netherhouse?"

Unsaid. *What wouldn't she do, for you?*

I rubbed the bandaged nub where my pinkie used to be. "I have a lawyer. I could beat the charges."

"Gayle? Really?"

The white-noise machine rattled overhead, the state money machine failing to keep even fabricated relaxation in working condition. Of course, once they convicted me and shipped me off to Huntsville, a broken white-noise machine would be hamburger and beer. A steak and a blowjob. Things beyond my reach.

Ellen didn't do partners.

I couldn't help Jamie from behind bars.

"Tell me about the strings," I asked.

* * *

Mak had the agreement in hand when she visited. Ellen's juice didn't extend to my partner, so we talked to each other through Plexiglas and wire mesh. Her eyes avoided mine. She didn't look angry or sad or disappointed. She looked like she'd made a stop at the post office.

Ellen had couriered the papers to Mak. Felt the acquisition of Netherhouse was best handled at a distance. Such separation reduced the odds of emotion getting in the way. Of course, no sale would be final without Mak's signature, us being equal partners and all. Ellen hadn't seemed concerned that Mak would sell, not once I'd signed.

I remembered Mak angling for Donny's desk almost since day one. I wasn't so sure she'd sign.

Mak read the contract in front of me, even though she must have read it before driving over.

"It's not a desk job, is it?"

She kept her head down, showing me the ragged part in her hair. "I work in the field," she said. "Period."

"Ellen wants you for your recovery skills. It's not a desk job. You'd do the same kind of work you do now."

After I said the words, I realized Mak might not consider present circumstances a template for future success. She didn't visibly react. "You're staying on?" she asked.

"Freelance consultant, on retainer."

"Unusual. Ellen doesn't have much respect for normals. You must have done something to impress her."

Vague mention of a role uniquely suited to my talents. Ellen had stared at me blandly as she made the proposition, knowing I'd take whatever I was offered.

"She wants my relationships," I said. "With Augments and normals. She told me she's buying the talent and the name."

"The talent." Mak rubbed at her temple. I couldn't be sure in the fluorescent light of the visitation room, but I saw a grey hair. It hadn't been there before. "Nice of her to say. Ellen's always been very considerate of my feelings. Kind of like you."

In all the time I'd known Mak, she'd thrown lots of barbs my way. About the pay, about the hours. Mostly, I'd taken the comments as good-natured ribbing, but this one hurt. The idea that Ellen and I were the same.

Mak read the sheets one after the other, the paper rasping like a file against bone. I told myself I could endure. We'd still be working together. Mak and Gayle. Gayle and Mak.

After Mak finished reading, she stacked the papers like she was making a book. Her face came up, and the forgiveness I'd seen at Big Fight was as far away as Antarctic snow. As remote as an Australian beach.

"You sure Ellen won't leave you in here to rot?" she asked.

"That's not her style; you know that."

"I guess I'll learn her style. Over time."

"You didn't have to sign."

"Didn't I?"

I waited.

"Don't give up." Her voice level, although the muscles in her jaw were tight. "That's what we said. We said we'd fight."

"I'm in jail, Mak."

"You were in Bonnell. You were in the hospital. We were surrounded by a gorilla and Doctor Dimension, had one of the most powerful augment devices in history pointed right at us, and we never gave up. But Ellen squeezes you for five minutes, and you roll over."

"I had to protect what we had left."

Mak folded her arms and looked at me. After a few seconds, she collected the contract. She stood with the papers clenched between her fingers, and she put her arms out straight, and she dropped the entire stack on the steel table. The impact turned heads.

"We don't have anything," she said.

When Mak left, we had a full minute of visitation remaining. I watched her walk to the door. I saw the guard buzz her out and I kept my eyes on the back of her head as she passed through the doorway. I'd lost my company and my mentor, lost a pair of fingers and what little respect I'd had in this town. But if Mak turned around, it meant she still cared. It meant I still had my best friend.

In this business, anything was possible, and I had to believe Mak would forgive me.

She had to turn around. She just had to.

* * *

My daughter opened her eyes and everything changed. She looked different. She used to have brown eyes, and now they looked blue. She used to squint like a suspicious cop, and now her eyes swelled larger than a lion's. Her cheeks were full. Her smile was bright.

She was cancer-free.

Charlie and I stood side by side at the Cancer Center, a miracle in and of itself. She'd asked about my hand, and all I'd been able to say was I didn't want to lie to her anymore.

"Dad?" Jamie said.

Her smile tugged at me. I found myself feeling happy and sad in equal amounts. Teary-eyed for reasons both clear and undefined.

"Your daughter is in full remission," Lady Laser said. "She'll need a recurring course of treatments and checkups, but at the moment, the cancer cells have been neutralized."

Lady Laser. *The* Lady Laser. She stood there in her full glory, optical fibers and flesh-colored endoscopes extended from the sheaths at her wrists. Her initial consultation cost more than a year of Netherhouse's operating overhead. But her entire fee had been covered.

"Mom?"

Jamie blinked. Rubbed her chest where the portacath used to be.

Charlie grabbed my hand. Squeezed and let go.

"You're a good man," she said. "To do this."

She knew how we were paying for the treatments.

"Now, don't worry." Lady Laser made a fist and retracted the endoscopes. "The treatment and the follow-ups are fully covered. It's all been arranged. Your daughter's health will be completely restored, at no cost to you."

I smiled, hardly having to fake it. My daughter on the path to recovery. Free to live a normal life.

Jamie yawned. I reached down to brush a hair from her face. And the words rattled around inside me until they brushed the tattered remains of my soul.

No cost.

Sure.

* * *

Texas Recovery occupied the fifteenth floor in the behemoth that was Frost Bank. Floor-to-ceiling windows cast natural light throughout the space. Exposed ductwork and vases full of tall sticks lent a classy touch. The receptionist was a bright blue humanoid claiming to be from a subatomic civilization destroyed four million years ago. She directed visitors to a line of couches with no backs. She made minimum wage.

Ellen made me enter through the lobby. She swung open the large doors with the firm's name etched in the frosted glass. She marched toward a private elevator and didn't pause for chitchat. I followed her into the elevator car and listened to the cold hiss of the doors sealing shut. We dropped for a few seconds and then the doors opened on a garage full of reserved parking spaces. Replaceable magnetized nameplates clung to square-topped metal signs, the names all famous Augments on Ellen's payroll. Squid. The Riding Revenge. A few of the plates were new, Ellen always dealing with turnover, the Augments who couldn't handle the pressure of working at a top-tier recovery firm. One new plate caught my eye, the ink shiny, the name long coveted by the firm's owner.

The name on the plate was Makareta Black.

We walked on.

More plates went by and then we reached the space at the end. Wider by far than any other, there were no signs and no nameplates. A long black Lincoln Town Car was parked diagonally across the space. The vehicle was decadent. Ominous. Anyone entering the garage would know immediately the car was Ellen's.

She approached the car. Strolled from the back to the front and paused at the hood ornament. Turned and looked pointedly at me.

There was a nametag sitting on the hood. A perforated card had been slid into the plastic housing, displacing the old card and the old name. Ellen's previous driver, name and face now verboten. Skylark had been fired after the Dimension incident. There was a new driver on Ellen's payroll.

I picked up the nametag.

The name on the card said *Gayle Harwood*.

"See that you have the car washed," Ellen said. "Once a week at minimum, and immediately following any inclement weather."

The nametag weighed a million pounds. And of course it did. It contained my get-out-of-jail-free card. My living wage and the health care for my daughter. The augmented health care that allowed Lady Laser to scour the cancer from Jamie's body.

"Is there a problem, Mr. Harwood?"

Ellen stood at the rear door. Waiting.

I looked around the lot. Wondered if any of the other augments on Ellen's payroll might stroll through soon. Drive up in their fancy hovering cars. Fly over on augmented jetpacks. Or simply roll in under the power of a 495cc engine.

Mak had to forgive me. She just had to.

Given time.

I pinned the nametag to my brand-new dress shirt.

"No, Ms. Clovis."

I opened the door.

ABOUT THE AUTHOR

Image credit Karen Macfee

Jeff Macfee is a writer whose work has appeared in *Needle: A Magazine of Noir*, *Shotgun Honey*, and the anthology *Killing Malmon*. He wastes time on Twitter at @ jmacfee. For more information about his work, visit his website jeffmacfee.com.

FOR NEWS ABOUT JABBERWOCKY BOOKS AND AUTHORS